Also by Jen Klein

Jillian Cade: (Fake) Paranormal Investigator

SHUFFLE, Repeat

JEN KLEIN

Random House New York

Text copyright © 2016 by Jen Klein
Jacket and interior spot art copyright © 2016 by Sarah Coleman
Jacket photo © Getty Images/PhotoAlto/Frederic Cirou

Visit us on the Web! randomhouseteens.com

Educators and librarians, for a variety of teaching tools, visit us at RHTeachersLibrarians.com

Library of Congress Cataloging-in-Publication Data
Klein, Jen.
Shuffle, repeat / Jen Klein.—First edition.
pages cm
Summary: "When Oliver and June are forced to ride to school together each morning, no one is more surprised than this odd couple when a friendship—and then romance—develops"—Provided by publisher.
ISBN 978-0-553-50982-3 (trade)—ISBN 978-0-553-50984-7 (ebook)
[1. Friendship—Fiction. 2. Love—Fiction. 3. Dating (Social customs)—Fiction. 4. High schools—Fiction. 5. Schools—Fiction.] I. Title.
PZ7.1.K645Sh 2016 [Fic]—dc23 2015012725

Printed in the United States of America
10 9 8 7 6 5 4 3 2 1
First Edition

For Josh

PROM NIGHT

The car jams to the curb and I hop out before the valet can reach my door. I'm in the biggest hurry of my life and I don't care who knows it.

I'm alone when I run up the front stairs, and I'm alone when I cross the vast empty lobby of the hotel and step into the glittering ballroom. Hung with twinkling strands of light and dotted with white-draped tables, it is crowded with people I have known for years. And that's the moment I feel the most alone of all: when I enter my senior prom.

It's my own fault, of course. Sure, it was a boy who broke my heart, but I am the one to blame. I am the one who broke a promise.

Still, I hold my head high, because I have a reason to be here. I have a grand romantic gesture to make, an epic speech to give, a heart full of regret to bleed out over the scuffed vinyl.

When I scan the dance floor, I see him standing on the edge, swaying back and forth in that way guys do when they don't want (or know how) to dance. He isn't looking for me, but that makes sense, since he's here with another girl. She's right beside him and their fingers are twined together.

Nothing about tonight is going to be easy.

FALL

Chapter 1

Even though I'm clearly visible on my new front porch, my unwanted ride heralds his arrival with a sharp honk, loud enough to cut through the Damned, playing in my earbuds.

Oliver Flagg is the kind of guy who likes to make an entrance.

I wait until his gas-guzzling behemoth is completely stopped before I kill my music and trudge toward it. Whatever Oliver is listening to—I can hear drums and guitars—abruptly cuts off as I approach. Even though I'm a perfectly reasonably sized person at five and a half feet tall, I practically have to take a running leap to get into his vehicle, because it's so monstrously huge, but eventually I am strapped in with my backpack on my lap. Ready to get this ride—and senior year—over with.

"You're ten minutes early," I tell Oliver. Just because our moms are BFFs doesn't mean we have to be.

"You were ready," he says mildly. "Waiting outside and all dressed up for the first day of school."

Since I'm in one of my standard outfits—jeans, Chucks, a black tank layered over a white one—I know he's being facetious. I also know he probably doesn't comprehend the word "facetious."

"I was listening to music. I was embracing the *solitude*."

"Now you can embrace hanging out." He flashes his patented hot-popular-jock grin in my direction before reversing onto Callaway Lane. "Besides, you're *supposed* to show up early for the first day of school. These are the glory days, Rafferty."

"Glory days." The words come out of my mouth in a flat line. As far as I am concerned, high school is something to get through and get over. I don't need to roll around in the overblown tradition of it all.

But this is Oliver Flagg. He wallows in window dressing. He festers in frivolity. If there's the remotest chance that something will involve a sign-up sheet or a spirit banner or a dude dressed up as a bird (our school mascot is a robin), Oliver is in.

Simply put . . . he loves that shit.

And I hate it.

I *really* hate it.

We pull onto Plymouth and rumble west in stiff silence as pastures and maple trees and farmhouses slide past us on both sides. Crazy that this much rural country exists only twenty minutes outside the city.

I finger-comb my hair, which is not quite brown and not quite blond, not quite straight and not quite curly. Not quite anything . . . just like me.

I apply lip gloss. I squirm in my seat and accidentally send the dozen empty plastic water bottles at my feet rattling against each other. Finally, I'm not able to take it anymore and I blurt out what we're both thinking. "Look, I get it. It's not like our moms consulted us when they came up with this little plan." Oliver glances at me but doesn't say anything, so I keep going.

"It's cool. You've got better things to do." His eyebrows squinch together in the middle. "Drive me a couple more times so they won't get all pissy, and then we'll come up with an excuse. We'll tell them you have practice and I'll take the bus."

This time, Oliver's eyebrows jolt upward. "Practice?"

"Throwing or kicking or dribbling or whatever you do. Seriously, it's fine."

Oliver's lips twitch into a half smile. "My, uh, dribbling practice is after school. It's no big deal to drive you in the mornings."

"It's no big deal to take the bus."

"Except that the ride is an hour and a half long. The bus goes all the way out before coming back to school."

He's right, but I hate being his charity case. "I know you have amassed a certain amount of nice-guy cred, but you don't really have to pick me up. It's egregious. It's excessive." Belatedly, I remember that Oliver might not follow my advanced vocabulary, and I dial it back so he'll understand. "It's too much."

"I don't mind."

I shift again in my seat to observe his profile. There are girls in our class who would trade places with me in a hot heartbeat. Those girls place a lot of weight on tan skin and tight muscles and chocolate-brown eyes (I've heard Zoe Smith refer to them as "bedroom eyes"), but none of that does anything for me. I'm a brains girl, all the way. "Of course you mind. Who would want to be responsible for getting someone else to school every single day?"

Oliver lets out a tiny puff of laughter. "You and your mom moved five minutes from my house and I literally pass right by you"—I feel a stab of gratitude for his correct usage of the word "literally"—"so chill, Rafferty. It's no big deal to swing by and pick you up."

It's a nice thing to say, which I do appreciate despite evidence to the contrary, but it doesn't stop me from being . . . *me*. "It's a little weird, don't you think?"

"Not until you said that." Again with the laughter as we cruise through a green light and merge onto the highway heading toward Ann Arbor. "Tell you what, let's just do what people do."

I have (literally) no idea what he's talking about, so I wait.

"Okay, I'll go first," says Oliver. "Who do you have for homeroom?"

Ohhhh, now I get it. Conversation. Fine. I can make an attempt. "Vinton. Who's yours?"

"Webb. I had her sophomore year. She's pretty cool."

I run through other topics in my head, finally coming back to the only thing Oliver and I have in common: school. "What electives are you taking?"

"Photography and family sciences."

I'm amused in spite of myself. "By 'family sciences,' do you mean 'home ec'?"

Oliver shrugs. "It's a cooking class, but if you want to use an outdated term, sure."

"I'm just surprised." Meatheads like Oliver usually take electives like grunting. Or lifting heavy objects. Or freshmen-intimidation techniques.

"And I am equally surprised by your misogyny," he says.

8

"Whereas I am now surprised that you know the word 'misogyny.'"

Oliver winks one of those brown bedroom eyes at me. "Isn't life a series of grand eye-opening revelations?"

Huh. A jock with a vocabulary.

A jockabulary, if you will.

"To be honest, I'm only taking the class because of this dumb thing with Theo," Oliver tells me. "We had a bet. I lost. Now I'm taking family sciences."

"What kind of bet?"

"Just a stupid guy thing."

I settle back in the leather seat. In all fairness, even though I've technically known Oliver from birth, it's not like I really *know* him. We haven't spent any time together since kindergarten, when we got married under the monkey bars in a ceremony officiated by Shaun Banerjee. Our relationship was consummated with a sticky kiss and then annulled a couple hours later when we got into an argument during art class. It culminated in our sitting in the principal's office, dripping in blue paint, waiting for our moms to bring us clean clothes.

Who knew that since then, Oliver had graduated from one-syllable words?

"How's Itch?" Oliver asks.

I'm a little thrown by the question. It didn't occur to me that Oliver would even know about Itch. Also, I don't know how to answer him.

"Fine," I finally say, because it might be true.

Probably.

Hopefully.

Itch—otherwise known as Adam Markovich—is my boyfriend . . . maybe. Before heading to Florida for the summer, he said it would be crazy for us to sit around and wait for each other, and that we should be free to date other people. I agreed with him—because what else could I do?—and assumed it was the beginning of the end. Then Itch called or texted nearly every single day, so I guessed he probably wasn't dating anyone else. Of course, I didn't exactly broadcast it when I kissed Ethan Erickson on the Fourth of July, so it's possible Itch cheated, too.

Since none of this is a matter of public record, I'm not sure why Oliver is asking. I angle my body toward him. "How do you even know who I date?"

"It's not like I live under a rock."

"Just under a helmet."

"You and Itch hold hands at school."

Double *huh*. I'm shocked that anyone outside my limited social circle has any idea what I do with my hands.

"It doesn't seem like something you'd notice."

Oliver shakes his head. "You know who my girlfriend is, right?"

Well, duh.

"Ainsley Powell." The smug face he pulls makes me want to defend myself. "But everyone knows that."

"Dude, it's our senior year. By now, everyone knows who everyone is."

I shift in my seat again, trying to get comfortable. The car is so huge I can barely see out the windows. "Right, senior year."

We take the exit and cruise onto Main Street, which has scattered gas stations and mattress warehouses and peeling billboards about mortgage rates at this end of it. I feel rather than see Oliver's glance. "Aren't you even a little bit excited?" he asks me.

"No."

"This is our last year. This is *it.*"

Ugh.

"Not to burst your bubble, but this is nothing," I say. "It's not real life."

"It's *better* than real life," Oliver informs me. "High school sets the stage for real life."

This time, I'm the one who laughs. "Please. Nothing we do right now matters."

Oliver's mouth drops open. "Are you kidding me?"

"I'm totally not. Think about it." I turn to face him more fully. "In the real world, in the grand scheme of *life,* this year is going to count for exactly nothing. These are the friendships that don't last and the choices that don't count. All those things we all freak out about now, like who's going to be class president and are we going to win the game this weekend—there's going to be a time when we can't even *remember* caring about them. In exactly three hundred and sixty-five days from right now, wearing your letter jacket or class ring will make you look like the lamest of losers."

Oliver blinks. "Man, you are bleak."

"I'm not bleak. I'm realistic." I mean it, too. I don't hate my life and I'm not unhappy. It's just that I understand the way the world works. I don't need to pretend.

We go in silence for a few more minutes, until, as we pass the sign welcoming us to downtown Ann Arbor, I decide I should smooth things over. After all, even though I might not be voluntarily hanging out with Oliver Flagg, it looks like we're going to have these early mornings together five times a week for the foreseeable future. "I'm not trying to be a dick," I tell him. "You can have fun in high school. I just don't think we should pretend it means more than it does."

Oliver doesn't say anything. He keeps driving as brick houses appear and then hunch closer and closer together. A half mile past the sign, it starts to actually look like a downtown, with restaurants and banks and four-story buildings and shops with awnings. That lasts only a handful of blocks and then we're crossing Madison and driving through the university area, where houses are bigger, lawns are greener, and cars are shinier. Oliver remains quiet as we pass the stadium and a golf course. It's not until we drive through Robin High's main gate and enter the senior parking lot that Oliver speaks again: "For the record, I don't think you're a dick."

"Thanks." I don't really care what the King of Everything thinks of me, but Mom raised me to know it's polite to say something in return.

Oliver maneuvers his gigantic beast into a spot between two older sedans before killing the engine and turning to face me. "But I do feel sorry for you."

"Feeling sorry for me is pretentious," I inform him.

"Calling me pretentious is pretentious!" Oliver says it with a grin, but I think he means it. "Look, June . . ."

Ah, my first name. He must really want me to pay attention.

"In the world of schools, ours is pretty cool. But instead of appreciating it, all you want is to get out. All this stuff you're pretending is stupid—it matters. Everything we do *matters*."

I stare at him. The judgy thing is annoying, but who knew Oliver was capable of such intellectual discourse? Of getting passionate about something not involving a ball or a score? I don't have to agree with his thesis regarding the importance of adolescence, but maybe these mornings can be more interesting than I originally presumed.

I'm about to say as much when a heavy thump on the rooftop makes me jump in my seat. Theo Nizzola—self-heralded Chick Magnet of Robin High (except he doesn't say "chick")—lurches into view by the driver-side window. "Besticle!" He pounds on the car again. "C'mon, get out here!"

" 'Besticle'?" I say the word in a tone that makes no secret of my contempt.

The glance Oliver throws at me might be apologetic. "It's a Theo thing. It's like bestie and—"

"I get it. Thanks for the ride." I open my door and clamber down, hoping for a quick getaway, but of course Theo immediately lumbers around to block my path.

"Hafferty, what's up?"

Yes, he knows my last name. No, he never says it correctly.

"Not much, Theo."

He looms closer and holds out his thick arms. The smell of spicy deodorant wafts out from under them. "Why aren't you giving me a good-morning hug?" He rotates his pelvis in a way that somebody somewhere must think is sexy.

I look him straight in the eye. "Because you're gross and kind of stupid."

Theo throws his head back and roars with laughter. It's what he always does. This is our long-standing tradition. He makes disgusting motions, I shoot him down, and then he laughs really loudly. It's also a big reason I don't worship Oliver like other girls do. At the end of the day, he's still a guy who surrounds himself with oafs.

I mean, besticles.

Theo bestows me with a final pelvic shimmy just as Oliver rounds the car and punches him in the arm. "Knock it off, jack-ass." He nods at me. "See you tomorrow, Rafferty."

"Great." I hang back to put some distance between us. I don't want to kick off the school year with those assholes.

• • •

The school lobby smells the same way it did at the start of last year: like beauty products and new sneakers and hormones.

God, we're predictable.

I squeeze through the crowd—occasionally making eye contact or trading smiles—and am almost to the curved stairway when I hear my name called from across the lobby. It's Shaun, bounding toward me like a gazelle, waving his arm frantically back and forth.

I love that kid.

Shaun catches me in a bear hug that ends awkwardly, knocking his glasses askew against the side of my face. He pulls back to adjust them and I take in his First Day of School outfit: preppy, from his polo to his oxfords. "Shopping spree?" I ask.

"You know how I feel about the Banana."

I groan at the double entendre, but before I can throw a witty comeback, Shaun pulls me to the side of the stairway and crowds me against the wall in the shadows. It's what a straight guy would do if he wanted a fast make-out session before homeroom.

"No, seriously," Shaun says in a super-earnest tone. "How are you and I adore you and all that, but first listen to this." He pauses dramatically before telling me. "I met someone."

"At business camp?"

"Don't mock. Behold." Shaun pulls out his phone and starts scrolling around. He tilts the screen at me and I stare at the photo of an extremely buff dude posing by a pool. He's wearing rolled-up khaki shorts and nothing else. He looks like he could be—

"He's not *actually* a Banana Republic model, is he?"

Shaun shakes his head, satisfied. "No, but I *know*. His name is Kirk. Isn't he amazing?"

I whap him on the arm. "What's amazing is that I'm just now hearing about him!"

Shaun gives me a look of mock offense. "Important news should not be shared in a *text*."

I try to remember what Shaun told me about the Rutgers summer business program he went to. "Weren't you only there for like a week?"

"Six days, but get this: afterward, I told my parents I was visiting my cousin Wajidali at Syracuse, and Kirk said he was visiting his sister in Queens."

I feel my eyebrows shoot up and disappear under my thick bangs. "Where did you really go?"

"A gay youth hostel in Manhattan." Shaun lowers his voice. "Technically speaking, in Chelsea. And technically speaking, not gay so much as gay-friendly, but . . ." He draws in a deep breath. "It was life-altering, June. I am in love."

I reach for his phone to assess the photo again. There are no two ways about it: Shaun's guy is so hot as to be almost painful. "*I* might even be in love."

"I know, *right*?" We grin at each other and then Shaun asks what I knew he would ask. "Have you seen Itch yet?"

I shake my head.

"Did you ever tell him about . . . ?" Shaun makes a conspiratorial face, which is code for the twenty minutes I spent behind the 7-Eleven with Ethan Erickson's tongue in my mouth. I shake my head again and Shaun nods approvingly. "Good. That news was *never* important enough to be shared."

"I hope you're right."

The early bell rings and Shaun links his arm through mine. "Time to get our senior on."

I allow Shaun to guide me up the stairs and onto the second floor, where we part ways to find our lockers. Mine is halfway down the hall and—like the rest of the twelfth-grade lockers—shellacked in blue. We've been told it's the exact same color as a robin's egg, but I suspect the real thing features more cute little speckles and less chipping paint. I shove my backpack inside, slam the door, spin the dial, turn . . .

And there's Itch.

He's weaving through the crowd toward me, like in a scene at the end of a romantic movie. His flop of almost-curly hair is longer than it was the last time I saw him, and his skin is sun-roasted. He keeps his hazel eyes locked on mine as he comes closer, and for just a second, I have that fainty-heart feeling that I used to get when we first started dating last year. Then he's right here, and before I can even consider, he's got his arms around me and I'm tilting my head back. His mouth is soft and waxy and familiar. When we part, he smiles his lopsided, lazy smile down at me. "I missed you," he says.

I choose to believe him.

• • •

Lily and Darbs are already unpacked and eating lunch when I arrive at the west end of the bleachers where we sit, halfway between the top and the bottom. Not in the center, because that would imply social dominance, and not on the first row, because that would imply citizenship of LoserVille. We sit off to the side, but far enough up to make it clear that we belong.

At least, we belong to each other.

Lily only says hello when I plop down beside her—we already saw each other in homeroom and AP English—but Darbs squeals and surges across the bleacher to hug me. "June! Holy crap, I've been looking for you all *day!*" We compare schedules for the trimester and discover we have Spanish III together right after lunch. This sends Darbs into a joyful delirium, during which she hugs me again. I am unable to resist touching her shoulder-length ponytail, which is currently a deep violet with bright pink underneath. I would never dye my own hair, but I love it on Darbs.

When we break apart, Darbs tells us about the new girl in her English class. Her name is Yana Pace, she wears a tiny golden confirmation cross, and she was no-question-about-it, absolutely *vibing* Darbs. Lily and I exchange glances over our sandwiches. This is how it always goes with Darbs. Big crushes, big heartbreaks. It's tough being a bisexual Christian. The gays don't want her, and neither does our school's God Squad.

Lily and Darbs are amused by my new carpool arrangement.

"What's the inside of his car like?" Darbs asks. "Is it filled with cheerleaders and beer cans?"

"Totally," I tell her. "The cheerleaders are stacked in the backseat and I have to rest my feet on a keg."

Darbs nods like she believes me. "At least he's reasonable to look at."

"*Very* reasonable," Lily agrees. "But what do you *talk* about?"

"I'm trying to avoid too much conversation," I tell them.

"Good call," says Darbs.

The cafeteria must have been slammed, because the three of us are almost done eating by the time Shaun bounds up the bleachers with his tray, Itch loping behind him. Lily makes a big fuss about how Shaun is *deigning* to sit with us on the first day of school. She raises her dark arms—almost impossibly toned from all her violin practice—to the sky. "We've been blessed with a presence! We've been graced by royalty . . . *ow!*"

Shaun tugs on one of her dreadlocks and tells her to quit it. "I can't help being so cool. Everyone loves me," he says.

"Since when are chameleons cool?" Itch asks. He and I share the same opinion about trying to fit into school hierarchies: it's dumb and pointless.

"Chameleons *change* their colors," Shaun says, adjusting the collar of his striped polo shirt. "I float from group to group because my colors are constant but abundant. I am a rainbow."

"You are a cliché," I say, teasing him. He elbows me but I know he knows I'm joking. Kshaunish "Shaun" Banerjee very well might be the *least* cliché person at our high school.

Itch raises his hand and Lily points a finger to call on him. "Mr. Markovich."

"Stupidest high school tradition: go."

I don't even have to think about it. "Prom."

It earns me a pout from Darbs. "Prom is *romantic*," she says.

"Prom is *lame*," says Lily.

"I can't wait until prom," I inform them all. "But only because then it will be over. It's the last stupid high school tradition before real life begins."

"You should go ironically," Darbs tells me.

"I won't go at all," I tell her. "There's no way." Belatedly, I realize I should have checked to see if my boyfriend felt the same way, but Itch is already nodding in agreement.

"Prom is stupid, but not the stupidest," he says. "Try again."

"Streak Week?" Shaun asks.

"No one's done that in years," Itch tells him.

"True, but it was the dumbest of dumb. I heard about this one guy who lost a pinky toe from frostbite."

"Gross!" We all throw napkins at Shaun.

"Ooh, I got it!" Darbs bounces up and down. "The mascot laying an egg at center field during halftime!"

We crack up, because of course it's one of the most ridiculous things at our school, but it's still not what Itch is going for. "All definitely stupid, but not quite as stupid as the stupid senior prank."

Every year, the seniors do something obvious and obnoxious, like hang the principal in effigy from the big maple tree or sandblast their graduation date into the sidewalk in front of the school. It's usually illegal and it's always destructive.

Itch tells us there's a plan in motion for this year. "I don't know the details, but apparently it involves a cow, the third floor, and laxatives."

"Ew!" Darbs makes a face like she can already smell cow poop.

"I know," says Itch. "It's only September and already the losers are planning for that crap. Get a life."

"I still think prom is worse," I tell them.

"Who's in charge of the prank?" Shaun asks.

"Who do you think?" Itch says.

"The athletes," Lily and Shaun say together.

Prickles of annoyance scuttle over me. "Of course they are." The same way Theo thinks it's okay to jut his disgusting pelvis at me, his cohorts think it's okay to take control of an inane piece of tradition that is—no matter how stupid—supposed to represent the entire community. They think they *own* the school. "Like they're more *senior* than us or something," I say out loud.

"Assholes," Lily agrees.

Itch leans over and kisses me. Darbs makes a gagging sound. "Get a room."

"We don't need a room," I tell her. "The world is our room."

This time, everyone gags.

• • •

Itch drops me off at the foot of my driveway. I ask him to come in, but when he sees Mom's Volkswagen, he says no. Itch is not a fan of polite, superficial conversation, which is what he feels is the best one can hope for with the parents of one's girlfriend.

Or, in this case, the parent.

I smell the garlic even before I open the screen door. It gets stronger and more fragrant as I wend my way past piles of neatly stacked two-by-fours and planks of wood leaning against the bare walls. Although we've been in the farmhouse for a month, it looks like we just moved in. Mom has been renovating the place for almost a year, ever since my grandfather passed away and bequeathed it to us, but it's still not done. This summer, she decided it didn't make sense to pay for two homes anymore and—since the plumbing was finished—we should go ahead and move in. I'm sure it was a smart financial move, but it's complicated my personal life. I used to jump on a city bus and make it to school in ten minutes, or else Mom would drop me off on her way to the University of Michigan, where she's an associate professor of art. Now, however, Mom's studio hours are earlier and our living situation is farther away, which means I'm stuck with Oliver Flagg every morning.

I find Mom at the stove, stirring a pot of tomato sauce. Her cheeks are pink from the heat and an embroidered headband holds back her straight brown hair. She looks up when I walk in. "June! Taste?"

She pulls her wooden spoon out and taps it against the edge of the pot before offering me some. It is, of course, divine. Everything my mom cooks is divine, with the exception of the things she made during the brief span of time when she was experimenting with scallions. She put them in everything, even cookies.

"The tomatoes are from Quinny," she tells me. "Her garden is producing like crazy and since ours won't be much of anything until next summer . . . How was your day?"

That's how my mom talks. She trails off from one subject and leaps to the next one without missing a beat. I think her brain must be like that, a patchwork quilt of ideas and questions and thoughts. Mine is more linear. Point A to point B. Clear directions, clear focus. Mom says she doesn't know how she and my father managed to produce such a brilliantly book-smart daughter, but she's thankful for it.

I think it's the *only* reason Mom is thankful for my father.

"It was fine. Mostly getting syllabi and hearing expectations. I think calculus is going to be hard."

"You'll be fine. You're really good at math and . . . How are your friends?"

"Darbs has a crush. Lily got a special waiver for two study periods so she can practice violin. Shaun is in three of my classes."

"So the same," Mom says with a smile. "How about Itch?"

"Good, he drove me home."

"That's . . . Oh, how was Oliver this morning?" I pause for only a second, but Mom reads into it. "You don't get along with him?"

"It's fine, Mom. We get along fine."

"I have an idea," she says in this super-casual way, which I know means it didn't just come to her. She's been thinking about how to say this for a while. I watch her turn down the burner and give the pot a few more stirs. "I need Saturday afternoon for studio time, but I'm around in the morning. Maybe we could do some practice driving."

My heart catches. Panic swells thick at the back of my throat. I do what I always do—take a deep breath and wait it out, sinking beneath the waves so the feeling can surge over and past me—and then swallow the panic back.

"I can't." I say it in a casual tone to match my mother's. "I already have plans with Itch."

It's not true, but Mom doesn't know that.

Or maybe she does.

Chapter 2

"No cows!" I squawk at Oliver from my side of the behemoth as he trundles us down Main Street. We've already been arguing for a full ten minutes and I'm not making any headway at all. Also, I feel like I keep sliding down in my seat, because his car is so damn huge. I decide to change tactics, and I push myself upright, adopting a calmer voice. "I don't want you guys to get hurt."

Oliver lets out an exasperated puff of air. "It's not a bull," he tells me. "We're talking about a dairy cow. They're big and dumb and they make milk."

"Just like you guys, except for the milk part." He can't blame me for hitting a softball when it comes in that low and slow.

"We're not going to *hurt* it," Oliver tells me.

"Oh, really? Medicating it with drugs intended for human consumption just to provide entertainment for a bunch of pumped-up boys isn't *hurting* it?"

Oliver lifts his right hand from the steering wheel and slowly—veeeeery slowly—flexes his biceps. He throws me a sideways glance. "What I've taken from this is that you think I'm pumped up."

It's not that I'm *trying* to look at his muscle, but it's right there, pushing against the sleeve of his T-shirt.

"Not funny."

"It's a little funny."

I roll my eyes and then, since Oliver is looking at the road and didn't see, I lean across the center seat so I'm in his peripheral vision, and I roll them again. Dramatically.

Oliver laughs. "*You're* funny. I didn't know that." I feel a small stab of satisfaction to have surprised Oliver the way he surprised me yesterday with his vocabulary. "Nothing's set in stone. I'm sure we can come up with something that doesn't involve prescription drugs or force-feeding."

"I don't get why you have to come up with anything at all."

"This again." He darts a quick glance at me before looking back at the road. "Your lack of school spirit is—"

"I know, I know. Sad."

"*So* sad. Tell me this, Rafferty. What kind of prank *would* you deem appropriate?"

"None!" My arms fling into the air all on their own. "I don't want to be involved in *any* senior prank! It's an irrelevant way to leave a legacy! It's *not* a legacy!"

"Because high school is not where legacies are made," Oliver says in a snippy version of my voice. "Because nothing we do now matters."

"Mock away, but we're only waiting until real life begins."

"But these are the memories you take with you into real life! Pep rallies and parties and prom—"

"Prom is the worst," I tell him. "It's the epitome of everything that is wrong with high school. An expensive dance with bad music that puts girls in the subservient position of hoping a boy will ask them to go."

"How do you really feel?"

"I hate it!" I explode, and Oliver laughs.

"Yeah, I got that. Okay, so traditions are stupid. Fine, I'll buy that your opinion has merit even though I disagree. But what about your boyfriend? He matters, right?"

"Itch? Yeah, but it's not like I'm going to freaking *marry* him."

"What if you are?" Oliver swings us past the front of the school and toward the parking lot.

"I'm not!"

"But *what if*?" Oliver's getting a little worked up. "What if it's meant to be and you can't even look beyond your version of what matters! It's sad!"

An underclassman with a trombone case steps off the curb in front of us and Oliver slams on the brakes, a little too hard. "Watch it," I tell him.

"I'm watching it." He waits for the underclassman to cross. "I'm watching everything. I care about every single minute, because I know that everything here *does* matter. It has to, because otherwise what's the point, June?"

There we go. My first name again.

Oliver steps on the gas and we pull through the lot and into a spot. I turn to him. "You know what's sad? Pretending is sad." I hop out and slam the door.

Final word. Suck it, Oliver.

Except Oliver is an athlete with lightning-fast reflexes,

which means he's by my side before I'm ten feet away. "I'm not done—"

I groan out loud. "What do I have to say to end this conversation?"

He catches me by the arm and swings me around to face him. Those overly hyped brown eyes peer earnestly into my own. "Say you know that something, anything, about this year will matter!"

I stare up at him and notice that the outer rings of his irises are dark. They're gray—close to black, even. They almost match his pupils. I am once again acutely aware of all the girls who would want to stand in the grip of Oliver Flagg's strong fingers, to gaze up into his remarkably gorgeous face. I'm about to throw him a bone, give him just an ounce of agreement, when we are interrupted by the voice I enjoy least in the world.

"Does Ainsley know you're getting a little Rafferty in the mornings?" Of course it's Theo, and of course he's hulking right up on us with his sneery smile.

"Ainsley knows I drive June to school." Oliver says it evenly.

"Yeah, but why?"

"Because she needs a ride."

"I'm right here," I remind them both, and then speed up even more. I really don't want to go down this particular road with either of these particular guys. They don't try to keep up, but I hear Theo's question before I'm out of range.

"Why can't she drive herself?"

Jerks.

• • •

Other than homeroom, Itch and I don't have any classes together. However, we're in the same building for third period, so it's easy to meet during break. We barely have any time between all our other periods, but they give us ten glorious minutes between second and third. We're supposed to go to the bathroom or eat a healthy snack—most of us use that time to socialize. Just like last year, Itch and I spend it huddled together in a stairwell, kissing.

"When can I come over?" he asks.

"You could have come over yesterday, but you opted out."

He slides the tip of his finger under the hem of my screen-printed T-shirt and I push it away. "This is an institution of education. Hanky-panky is not permitted within these hallowed halls."

"Education is overrated," he says, and dives in for another kiss.

I briefly allow it and then pull back, unable to shake my morning conversation with Oliver. "Do you think any of this matters?"

Itch squints at me. "What do you mean?"

"This." I make a wide, sweeping gesture. "School. Traditions. Us."

Itch's lips curve upward and I notice there's a sliver of dark dots along the left side of his mouth that he missed when shaving. "Tell you what. I'll come over this weekend and *show* you what matters."

This time when he kisses me, it's with tongue.

• • •

I'm heading into my third-period class—physics—when I feel a nudge from behind. It's Oliver. "Looking forward to all the nonessential information we'll learn today?"

"I'm just here to collect my A."

"Only an A?" He grins down at me, so I nudge him back, since apparently he's not still mad about our argument.

"Make that an A-plus."

Oliver looks like he's about to say something in return, but Ainsley Powell squeezes between us and our conversation is over. She rises on her toes to kiss him before gifting me with a brilliant smile. "Hi, June."

Ainsley smells like summer peaches, and her hair, thick and curly and wild, is the color of beach sand. Her wide emerald eyes gaze into mine, and even though I'm painfully straight, I almost want to kiss her myself because she's so damn gorgeous. Instead, I manage a smile and a "Hey" before heading to a lab table in the front row.

Itch thinks I'm insane for taking *two* sciences during my senior year, when I should be slacking off, but this is the only one that feels like work. Environmental science, which I had right before the break, is super interesting. Plus, because of our school's partnership with the University of Michigan, it qualifies for dual enrollment, so I'm getting college credit for it.

Physics is another story. Today, for example, I'm having a tough time paying attention to whatever Mrs. Nelson is saying about the subdisciplines of mechanics, because I keep replaying things I *should* have said to Oliver. I sneak a furtive glance toward the back of the room, where he's sitting with Ainsley. They're holding hands and Oliver is looking straight at me.

I whirl back around and start scribbling notes about translational motion and oscillatory motion and rotational motion until I make the ironic realization that I am—quite literally—going through the motions.

Why did I look at him, anyway?

Chapter 3

The next morning, I'm on a mission when I get into Oliver's car. "I have an idea," I inform him, tossing an empty water bottle from the passenger seat into the back as he pulls us out onto the street. "A way to make this drive much more tolerable."

"Twenty questions?"

"No."

"The license plate game?"

"That's for little kids."

"Don't take this the wrong way," says Oliver, "but you're not very big."

I sit up a little straighter, even though I'm 100 percent normal size. It's Oliver who has a skewed perspective, because he's so tall. Just like his girlfriend.

"We've been going about this all wrong," I tell him. I flip my backpack around on my lap so I can unzip the front pocket. "We obviously both have deep-held convictions that support our individual life philosophies."

"Huh?" says Oliver.

"What I mean—" I start, but he interrupts.

"I'm kidding. I know what you mean." He shakes his head and I can't tell if he's amused or annoyed.

Right.

"I don't think these morning drives have to be . . . like this."

"Like what?"

"All fighty and crabby."

Oliver's head tilts. "I thought we were making conversation."

"I think . . ." I pause, formulating exactly what I want to say. "I think we are very different from each other, and we don't see the world the same way, and that's okay. But it's also no reason for us to start every day miserably." Oliver keeps his eyes on the road ahead of us. "I have a solution." I pull my phone from the backpack. "After a brief exchange of pleasantries in my driveway, we can stick to music."

"Music."

"Loud music."

"Loud music?"

"*Really* loud."

Oliver considers before nodding. "If that's what you want."

"It is."

"Then okay."

"Good."

"Lovely."

Satisfied, I scroll through the playlist I made last night after coming up with this stroke of peacemaking genius. I think I'm in the mood for something classic—the Clash or maybe a little Ramones—but then I see Alesana and know that's it. I hunt around on the console for a speaker wire like in my mom's car, but I don't see one. I flip open the middle compartment lid only to find it empty. "Hey, where's your—"

Unfortunately, the rest of my sentence is drowned out by a rush of piano chords. My hands drop the phone and fly up to cover my ears.

"Where is that coming from? How are you—" I stop as a man's voice throbs through the behemoth's speakers. It's earnest and it's passionate and it's loud and . . . "What is this, Bon Jovi?"

"Survivor!" Oliver yells over the lyrics.

"It's terrible!" I scream at him, frantically searching the dashboard for a way to turn it off.

Oliver brandishes his phone. "Wireless connection!" he shouts.

"It's killing me! Turn it down! Turn it off! Make it"— the song abruptly cuts off—"stop!" I clear my throat. "Thank you. No offense, but that was the worst."

Oliver grins like it's a giant joke. "You clearly have no appreciation of fine music."

"What are you, a twelve-year-old girl?"

"It's a power ballad, June. They were wildly popular."

My eyes widen. "Are you a twelve-year-old girl *in the eighties*?"

He laughs out loud and I can't find the humor, because I'm so shocked that *Oliver Flagg* likes awful hair-band power ballads.

He reaches over to pat my bare knee. "It's okay. Not everything fits into one of your neat little boxes."

My mouth drops open. "What is that supposed to mean?"

But Oliver isn't bothered. "What do you listen to? Share."

"I don't know how to jack into your system," I say, still offended.

"Just play it from your phone."

"Fine," I say, and touch my screen. It's not as loud, since it's not connected to the speakers, but my phone packs a punch. The opening drumbeats reverberate fast in my ears, scrubbing away the pulsing banality of Oliver's terrible music.

Yeah.

That's more like it.

Beside me, Oliver's right hand sails off the steering wheel. It lands on the compartment between us and opens the lid. Scuttles around inside.

Still empty.

We stop at a red light, and he reaches across me to open the glove box, which is crammed full of napkins and ketchup packets. "What are you looking for?" I ask over the music.

"Aspirin!" he yells back. "This is breaking my brain!"

I glare at him before touching my screen to kill the song. The light turns green and we cruise through it. "Ha-ha," I say. "You're hilarious."

"No." He says it with yet another of those smiles. "*You're* hilarious. What is that screamo?"

"*Screamo?*" He knows nothing—*nothing*—about what constitutes good music . . . or good friends . . . or good anything. "It's Alesana. Pop-metal out of North Carolina, and they're actually amazing."

"Amazingly shitty," Oliver says. "It hurts my ears. It hurts my *soul*."

"Their sound is rough, but that's the *point*. It means something. It's *real*—"

"Real awful. How do you even find stuff like that?"

"My dad turned me on to it."

Oliver looks surprised. "Your *dad* listens to screamo?"

Of course it would be weird to someone who looks and lives like everyone else. "Yeah, he taught me not to just scratch the surface," I tell Oliver. "It's *easy* to find mainstream music. You don't even have to look. It's just there, in your face all the time, on the radio and TV. There's no thought to it. No *discovery*."

"You make no sense," Oliver informs me. "Try getting beneath the surface of *my* music. Look a little deeper, be a little less obvious and you'll see what's underneath."

"Underneath?" I practically explode. "There's nothing underneath. Your music is overly produced and overly cliché!" I point a finger at him. "It totally makes sense."

"How's that?" Oliver still doesn't seem mad. Only amused.

"That you would be into that. It's manufactured and it's fake!"

Oliver's lips press together. He doesn't look amused anymore. We drive a few more minutes and then he says, "Maybe we shouldn't listen to music after all."

"Fine," I say. "We'll suffer in silence."

• • •

The next morning the score is as follows:

Suffering = 1. Silence = 0.

We haven't even gotten to the highway yet and Oliver has made (almost) every sound a human body can make. He started with humming and moved on to whistling. After a little of that, he switched to clicking his tongue. It went on for at least a full minute and now he's singing one of those power ballads under his breath.

I'm not sure why Oliver is trying to torture me, but he's clearly enjoying the process. I close my eyes and breathe slowly. In through my nose, out through my mouth.

I hear a pop and my eyes fly open. Oliver is cracking his knuckles, one by one. He gets to the last and then looks at me. I scowl and he grins big.

Really big.

I might kill him.

I close my eyes again and lean back against the seat, trying to envision myself anywhere but here. A snowy mountain. A desert at night. A sunny expanse of beach.

I hear a chomping sound and I can't stop myself from peeking at Oliver. He's chewing a piece of gum. With his mouth open.

I glare at him and decide I don't even need the mountain or desert or beach. I could be happy in a pit of burning coals as long as Oliver isn't there with me.

Oliver slides a second piece of gum from the pack. He pops it into his mouth. Chews. He glances over before adding another piece. And another. And another.

Killing. Me.

There's one piece left in the pack. Oliver holds it toward me—an offer of faux generosity. I snatch it out of his hand and shove it into my backpack. I don't want his stupid gum, but I surely don't want to hear it in his mouth.

That only makes him smile more widely before turning back to the road.

Oliver cracks his gum. He blows a bubble. It pops and he reaches up to swipe the gum off his upper lip and shove it back into his mouth.

I turn to look out the window.

Thank God it's Friday.

• • •

Even though I already know our planet is unique in the solar system, that it is nearly magic how we have water and oxygen and creatures that evolved from tiny one-celled organisms, I still feel awestruck in environmental science when Mr. Hollis takes us through the process of its creation. Since there are only twelve of us, we move along quickly and have plenty of time for discussion and questions. We get all the way through the Proterozoic era before we're dismissed for break.

I'm heading toward the stairwell where Itch is waiting for me when I hear Oliver's name squawked from the family sciences room. I guess if a class has "science" in its name or uses open flames, this is where the school puts it.

I slow down to make way for the kids trickling out the open door. Oliver is standing before Mrs. Alhambra's desk. She wags her finger at him. "All you sports-minded boys are the same." Oliver's shoulders droop. He shuffles his feet. He doesn't say anything. "You think you don't have to work at anything. You think you can skate through life on your looks," she continues. "Well, not here. You need a *brain* to pass family sciences. You need to *use* it!"

"That's what I'm—"

"Salt is not the flavor. It's the flavor *enhancer.*" Mrs.

Alhambra holds up a red plastic bowl—like the kind you buy for a picnic—and shakes it at him. "You're going to give someone a heart attack with this!" The bowl and its contents make a loud *chunk* when they drop into the trash can.

"Yes, ma'am," Oliver says. He heaves a sigh and turns in my direction. I jerk my gaze away, speed-walking past the classroom and down the hall.

If today was the first day of school, I would probably be on Mrs. Alhambra's side right now. But I'm not. Sure, Oliver surrounds himself with helmets and muscles, but it doesn't mean he's exactly the same as those Neanderthals. He seems different.

At least, a *little* different.

Three minutes later, I'm in the stairwell with Itch, whose hands are again trying to tease beneath the hem of my shirt. I kiss him before pulling away. "I have to get to class."

He frowns. "Don't we still have time?"

"I don't want to be late to physics."

"You and your good-girl ways," he murmurs.

I reach up to ruffle his shaggy hair. "I'm not a good girl about *everything.* Are you still coming over tomorrow afternoon?"

"Is your mom still going to be out?"

"As far as I know."

"Then I'll be there." He drops a last kiss onto my mouth before heading for the steps. "See you at lunch," he calls back over his shoulder.

• • •

I am already seated when the bell rings and Oliver rushes in at the last minute. Even though I'm staring straight ahead at the whiteboard with my hands folded primly before me, I can see him trudge past in my peripheral vision. Mrs. Nelson pushes up from her desk and asks us to take out our books. There's a rustle of paper and the creaking of chairs as everyone does what she asks.

This time, I don't need to risk a glance back to confirm that Oliver is looking at me. After all, I know that when he arrived at his lab table, there was something sitting in the very center of it.

Something I placed there.

A peace offering.

Or rather a *piece* offering.

It's Oliver's last piece of gum. The one he gave me this morning.

• • •

"I was wrong about the prank," says Itch. We are sitting in our place on the bleachers—all of us but Shaun, who is eating onstage with the theater kids—and watching what's happening on the field. "*This* is the stupidest tradition at our school." I have to agree with him.

"This is the stupidest tradition at *any* school," says Lily.

Darbs and I both nod vigorously as a hundred upper-classmen cheer and pump their fists in the air from the center of the bleachers. The graduating football players are busy march-ing five younger guys into the center of the field for what's affec-tionately known as shearing: when the senior football players cut the hair of their newest varsity teammates, who—this year—are all sophomores.

A row of chairs has been set up, and the cheerleaders are

showing off their supremely helpful skills by placing buckets of soapy water by each one. Ainsley settles one of the sophomores into a chair before squeezing a sponge over his head. Water drips over his hair and darkens his shirt. We can hear Ainsley's laugh all the way up here. It sounds high and sweet and clear. The wet sophomore even laughs along with her.

"God, I hate that," says Lily.

"PMGO," Darbs adds.

"What?" says Lily.

"It's something I'm trying out," Darbs tells her.

I can't take my eyes off the sophomores. "Look how they suck up even while they're in the act of being demeaned."

"Gotta be a good sport about it," Itch says.

"Or it only gets worse," I say.

Oliver is down there, of course. He's watching Theo goose-step the smallest sophomore to a chair and plop him into it. When Theo waves him over, Oliver obliges, plunging his hand into the nearest bucket for a sponge.

"They don't even use warm water," says Darbs. "It's ice cold."

"In good news," says Itch, "it's hot today."

"Nothing about this is good news." I watch Theo hold out his hand to Oliver, who gives him a can of shaving cream. Theo assumes a widespread pose behind his victim. He shakes the can before his crotch in a suggestive manner.

"No," says Lily.

"Please don't," says Darbs.

Theo lets out a theatrical groan and squirts the shaving cream all over the sophomore's head. Beside me, Itch gags.

"That is so gross," I say. I am disgusted by the way everyone casually accepts this public humiliation. I want to run down there and snatch the can and punch Theo in the mouth, but I'm smart enough to know it wouldn't change a thing. It wouldn't save the sophomore and it wouldn't break the tradition. It would only embarrass us both.

So much for Oliver being different.

Oliver hands Theo some sort of shaving device so he can get to work on the hapless head. Theo starts over the ears, and—thank God for small favors—at least he's going slowly so as not to cut the sophomore. All the others appear to be just hacking away at the hair of their victims, but Theo seems to have some sort of plan.

"He's an artist," Itch says. "He's Picasso."

"He's *Dick*asso," I say.

"Salva*dork* Dali," says Lily.

"He's Leonardo da . . ." Darbs's voice trails off. "Damn. I had one and then I lost it."

There are hoots from the audience as Theo gets closer to the center of his guy's head. Lily and I realize what's happening at the same time.

"Ew!" Lily says while I make a disgusted noise.

Itch shakes his head. "You have got to be kidding."

"What? *What?*" Darbs scans the field below us.

Itch nudges her. "June had the best name."

"What—" Darbs stares at Theo's victim. She makes the connection. "Ohhhh . . ."

Theo did, in fact, have a plan. It is becoming horribly clear that he is in the process of shaving the silhouette of a penis and balls onto the unwitting sophomore's head.

That's it. I can't watch any more. I shove the second half of my sandwich back into its reusable wrapper, and I surge to my feet. "I'm going to the library."

I guess the sudden motion attracts Oliver's attention, because suddenly he's looking up at me from where he stands beside Theo. We're far enough away that his expression isn't clear, but I can tell he's definitely staring at me staring at him.

Surely my stance alone tells him how pissed I am.

I lean down to kiss Itch. "I can drive you home," he says.

"I'll let Mom know not to pick me up." I straighten and shoulder my backpack. Against my better judgment, I look at the field one last time.

Oliver has taken Theo's place behind the sophomore.

I'm going to leave. I want to leave. I need to leave.

And yet I don't.

I stay and watch as Oliver wields the razor above the sophomore's head. It's a show of strength. An act of assholery. The crowd goes wild, clapping and stomping as he flicks his hand first to one side, then the other. He's warming up. He's playing to his fans.

I feel sick.

Oliver sets the razor on the side of the sophomore's head, and he pulls it in a deliberate, straight line from front to back. I see the look on Theo's face as Oliver quickly switches sides and repeats the motion.

The corners of my mouth turn up of their own accord.

Oliver has rendered what was a silhouette of male genitalia into merely . . . a Mohawk. He castrated the original design.

He neutered Theo.

41

Theo's roar of indignation carries all the way up to us. My smile widens. Below, Oliver hands the razor back to Theo before giving the sophomore a high five.

The glance he flashes up at me could be a peace offering, like my gum, or it could be an apology.

Either way, I accept it.

Chapter 4

Itch is suffering through conversation with my mom. I could have told him to show up later, but he spent an entire summer in Florida not talking to his girlfriend's mom. Ten minutes of polite chatting now won't kill him.

"I bet your grandparents were thrilled to have you around," Mom tells him.

"Yeah."

"Do you help them in the yard or the house or . . . Do you cook?" Mom cocks her head at him like an inquisitive sparrow.

I answer for him. "He bakes. What were those things called, Itch? The little pastries?"

"*Kiflice.*" He glances at Mom. "They're basically Serbian croissants."

"That's so nice!" Mom exclaims. "Maybe we can exchange recipes . . . June, did you see where I put the paint samples?"

She jumps topics so fast it takes me a second to catch up and realize someone is knocking at the front door. "I think they're on the buffet."

"Cash is here," Mom says.

Itch looks at me and mouths the word: *"Cash?"*

"Her contractor," I say out loud.

"My *friend,*" Mom says, and then calls out, "Come in!"

A couple minutes later, Cash the contractor has greeted us, found the paint samples, and deposited Mom into the passenger seat of his old putty-colored pickup truck ("Made right here in Michigan!" Cash said when I first met him). Itch and I wave from the porch as they drive off in a cloud of road dust. The minute it dissipates, Itch pulls me in for a kiss.

I know some parents won't leave their kid alone in the house with a significant other because of STDs and teenage pregnancies and whatnot, but my mother has a different strategy. Her weapon of choice is conversation. She talks to me about sex every chance she gets.

Every. Chance.

Mom says I am in charge of my own body and what I do with it is my business. She gave me The Talk way earlier than any of my friends got it, and she also put a box of condoms in my nightstand before I'd even kissed a boy (other than Oliver in kindergarten). She believes it's better to have them early than too late. Turns out there is such a thing as *too* early, though, because by the time I needed those condoms toward the end of last year, they'd expired.

Luckily, Itch had some of his own.

All that being said, it's not like Mom lets me spend the night with Itch or anything. A few daylight hours in an empty house is about the most I can hope for. She's not a total hippie.

Itch and I drag two quilts and a pile of pillows onto the family room floor to fashion a fool-around nest for ourselves, and then he dorks around with the remote control until he finds a horror

44

movie. Both of us know we're not actually going to watch it, but this is how we've always prefaced our physical interactions: by first pretending we're going to do something less intimate.

"What do you think of the house?" I ask once the movie is playing on mute.

"It's cool. Way bigger than your last place."

"Yeah, I actually have my own bathroom here."

"But it sucks that it's so far away."

"Only twenty minutes from school."

"*Thirty* minutes from me," he says, and I am reminded that he wants me near, that my proximity is desirable. The way he wants me makes me feel worthy of being wanted. It makes me want him. I'm starting to tug him toward me when he says something else. "And now you have to drive with that douchebag every morning."

I have an errant flash of protectiveness, a desire to defend Oliver. After all, there was the Mohawk. "He's not that bad." Itch makes his snorting sound that means he's not buying something. "No, really. I don't think he's like all the other muscle heads. He's definitely smarter than I thought."

"Really." It's not a question the way Itch says it. "Because I haven't seen him around the AP classes."

"I haven't seen *you* around the AP classes." I kiss him on the neck so he knows it's a joke. He doesn't answer, because he's more interested in rolling on top of me and *not* watching the movie.

This is why teenagers get a bad rap.

Chapter 5

This time, it's Oliver who has an idea when I climb aboard. "We disagree about music, right?"

"Very much so."

"And also about what constitutes *meaning* in our high school life."

"Does Theo know you use big words when he's not around?" Oliver flicks a gum wrapper at me and I flinch backward with a squeal. "Really, what do you *see* in that dipshit?"

"We've been friends since middle school," Oliver tells me. "We have a history."

"Our country has a history of denying women's rights and smoking on airplanes and allowing cousins to marry. Doesn't mean we still adhere to those things."

"Are you going to behold my genius or what?" Oliver unlocks his phone and hands it over.

I take it with a show of trepidation and tap the screen to find that his music app is open. In the center of the screen is an icon with the title Sunrise Songs. "All I behold is a cheesy name."

"Open it."

I do, but it's empty, which doesn't make any sense. "Explanation, please."

"This is the solution to all our problems. This is the grand prize for the person who proves that their life philosophy is true."

"This is a playlist," I tell him.

"Exactly."

"Are you high?"

Oliver shakes his head. "Keeping my body pure for the football field."

"Please don't flex your muscles again."

But of course he does.

"It's our morning playlist," he says. "We'll listen to it on the drive to school."

"And yet there are no songs on this playlist," I tell him. "It's empty."

"That's the part where I'm a genius."

"That's the part I find most hard to believe."

"Listen," he says. "Learn."

"Lame," I say, but wait for him to explain.

"You think high school doesn't matter. I know that it does." Oliver pokes me lightly in the arm. "Anytime one of us can find a reason to support our side of that particular conversation—"

"Argument."

"Whatever. We get to add a song to this playlist. Then we can let it shuffle and repeat in the mornings. More wins for you means more of your screamy music on the list."

I'm skeptical. "But the argument—"

"Conversation."

"It's subjective. There's no definitive answer. I will naturally come up with brilliant ways to prove that I am right"—Oliver snorts—"but that doesn't necessarily mean you'll concur."

"We'll have a gentleman's agreement."

This time, I am the one who snorts. "You hang out with people who shave male *parts* onto people's heads. Nothing about you is gentlemanly."

He gives me a look of mock offense. "*Everything* about me is gentlemanly. But fine. We'll just find someone who can be objective."

"I nominate Itch," I say.

"Then I nominate Ainsley."

I sigh. "Obviously my answer is no."

"And obviously mine is the same."

I look down at his phone again. It's a fun idea; I'll give him that. It adds a little competition to our morning routine. I mull over the details. "I have some additional rules."

"Hit me."

"Don't tempt me." I hold up a finger. "Proofs may only be given on school premises and during school hours. First bell to last bell. I don't want you drunk-texting me in the middle of the night."

"What about football games?" Oliver asks. "School dances? Pep rallies?"

"Approved." It's an easy give, since I wouldn't be caught dead at any of those. "If we are both present at a school-sanctioned event, it can be considered legitimate grounds for offering a proof."

"I have one more rule to add," Oliver says. "One shot per day. I don't want to be overwhelmed by your screamo." I smile at him. "What?"

"You think I'm going to win."

"In your dreams, Rafferty."

• • •

I'm waiting outside the family sciences room when Oliver emerges. He looks surprised to see me. "What's up?"

"Oh, nothing," I tell him. "Except for this: college."

Oliver blinks. "College?"

"College. Classes are harder. Relationships are more important."

"That is subjective."

"Also, you can drink openly at a bar. My point is that everything happening now will just happen *again* in college but will be bigger and better. Don't you see? College itself nullifies the importance of high school. . . . What?"

Oliver is shaking his head. "Really? This is your opening shot?"

"It's legit!"

"It's weak."

I glare at him. "You said you were going to be a gentleman about this."

"We need a judge."

"An *impartial* judge," I remind him.

"I'll ask around. Please consider your first proof as remaining unconfirmed."

He heads down the hallway. "Not Theo!" I call after him, and he waves back at me over his shoulder.

• • •

Over lunch, Darbs regales us with a description of how Yana-the-new-girl is *definitely* vibing her. "It's her hair," she tells Itch and Lily and me.

I'm sure everyone else's look of confusion mirrors my own. I search my memory. "Blond, right?"

"*Honey* blond," Darbs says dreamily. "*Golden* blond. Long and straight but not *too* straight. A little tangled, like she's been at the beach, lying out in the sun . . ." Her voice trails off. Lily and I exchange glances. Darbs shakes out of her reverie. "Except get this: today she comes into English and she picks a new seat. There are plenty of open chairs—plenty—but she doesn't go to the one in the third row by the windows, where she's been every other day. No, she turns left and she walks past the bookshelves, and she sits directly in front of me."

"Is there any chance," Itch asks through a mouthful of pizza, "any chance at all that she simply wanted a different vantage point?" I elbow him in the ribs. "What? It's a legitimate question."

"You're a legitimate asshole," Darbs informs him. "She made a deliberate choice to be near me. I could tell."

We're all thinking the same thing, but I'm the one who says it. "How?"

"I'm glad you asked," says Darbs. "We didn't make eye contact—"

"Huh," says Itch.

"Shut up," Lily tells him. "Go on, Darbs."

"—but right after she sat down, she kind of moved her head

50

a little so her hair would swing around. You know, so she'd have my attention."

Darbs is definitely a little crazy, but she's also my friend. She deserves respect. "Then what?"

"She's got like five elastic bands around her wrist. She slides the purple one off . . ." Darbs gestures to her indigo head. "Purple."

"Hold on," Itch says. "If she's sitting in front of you and facing forward, how can you even see any of this?"

Darbs gives him a solemn look. "She's angled in her seat. Like just a little diagonally."

We all sit in silence for a moment, until Lily points something out: "You were tilted forward, weren't you? You craned."

"Fine." Darbs shrugs. "I craned, whatever. Anyway, she lifts her hands back to her hair, and she does it all slow and sexy-like. She pulls her hair up into a ponytail and guess what?" Darbs pauses theatrically.

"What?" This time, Lily and I both ask. Itch only shakes his head.

"Like four or maybe even five strands of her hair underneath are dyed."

"Purple?" I ask.

"Well . . . blue," says Darbs. "But *dark* blue. *Navy* blue. In the rainbow, it's next to purple." She sits back and folds her arms. "Totally vibing me."

"Totally vibing you," Lily and I agree.

"What the hell," says Itch.

I turn to admonish him, because that's just *rude,* but I see that he's not talking to us. He's looking at something.

It's Shaun, making his way up the bleachers toward us, which would be totally normal, except that Oliver is following him.

Holding a tray.

For no reason whatsoever, light heat prickles up my neck and into my cheeks. I duck my head and take a bite of my sandwich to camouflage my (ridiculous) reaction.

Even the losers on the first row are watching with curiosity as Shaun and Oliver plop down with us. Shaun gives a general wave to the whole group, but Oliver greets everyone individually by name, except for Darbs. He juts out a hand to her. "I'm Oliver. I don't think we've ever actually spoken."

Darbs doesn't take his hand. "I know who you are."

Oliver lowers his arm. The moment stretches into a standoff, both of them unmoving, staring straight at each other. I catch myself wondering if Darbs is noticing the gray part of his eyes also.

She points to her head. "How do you like my hair?"

He looks her over. "Cool. Last year was green, right?"

"Turquoise." Darbs holds out a bag. "Chips?"

"Thanks." Oliver takes one and the moment is over.

Shaun clears his throat. "Everyone done peeing on the bleachers?"

"I am," says Darbs.

"Me too," says Oliver.

"I don't have to pee," says Lily.

Itch and I don't say anything.

Shaun gestures at me. "Oliver asked me to settle a bet between him and June."

I feel two things: Itch's stare and my cheeks blazing up again.

"June," says Oliver, "will you accept Shaun as our impartial judge?"

"It's just a game," I say. "And sure. Shaun is fine."

Shaun reminds everyone of our morning carpool arrangement. Lily shakes her head. "No, really. What do you *talk* about?"

"They don't," says Shaun. "That's why there's a game." He turns to me. "When are you going to get your license, anyway?"

I'm unprepared to answer that question, so I say the first thing that comes to my mind. "I'll get to it."

"When?" asks Itch.

"When I'm ready," I tell him, irritated. "It's not like I even own a car."

"You worked at the nature center all summer," Lily says. "You've got to have some cash."

"She spent it on hookers," says Oliver.

"And blow," I agree.

Lily and Darbs and Shaun all laugh. Itch doesn't. "You should get on that," he says.

"Eh." Oliver shrugs. "It's just a license."

Shaun claps his hands really loudly and we all quiet down to pay attention. He explains the game and I lay out my first proof, just like I did this morning by the family sciences room.

Shaun mulls. He considers. He strokes his chin and says "hmmm" until I kick him in the shin. "Ow!"

"Come *on*. Lunch is almost over."

Shaun takes a deep breath. "Okay, I have completed my deliberations."

"Tell us, O Masterful One," says Lily.

"Seriously?" I ask her.

"Sorry." She grins at me. "This is hilarious, you know."

Shaun clears his throat. "It should be recognized that all decisions of the judge are final. No additional discourse shall be allowed once a verdict has been rendered."

"Agreed," says Oliver.

"Agreed," I say.

"In the case of June Rafferty versus Oliver Flagg, I hereby pronounce in favor of . . ." We all wait while Shaun does some additional throat clearing and head bobbing. "Oliver Flagg."

"What?" The word squawks from my mouth. "You're supposed to be *my* friend!"

"I have been retained as an impartial judge," Shaun reminds me. "And in this venerable magistrate's opinion, it's just crazy-pants to think that something repeating in the future negates what's happening in the present. Tomorrow, I'm going to have lunch. That doesn't mean I didn't have lunch today."

"He's got a point," says Lily.

I know she's right but it's super irritating. Still, I try to defend myself.

"But tomorrow's lunch might be better than today's," I tell Shaun. "I could have more money. I'll be able to afford better ingredients."

"Or you might not," he says. "You might be back in the cafeteria eating wilted salads and dry spaghetti."

"I won't."

"But you *might.* And in other news," Shaun continues, "I believe Oliver has a proof of his own to share."

My eyes narrow. I whip my head around to glare at Oliver. "Really."

"Why, yes. And I have you to thank for it." Oliver gives me the sweetest of smiles. "What you said about college really hit me. You're right, you know. All that cool stuff *will* happen in college. However"—he leans in close—"you know what determines what college you get into?"

My shoulders slump and I know I've been defeated. "High school."

Oliver doesn't say anything. He just raises both hands in the air and starts snapping his fingers and moving his shoulders in time to an imaginary beat.

"You have no rhythm," I tell him.

"He's not so bad," says Lily, starting to snap along. Darbs grins and joins in. Shaun, too.

"This is the worst," I inform everyone as, in the distance, the bell rings.

Oliver rises, still snapping. "Foreigner," he says as he jumps one bleacher down from where we are. "Poison." He jumps down another. "Warrant."

"What are you doing?" I ask, exasperated.

"Torturing you," Itch tells me. "Those are the names of crappy bands."

Below, Oliver takes several leaps in a row, calling out more inscrutable words with each one. "Whitesnake! Starship! Night Ranger!" He reaches the bottom and turns to face me. "Bad English!" he yells before taking off toward the school.

I shake my head and turn to Itch. "I hate my life."

"You should," he says.

Chapter 6

When I step out onto my wooden porch, the behemoth is already parked in my driveway, with Oliver standing beside it. He sees me and immediately opens the passenger door with great ceremony. "Your chariot awaits," he calls. "Your sweet, sweet musical chariot."

I plod toward him, trying not to smile at the ridiculousness of it all. "Stop it," I say as he takes a deep bow, gesturing toward my seat.

I swing my backpack into the car and am about to scramble aboard like I always do, when I feel Oliver's hand on my elbow. It's warm and it makes my skin even warmer where it's touching me. I know we must have touched before—besides that kiss in kindergarten—because surely we have collided in the halls or brushed past each other in the cafeteria.

Yet this feels like the first time.

We're waiting at the Plymouth stop sign when Oliver turns to me with a giant smile.

"This is the moment, isn't it?" I ask him.

"Oh yes," he says. "This is the moment."

And then music—if you can call it that—blasts from his speakers. I am not exaggerating when I say that it is the worst, most egregiously sappy, power-chorded, ridiculously overly romantic rock ballad that has ever had the painful misfortune to grace the earth. That would be bad enough, but as I immediately discover, Oliver knows the lyrics.

All of them.

And he sings along.

With feeling.

When the song finally comes to the bridge—which is a marginal improvement due to the lack of drippy words—I yell at Oliver over the electric guitar chords. "Any part of me that has managed to achieve sophistication, any little shred of my being that has understood something greater and somehow risen above the huddled masses . . ."

"Yeah?" Oliver yells back at me.

"Right this minute, that shining piece of me is being slowly throttled by this unrelenting stream of sentimentality!"

Oliver holds up a finger. "Wait for it!"

"For what?"

The guitar solo builds to a melodramatic crescendo. "For this!" he shouts . . . and then he's back into the chorus, waving one arm around and making wide-eyed faces at me anytime we're stopped.

The song—annoyingly named "When It Matters"—plays a total of six and a half times before we arrive at school.

Oliver doesn't miss a word.

• • •

I know I have to wait for the first bell to ring before I can nail Oliver with a proof, but even though we walk onto campus together,

I lose track of him before homeroom . . . or maybe he loses track of me. I look for him afterward, and then again before second period, but he's as elusive as Itch when my mom is around.

However, it's impossible to hide forever when we share a physics class.

Oliver again charges in right as the bell is ringing. I make a swipe for his arm as he blows past my desk, but he doesn't even glance at me.

Oh. Hell. No.

I turn around in my seat and wait while he plops down and pulls out his materials. When he looks up and finds me watching him, he cringes. I smile and hold up a folded piece of paper. He can't avoid me forever.

Minutes later, Mrs. Nelson is explaining the principles of thermodynamics and my note is stealthily wending its way back across the classroom—being passed from person to person—toward Oliver Flagg.

> Dear Oliver,
> 1. My parents met in college.
> 2. Your parents met in college.
> Sincerely,
> June

It's simple. Easy. I assume that all four of our parents had high school relationships with other people—even if they were merely crushes or flirtations—and all four eventually moved on from them. Yes, I guess you can say it's an *example* more than a *proof*, but for the purposes of our little game, it should work.

Anything to cut down on the number of times I have to hear that dreadful "When It Matters" song.

I anticipate Oliver's arguing the validity, since my parents ended up divorcing, but I plan to come back with the fact that they stayed together long enough to procreate, and that's one of the most life-altering, meaningful things that two people can do together.

It's close to the end of class and Mrs. Nelson is jotting a stream of symbols across the whiteboard when a familiar folded paper wings onto my table.

Dear Oliver,
1. My parents met in college.
2. *Your* parents met in college.
Sincerely,
+1 song — June

Approved

Dear June—
1. Your handwriting is creepily perfect. Like a serial killer's.
2. My uncle Matthew met his wife, Ellie, in high school. Our neighbors Anna and Brian did, too. Some people *do* meet their soul mate young, and you can't discount that.
Even more sincerely,
Oliver

Huh.

I guess there's no refuting that. The second part, that is.

Since Oliver is being fair about it and not calling in Shaun for something that obviously needs no judgment, I pick up my pencil and write a response (in my creepily perfect penmanship).

Dear Oliver,
1. My parents met in college.
2. <u>Your</u> parents met in college.
                    Sincerely,
        +1 song ← June

Approv

Dear June—
1. Your handwriting is creepily perfect. Like a serial killer's. Jerk!!
2. My uncle Matthew met his wife, Ellie, in high school. Our neighbors Anna and Brian did, too. Some people <u>do</u> meet their soul mate young, and you can't discount that.
                    Even more sincerely,
        +1 song ← Oliver

When the bell rings, I turn around to see if Oliver fully appreciates my last comments, but he's already heading for the door. Ainsley, however, is staring straight at me. For no reason that carries even a semblance of sense, I have a sudden flash of guilt, like I'm doing something wrong.

But I'm not.

• • •

Lily is meeting with her private music instructor, and Darbs is stalking Yana-the-new-girl, and Shaun is in the yearbook room, so Itch and I are enjoying a rare solo lunch. And by "lunch," I mean "make-out session."

Itch sits with his feet on the next bleacher down, and I am half reclined across his lap so all he has to do is tilt a little to reach my face. It's too warm and humid to be messing around on the metal bleachers, but we're doing it anyway. Itch's legs are sticky hot under my back, and I can feel my black-Converse-clad feet baking in the sun, but the whole thing is familiar and public and easy. Kind of like our relationship. I have a flash of remorse as I remember the boy I kissed over the summer, but I hastily pack it away. Itch didn't ask, so I didn't tell. It's not like I'm lying.

I hear clacks and feel vibrations beneath me. Itch removes his mouth from mine and a sigh of disgust puffs out of him. "Is this going to become a regular thing?"

I push off him and sit up. The clacks are the sound of high heels ascending the bleachers, and the person wearing them is Ainsley Powell. She's clearly headed toward us, because there's no one else anywhere near, plus her brilliantly green eyes are locked right on us.

"I'm out," says Itch. He starts to stand, but I lock on to his wrist and pull him down.

"Don't be rude," I hiss.

Itch settles back as Ainsley arrives on our row. "Hey, guys," she says in a voice that is somehow made for both shouting cheers over packed stadiums and whispering poetry into the ears of worshipful boys.

I tense up. Is she here to start something with me? I'm pretty sure she could take me physically—she's taller and probably stronger from cheerleading—but she *is* wearing those heels. Maybe I can catch her off balance. "What's up, Ainsley?" I ask like it's no big deal.

She gestures to the row in front of us. "May I?"

"Of course," I say graciously.

"It's a free country," Itch says, and I elbow him.

Ainsley lowers herself to a graceful sitting position like she's a peacock feather drifting to the ground. "Are you going to the first game?"

"The *football* game?" It comes out of my mouth in a tone of incredulity. Is she trying to figure out where to deploy her band of evil pom-pommed henchwomen to kick my ass? Or is she warning me away, staking her claim to anything sports-related . . . anything that involves Oliver?

Itch speaks for me. "We don't do tournaments of brutality."

Ainsley turns her dark-lashed gaze on him. "High school *is* a tournament of brutality."

Itch looks surprised at her comeback. "I'll give you that."

Ainsley taps me on the knee. "You should go."

"Why?"

"It's the first game of the season. We're trying to have a big crowd to show support for the team."

I somehow think there's a little more to this invitation than school spirit, but for the life of me, I can't figure out her angle. "Maybe," I tell her.

"There's a bonfire after," Ainsley says. "You guys can catch a ride with us."

"*Us?*" Itch repeats.

"Oliver and me."

"Like a double date?" I ask, and watch Ainsley's smile grow even wider.

"Exactly like that."

• • •

I guess Itch and I had to have our first fight sometime. I just didn't think it would happen in the middle of a Rite Aid.

I'm standing with my hands on my hips, watching him browse a rack of corn chips. "It wouldn't kill you," I tell him. "It wouldn't actually make your heart stop beating and your blood stop pumping."

"It might. You don't know."

"One game. One party."

Itch laughs and the sound comes out brittle, like it would break if it hit the ground. "That's how it starts," he tells me. "A game, a party, a bunch of booze. Then suddenly you're part of their crap and doing their bidding."

"No one's talking about doing anyone's bidding! It's football, not slavery."

"Keep telling yourself that." Itch swipes a bright orange bag off the shelf. "There's a reason we're not joiners, June. It's not because we're geeks and it's not because we buy into some sort of outdated hierarchy of popularity."

"I never said—"

"It's because we're better than it." Itch walks over and slings an arm around my shoulders, which are tensed up higher than they should be. "*You're* better."

He kisses me and I let him.

I always let him.

Chapter 7

The sun has barely risen and already there are two guys install-
ing a storage bench in the entryway. I nod at them as I go by
on my way to the kitchen, skirting a pile of boards and tools on
the floor.

I find Mom and Cash perched on stools, sipping coffee.
Cash stands when I walk in. "Sorry about the noise and the
mess."

"It's cool," I tell him. "The banisters look great."

"Thanks." He nods at Mom. "See you tonight?"

"Yes!" She says it a little too loudly and glances at me.
"Omelet?"

Uh-*huh*.

I nod and watch her start to pull out ingredients. "How long
until the house is done?" I ask.

"The entryway will be finished this week. Next is my studio.
Cash is going to redo the drywall and put in new flooring. We're
also . . . Sorry it's still crazy, honey. Sometimes things get messy
before they get good."

"You're so deep," I tell her, and she laughs. I realize that
Mom doesn't look messy at all. In fact, she's wearing coral lip

gloss and hoop earrings, so I ask the obvious question. "Mom, are you dating Cash?"

Mom flushes. "No!" I raise an eyebrow and she sets down her spatula. "We're friends."

"Friends," I say.

"And in the spirit of *friendship,* he's coming over tonight for dinner."

This time, I say it out loud: "Uh-*huh.*"

"Settle down," she tells me. But she flushes again, and this time her eyes sparkle, too.

• • •

School let out three hours ago, and I'm still in the main lobby. I've already organized my locker and done my English reading for the weekend. Now I'm sitting on the bottom step, braiding strands of my hair. And waiting.

When my phone vibrates—*finally!*—I check the text from Mom:

> at least 45 more mins
> sorry
> mtg still going
> dept chair droning on about budget
> wish you were old enuf to buy wine
> luv u

Damn.

If I'd known in advance, I could have asked Itch for a ride and lured him with the promise of an empty house. Or maybe

Shaun would have driven me. Or Lily or Darbs. Or *anyone*. If it at least was Monday, it wouldn't be so bad, but on a Friday? By the end of the week, I'm ready to get out of here.

I wonder if there's a chance Shaun hasn't left yet. He's not answering his texts, but it's a very Shaun-like thing to not check his texts. He keeps his phone on silent all the time, even when not in class.

I head out into the student parking lot. There are quite a few cars still here, but I don't see Shaun's. I trudge across to see if I'm missing any on the other side—maybe hidden behind a gas-guzzling behemoth like Oliver's, over there in the center, where he always parks and . . .

Oliver! That's a new idea. I didn't even think about checking with him. It didn't occur to me that I could ask him for a ride *home*. Oliver isn't a guy who leaves when the bell rings. He's always hanging around after school because of all the throwing and kicking and dribbling. I head toward the gas-guzzling behemoth, pulling out my phone to send him a text, and run straight into him.

Oliver catches me by the arms. "Hey, texting and walking. Not safe."

"I was texting *you*," I inform him.

"Really?" His eyes dance over me, and I suddenly remember I have these crazy little braids all over my head.

"Are you going home?" I ask.

"Yep. Need a ride?"

"Yes, please."

He gestures toward the car, and a minute later, I'm in the passenger seat, trying unsuccessfully to smooth out my hair, which has flown into a frenzy of static electricity. "Why are you still here, anyway?"

"I had to talk to Coach Rand after practice."

I assess him. Oliver isn't carrying himself in his usual jaunty, confident way. He's drooping a little and looks forlorn, sitting behind the wheel. "You okay?"

"Yeah." But I keep watching him and he doesn't *look* okay. In fact, now that I think about it, he seemed subdued this morning, too. He realizes I'm looking at him. "Coach is pissed because I'm missing two practices next week."

"You're not allowed to miss *ever*?" It seems extreme.

"Not really. And definitely not at the beginning of the season. We're supposed to be focused."

"But it's just a game." The minute it comes out of my mouth, I wish I hadn't said it.

"You sound like my dad."

We drive in silence for a few minutes before I ask the question. "Why do you have to skip practices?"

"Oh, you'll love this," he says. "I'm hanging out at a bank with my uncle Alex. He's supposed to teach me the joy of finances."

"That's *terrible.*" Again, I immediately wish I hadn't said it, but this time, Oliver laughs.

"Thank you. It *is* terrible." His smile drops away. "My parents aren't even coming to the game on Friday. Dad has a dinner with the partners."

"What about your mom?"

"She doesn't miss Dad's work dinners. They're a team."

I try to come up with something reassuring to say. "Next

year, you won't ever have to miss a practice if you don't want to."

Oliver shoots me a look. "No offense, but you really don't know anything about football." We come to a four-way stop and he trains his eyes on mine. "I'm high school good, June. I'm not college good."

I make a *pfft* sound. "Please. I'm sure you can handle a ball." I flush at my own unfortunate choice of words and hurry to cover. "A *foot*ball."

Oliver smiles, but the smile is sad. "It's cool. I'm not like you. Some people peak early."

I stare at him, not sure how to respond. It's the most openly painful thing I've heard him say, and it seems like I should say something open and honest in return.

But I'm not that brave.

A horn honks behind us and we both jump in our seats. "Oops," says Oliver, and he steps on the gas.

The rest of our drive is silent. Oliver doesn't start our playlist and I don't ask him to. When we crunch over the gravel into my driveway, Cash's truck is parked ahead of us and Cash himself is just trotting down the front steps. He waves an arm and I assume he's saying hello, but then he does it again and I realize he wants us to come over. "Who's that?" Oliver asks.

"My mom's contractor and not-boyfriend."

I introduce Cash and Oliver to each other, and Cash asks if Oliver can give him a hand with something. "I thought my guys would still be here, but they already took off for the weekend." He jerks a thumb toward his truck. "It takes two people to unload a generator."

"At least," Oliver agrees, and follows him toward his truck, stripping off his jacket.

I recognize that in this scenario my role is to watch for loose gravel in their path and hold the front door open, but with that recognition comes realization: Oliver is going to get a firsthand sighting of my house's messy, unfinished interior.

"Maybe you can just leave it on the porch," I say.

"Nah, we'll bring it in." Cash climbs into the truck bed. He slides a big box to the edge before hopping out and bracing himself alongside Oliver. "Ready?"

"Ready," says Oliver, and they lift.

I scamper to the porch and swing the door open, watching them move toward me. Even though I know it's cliché, even though I know it's superficial and ridiculous, my eyes are magnetically drawn to Oliver's arms. It's not that I'm one of those girls who's swoony-la-la-la about muscles, but when the muscles are doing all kinds of bulgy, strainy things against a tight shirt, one can't help but notice.

I'm cerebral. Not dead.

Cash and Oliver edge past me into the house, occasionally grunting and saying things like "watch it" and "almost there." I'm hoping they'll set it down in the entryway and get out, but Cash wants it in Mom's studio, so of course they have to go all the way through, walking past a stack of wall sconces and avoiding various tools scattered around.

"I'll tell my boys to clean up their mess better when they vacate the premises," says Cash, and I am re-horrified by the fact that he is talking about the mess in *my* house, *my* premises, and Oliver is right here to witness all the grimy glory of my life.

After all, this is a boy who lives in one of the pristine mansions at Flaggstone Lakes, who has two parents sleeping in the same bed every night.

My mom, on the other hand, trades paintings for vegetables and pottery for woodworking. Dad is an actor-slash-waiter in New York. I'm a senior who doesn't know how to drive, and we live in a house that is currently one giant art project. It's not exactly a bastion of normality and I'm not exactly thrilled to have Oliver in the middle of it.

Yet in the middle of it is exactly where Oliver is. Once he and Cash have the generator settled in the built-in unit where it's going to live, he's back in the entryway, looking around. All I can see is the mess, and all I can smell are wood shavings, so I give Oliver my brightest smile. "Thanks so much!" I chirp in my best imitation of Ainsley. "Have a great weekend!"

I sweep the front door open, but Oliver doesn't walk through it. In fact, I'm not sure he even hears me. He's running his hand over the storage bench, touching the heavy iron hooks installed above it to hold our bags and purses. "Did you make this?" he asks Cash.

"Yeah. It's nice, right?"

"Gorgeous. Is that antique beadboard?"

"Antique" is a nicer thing to say than "old" or "crap someone else threw out."

"Salvaged it from a place we were demoing down in Clinton."

"Salvaged." Try "trash-picked."

"Awesome," says Oliver.

"Thanks," says Cash, clearly pleased. I, however, am the opposite of pleased, especially when Cash points toward the opening leading to the rest of the house. "Want to see what we did with the banisters?"

"I'm sure Oliver has to go home." I say it hastily, but again I'm too late, because Oliver is already following Cash around the corner.

Crap.

By the time Mom gets home half an hour later, Cash and Oliver have embarked on a bromance that runs deep and hard and true and is based entirely on their shared appreciation of home renovation. They have argued the visual merits of stone penny tile versus ceramic. They've waxed poetic about cabinetry and crown molding. They've done everything except choose baby names together, and I'm no longer certain either one is even aware of my presence.

Which is maybe a good thing, because when I catch a glimpse of myself in the hall mirror, I appear to be wearing a fright wig. Neither Cash nor Oliver notices when I run upstairs to yank my hair into a ponytail and change into a clingy gray sweater with blue cuffs. Might as well look decent if we're going to have visitors at the house.

Mom is delighted to see Oliver. She tells him he's gotten so tall—which he seems to enjoy—and also reminds him that she used to change his diapers, which I definitely do *not* enjoy. The entire thing is super weird, and it only gets weirder when I'm trying to subtly urge Oliver toward the front door and he stops to browse a row of Mom's books lined up in the family room. "Sandburg," he says. "Neruda. Rilke. Your mom has good taste."

I gawk at him. "You know poetry?"

He places a hand over his heart. "At their core, my power ballads are poetry."

"At their core, your power ballads are schlock."

"You have no soul," he says lightly. "I happen to be an admirer of the well-placed word."

"I happen to have several words I'm considering placing," I tell him.

Oliver laughs, and I suddenly realize how much I like the sound of his laugh. "I'm going to say good-bye to your mom and her not-boyfriend."

I trail him into the kitchen, where Cash is opening a bottle of wine and Mom is chopping arugula. They smile when we enter. I hope Oliver is going to do the polite nice-to-meet-you thing and make a fast getaway, but instead, he freezes, pointing to something on the counter. "Is that what I think it is?"

I peer around him to see that it is—*fantastic*—a dirty hunk of old mushroom. This day couldn't be more humiliating.

Except that yes . . . yes it could, because Cash lifts the mushroom and holds it toward Oliver. "Want to smell?" To my vast horror, Oliver obligingly ambles right over to *sniff* the object held between the fingers of my mom's not-boyfriend.

Oh.

God.

I open my mouth to protest or to apologize or maybe to start opera singing, because that might at least distract everyone from the fungal horror show before us, but then Oliver looks at me with a face of pure delight. "June, you have to smell this truffle."

Truffle.

I know it's something culinary and fancy, but that's about all

I know. I'm pretty sure I've never tasted (or smelled) one before. Since everyone is waiting for me to do something, I walk over and take a whiff. The scent is earthy and rich and not altogether unpleasant. "Nice," I say, even though everything about this is decidedly the opposite of nice.

"Abruzzo's gave it to me," Cash tells us.

"The restaurant?" Oliver asks.

"Yep. I built them a new hostess stand and fixed their outer deck."

Suddenly, it's all making sense. Cash lives the same bartering lifestyle as my mom. Oliver must think we are absolute *gypsies.*

"That is the coolest thing ever," he says, and I try not to imagine how he's going to relay this whole experience later to Ainsley or Theo. "You guys are so . . ."

Bizarre.

Bohemian.

Weird.

". . . authentic," Oliver concludes. "I love it."

He sounds like he means it.

Cash glances at my mom and they have some sort of unspoken conversation through their eyebrows, because then he's inviting Oliver for dinner.

"It's risotto," my mother chimes in.

"With shaved truffle," adds Cash.

"I'd love to," Oliver says.

I look back and forth between them all. Apparently I'm the only one who's freaking out.

• • •

Against all odds, dinner is a huge success. The truffle risotto is to die for, and so is the apple-rhubarb pie we have for dessert (baked, of course, by Mom's friend Quinny after some complicated trade involving Mom, Quinny, and their friend Morgan). Oliver and I talk about our SATs and where we might go to college (me: maybe New York; him: no idea) and Mom explains to Cash that she and Oliver's mother were roommates a long time ago. I tell them about my volunteer work with the nature center, and Mom shares funny stories about the lengths some of her students will go to try to get out of their assignments. It's all very easy, and I can't help contrasting how the evening would have gone if our guest had been Itch instead of Oliver.

If Itch had been here, we would have taken plates into the family room. We would have eaten dinner in silence while watching a movie. After, we would have made an excuse to go up to my room or for a drive so that we could be alone. Then, when we were alone, we still wouldn't talk.

After dessert, Mom and Cash go upstairs to discuss the trim in the guest bedroom. The minute they're gone, Oliver waggles his eyebrows at me. "Discuss the trim, my ass," he says, and I whap him. "You know he wants to drop the 'not' from his 'not-boyfriend' status, right?"

"Yeah. That's what it looks like."

"Is that cool with you?" Oliver asks as I walk him to the entryway.

"What do you mean?"

"Your mom dating someone. Are you okay with that?"

I suppose it makes sense that he's curious. Oliver's parents have been together since forever, since college, since some

wild party where both of our moms flirted with Oliver's dad—
Bryant—and he ended up asking for the future Mrs. Flagg's
phone number. The way Mom tells the story, there was no fighting it. Marley and Bryant belonged together. They made sense
together.

"What about you and Dad?" I asked Mom once.

"He came later," she said. "And the only thing that ever
made sense between us was you."

"I'm fine with it," I tell Oliver, watching him push his long
arms through the sleeves of his coat.

"Good," he says, "because I think they're a thing."

Part of me is startled that he would check in with me. "You
know you just asked about my feelings."

"Friends do that," he says. "See you Monday."

Friends?

• • •

On Monday, I hop into my seat, slam the passenger door, and
immediately turn to Oliver. "Are we friends?"

He stares at me. "Where is this coming from?"

It's coming from him buddying up to my mom and her not-
boyfriend. It's coming from him acting like he gives a crap about
me. It's coming from me giving a crap back.

"Answer the question."

"Ye-e-e-e-s." His expression falls somewhere between
amusement and confusion. "We're friends."

"Cool." I fasten my seat belt.

Oliver shakes his head and pulls out of my driveway.
"You're weird."

"Here's the thing. I don't have straight, popular"—I pause, editing the word "hot" from my litany—"jock dude friends. I don't care about high school traditions and I don't hang with cheerleaders, and now my senior year is really different from how I thought it would be, especially the part where you and I . . ."

"Are friends."

"Right. That." I tuck a leg underneath me to get comfortable on the big seat. "As it turns out, you're reasonable to hang out with. You're nice to my mom. Your girlfriend even seems okay."

"Sounds like friendship."

"You're kind of like an extra gay boyfriend, except you're straight."

Oliver frowns. "Or I can be your straight guy friend . . . since that's what I actually am."

"It's just that it so rarely works."

"Why?"

"Because it's almost never even. Someone always wants to make out with someone else. The only way it really happens is if one of the two people is shockingly unattractive, which means that the shockingly unattractive one is attracted to the attractive one, but the attractive one is so far beyond the shockingly unattractive one's league that everyone knows it'll never go there." I suddenly realize the implication of what I've just said. Luckily, Oliver saves me.

"You, June Rafferty, are in zero danger of being shockingly unattractive."

He says it in an offhanded way, but it stops me in my tracks. And then, because I don't know what else to do, I return the compliment. "Back at you," I tell him in what must be the world's most obvious statement ever.

"So we're outliers?"

"Yes, we're outliers," I say. "And here's the thing—"

"I thought you already said the thing."

I mock glare at him. "Here's *another* thing. I can objectively ascertain that you're an attractive dude and . . ." As if on auto-pilot, Oliver preens and flexes his muscles. "Don't do that."

"Sorry."

"Your hair and your eyes and the muscles and everything. I mean, I get it. I get the Oliver Flagg thing."

Oliver looks surprised. "There's an Oliver Flagg *thing*?"

"Hush. I'm on a roll here. So you're attractive and we can both admit that, but since I am not personally attracted to you, it makes this friendship thing between us something that is man-ageable. More than manageable. It's *desirable,* because you can fulfill a role that no one else in my life does. You can give me the straight male honest take on things." Oliver waits until I flutter my fingers at him. "Okay, now it's your turn."

He makes a very solemn face. "You should know that there is one thing I will not do and one place I cannot go."

"What?" I'm a little worried about what he might say.

"If you ever—and I mean *ever*—ask me if you look fat in a particular article of clothing, it's a deal breaker."

I laugh and he smiles along with me. "Agreed. I promise to never ask you that. We need to draw the line somewhere."

"How about this," says Oliver. "How about we draw the boundary at truth in general. If you have a stupid fight with Itch or if you spill pizza on your shirt or get spinach stuck in your teeth or have toilet paper stuck to your shoe, I will absolutely tell you."

"How come I'm such a hot mess in this scenario?"

He holds up a finger. "Still my turn."

"Sorry."

"If I ever edge too far into douchey locker room territory, you will tell me."

"You mean if you act like Theo?"

Oliver smiles. "Yeah. If I act like Theo."

"All honesty, all the time. I like it." I thrust a hand toward him. "Let's shake on it. I mean, when we come to a safe stop at an intersection, of course."

Oliver shakes his head. "Too corporate. Let's fist-bump."

"Hitting awfully close to locker room territory already," I tell him, but I hold out a fist and he gives it a gentle tap with his own.

"Friends with honesty," he says.

"Friends with honesty," I answer, wondering how our social circles are going to react to this strange new arrangement.

He slides me a sideways glance. "Tell me more about this Oliver Flagg *thing.*"

"Shut up."

But as we head into the parking lot, I realize there's a thought jostling to move to the top of my brain—a thought that I keep trying to flick back into the subconscious shadows. When I pull my jacket tighter and exit the car, I have to acknowledge it, because it's right *there,* trying to escape to the surface.

It's a piece of the conversation we just had. A piece that keeps repeating over and over in the playlist of my mind.

It's the part when Oliver told me in no uncertain terms that he does not, in fact, find me shockingly unattractive.

I know, I know.

High praise, indeed.

• • •

"Frankly, I'm shocked," Shaun tells me as we push our way through the main lobby.

"Stop it. It's not *that* shocking."

"'Inane,' you've called them." He holds open one of the doors for me to walk through. "'Ludicrous.' 'Gratuitous.'"

"All right, all right. So I haven't always been awash in compliments. Cut me some slack."

"'A parade of hormonal insecurity swathed in violence and unnecessary ceremony.'" Shaun says it with air quotes and all.

"A girl's allowed to change her mind," I tell him. "Especially about something as insubstantial as football. Will you be my date on Friday?"

Shaun makes a big show of considering it, but of course he says yes. "Only because Kirk's not around."

"How's that going, anyway?" We round the corner of the school and head toward the parking lot. "Have you talked to him?"

"Only every day," Shaun says. "I don't screw around when I'm in love."

After that, I go quiet.

Chapter 8

I have a new tactic to allay the agony of Oliver's horrendous music: conversation. I've discovered that if we talk on the way to school, he turns the music down low, so I can barely hear the atrocity (two songs to my one that is currently on the playlist).

"You're actually nervous?" I ask in response to his comment. "I thought you people lived for Friday nights."

"We *people* do," he says, emphasizing to let me know what he thinks of my painting all athletes with the same brush.

But let's be honest: the brush fits.

"It's still a lot of pressure," Oliver explains. "If you fumble or something, there are literally hundreds of people watching."

"Yeah, but if you score a home run—"

"Touchdown."

"—then everyone cheers."

"That part isn't so bad." Oliver changes topic. "Do you know our moms are going out tomorrow?"

"Yeah. There's a new restaurant they want to try."

"Do you think they talk about us?"

That makes me laugh. "God, what else would they *have* to talk about?"

"Well, I'm sure your mother is a font of fascinating debate. My mom on the other hand . . . I don't know. Meat loaf recipes? The original Kinkade my dad bought her?"

"Your dad bought her a mixer?"

"That's a *Kitchen*Aid. Kinkade is an artist."

"Oh." It's a little embarrassing. After all, my mother is an artist, too. I should know these things. Also, Oliver has this big smile on his face because he's oh so amused at my lack of knowledge about the Fancy Ways of life.

Oliver sees my look. He reaches over and pats my leg. "Don't worry. You're cooler for *not* knowing Kinkade. Strip malls carry his work in bulk. Your mom's art is authentic. No mass productions, no marketing campaigns. I like her stuff."

"What do you know about my mom's work?"

"You do realize we've known each other since birth, right?"

"I guess. I just . . ." I stop and think about it. I suppose I do know quite a bit about Oliver's family. His mom, Marley, is my mom's best friend. His father, Bryant, is a developer of many gated communities, including fancy-schmancy Flaggstone Lakes, where they all live. His older brother, Owen, is now in college in North Carolina.

"What?" Oliver asks.

"I'm surprised you like my mom's art," I tell him. "Especially given your terrible taste in music."

• • •

Shaun wends his hatchback through throngs of students wielding giant foam fingers and parents carrying hand-painted signs. We find a parking space and he turns to me with a face that is all kinds of serious. "You love me, right?"

"Definitely."

"Here's the thing. I'm different at football games than I am with you and Darbs and Lily."

"I know, I know. You're a rainbow."

"*Such* a rainbow." Shaun pulls off his hat to reveal a giant mop of red-and-blue hair.

I gawk at him. It's supremely hideous. "Please tell me that's a wig."

"It's a wig. Isn't it fantastic?"

It takes me a second to find the words. "It definitely shows school spirit."

"Exactly," says Shaun. "On Friday nights, I have school spirit."

I look down at my own outfit: black tunic over leggings, high-top Chucks. Decidedly not spirited. "I can live with that."

At the gate, a twenty-something security guard rifles through my messenger bag. "What are you looking for?" I ask him.

"Drugs. Booze."

"I don't have either of those."

"Cool." He waves me through.

Shaun and I have to walk along the track to get to the bleachers. It's much louder and more crowded than I ever would have guessed. The marching band is already in their section, playing what I assume is a fight song. Ainsley and the other cheerleaders are out in front, waving and kicking and bouncing. We thread our way through packs of young kids eating hot dogs and parents carrying vinyl seat cushions and students vibrating with pep and anticipation. Everything smells like popcorn.

I let Shaun lead me to a seat in the center of the bleachers. "Wow, so this is what the world looks like from here," I say to him, and he elbows me in the ribs.

"Okay, turn to me," he orders. I do and his eyes rove over my face for several seconds. He looks very intent. "I'm seeing hearts."

"What?" If Shaun is turning straight or something, we are going to have to retool how our friendship works.

"I'm seeing balloons. I'm seeing a delicate bird stretching its wings to leap from a nest."

"I'm seeing a crazy person. What are you talking about?"

"The work of art that I'm going to paint on your face." Shaun whips out a pack of fat, oily crayons. "You're here, so *be* here already."

I open my mouth to say no—or more likely, *hell* no—but then I pause. Something about the trumpets and the cheerleaders' skirts and the stale popcorn in the air makes me reconsider. Below, Oliver is about to put himself out there in front of all the world to see his triumph or his defeat. Would it kill me to show a little support?

"No hearts," I tell Shaun. "No balloons, and definitely no delicate birds." I point to my right cheek. *"Go."* I point to my left cheek. *"Robins."*

A smile blossoms across Shaun's face. "That's my girl. Blue or red?"

"Surprise me."

• • •

It's somewhere in the middle of the third quarter and we're tied with Lake Erie High. I've been able to figure out which one is Oliver (mostly because he told me he'd have a number 2 emblazoned across his back) and have watched him do all sorts of running and catching. Two out of our four touchdowns were made by him, to much screaming and adulation from our side of the field. The marching band show at intermission ("halftime," Shaun corrected me) was loud and precise and clap-worthy, and it's been surprisingly interesting to watch the cheerleaders hop and scream and fling each other into the air. I'm wearing Shaun's letterman jacket (varsity tennis), because it's gotten chilly, and even that makes it feel like I'm at a weird, fun costume party.

There's no way around it: I'm having a great time.

Since I still don't really understand what's happening on the field, it doesn't occur to me to wait until the end of a play to admit this all to Shaun. I tug on his sweatshirt and he tilts toward me, his eyes still on the game. Everyone in the bleachers is chanting and stomping and clapping, so I bring my mouth up to Shaun's ear. "This is fun!" I yell, and pull back to see his reaction.

Except he's not turning to give me one of his wide, happy smiles. Instead, he's gasping and his hand is at his chest, squeezed in a fist.

In that moment, I realize that all around us, in every row, all the students and parents and little kids have also retreated into shocked silence. I whip my gaze to the field and zero in on the center, where one of the players lies in a crumpled heap while people run toward him from every direction.

Oliver.

That's when I gasp into the silent air, seconds later than

everyone else. That's when both my hands fly to my mouth and I lurch to my feet. I'm not sure what my plan is—to run down there or call 911 or something—but before I can do it, there's a death grip on my left elbow. Shaun pulls me back to the seat and tucks an arm around my waist. "Easy," he murmurs, and makes a fast, subtle gesture with one knuckle.

I follow his gaze to where Ainsley stands amid a protective circle of cheerleaders. She's tense, her arms wrapped around herself, watching the people clustered around Oliver. One of Ainsley's friends rubs small circles on her back.

"Right," I say to Shaun.

"Right," he says.

And then the awfulness is over, because Oliver is lifting his head; he's slowly sitting; he's shaking off assistance; he's pulling himself upright and waving to our side of the field, where the bleachers erupt into a stomping, screaming explosion of celebration. I feel like crying but I don't, because below, Ainsley already is doing that. Instead, I smile and I clap and I let my tears flow out of her eyes.

That's where they belong.

• • •

"I didn't realize," says Shaun as we stand around by the south entrance of the field, waiting for Oliver and Ainsley.

"What are you talking about?"

Shaun gazes at me, then leans over and kisses the top of my head. "Never mind."

• • •

The party is at a farm out near Dexter. Ainsley said it's the property of Theo's cousin, but then I heard Zoe tell someone the land belongs to the family of Cal Turman, who graduated last year, so who knows? Getting here was the first time I've ever ridden in the backseat of the behemoth, the floor of which is just as littered with discarded water bottles and trash as anyone would think. Right after the game, Ainsley was really worried about Oliver driving after his injury, but she appears to have been reassured, since now she and her posse are pounding beers beside a raging fire in the middle of nowhere.

Shaun and I sit on a wide stump together, sharing a beer from the keg and watching several dozen of our fellow students flirt and drink and slip off into the shadows to make out.

"Do you always come to these?" I ask Shaun.

"Bonfires are only for the first game of the season," he tells me. "I came last year, but it was on a different farm."

We sit in silence for a little while, both of us taking only tiny sips from the cup. Shaun knows he'll have to drive home after Oliver returns us to school, and I don't want to pee in a cornfield. Hence the moderation.

Shaun gives me a gentle bump with his arm. "Hey, are you okay?"

"Yeah. You?"

He heaves a deep sigh. "I miss Kirk."

Shaun drops his head onto my shoulder and I stroke his thick black hair. "I know," I tell him, even though I don't. When Itch was gone over the summer, I missed him being around, but I didn't miss *him,* if that makes any sense. It seems devastating to have your heart so completely undone for a single person. If they screw up, if they don't feel the same, if their life is too busy or too complicated or too far away to fit you into it, something inside you breaks. Even when it heals, there are scars.

There are always scars.

No thank you.

Someone shows up with a portable speaker and pop music fills the smoky night air. There's a sudden cheerleader stampede toward the patch of open dirt substituting as a dance floor.

I check out Oliver and Theo, who stand off to the side, watching the girls gyrate and twirl. Theo points to first one and then another, making comments I can't hear. Oliver smiles.

I can only imagine.

I nudge Shaun's head off my shoulder to ask if he thinks we can find an earlier ride home with someone, but I never ask the question, because he's beaming at me with this big, sappy grin.

"What?"

"Tell me you won't miss this." He waves a hand in the general direction of the party. "This is what we'll look back on when we're old and boring and sedentary."

I am about to say something about perception and hindsight when we hear my name yelled from the dance zone. It's Ainsley. She's pointing straight at me.

"I don't suppose I have a choice in this matter, do I?" I ask Shaun.

"Nope." He shoves me up from our stump. "Life is easier when you acquiesce."

Ainsley calls my name again. I shrug off Shaun's letter jacket and drop it onto his lap before pasting on a big smile and heading toward the dancers with as much buoyancy as I can muster. When I reach Ainsley, she holds out a hand toward me. "Phone."

"There's no reception," I tell her, and she cracks up.

"No, silly. Next song up on your phone is what we dance to."

No one told me about this delightful tradition. I glance back at Shaun but he's looking moody and tracing the rim of our plastic cup with one finger, no doubt thinking about Kirk.

Shit.

"Come *on*," says Ainsley, her hand still open and out.

"You're not going to like my music," I tell her, sliding my phone from a pocket and turning it over.

"Who do you listen to? Justin Bieber?" she teases.

If only.

I watch—hating my life—as Ainsley struts to the speaker. The current song abruptly cuts off. Cheerleaders pause midbounce with wails of protest. The night suddenly feels very thick and dark.

Ainsley throws an arm up to the crowd. "June Rafferty for music roulette!" she screams. There's an expectant hush as she plugs in my phone and touches the screen. I scroll through songs in my brain, trying to figure out the worst-case scenario. Dead Kennedys? The Sisters of Mercy? Maybe I'll get lucky and Ainsley will hit on a Cure song everyone knows.

I'm frozen somewhere between defiance and panic when I see movement from the edge of the dance floor. It's Oliver, headed toward Ainsley with determination etched across his face. But before he reaches her, drumbeats hit the air, followed by guitar chords. They're exuberant and light, like the cheerleaders.

The group hesitates as they all look to their leader. Ainsley's dark eyebrows wing together in a frown. She stalks toward me. "Who is this?" she demands.

I consider telling her it's Bieber, just to see if she'll buy it, but I don't want to press my luck when stranded in a nest of jocks.

"Pansy Division."

"Never heard of it."

"Queercore punk out of San Francisco."

There's a pause during which it could go either way, but then good old P.D. gets to the chorus, specifically the "Sex! Sex! Sex! Sex!" line, and Ainsley's lips turn up in appreciation. "I love it!" she shouts, and grabs my wrist, careening us both into the center of the crowd.

I catch a flash glimpse of Oliver at the edge, standing with his arms crossed over his chest and watching. But before I can figure out what he's doing or thinking, I've been launched into the lunacy. The bouncing escalates, the screaming intensifies, and against all odds . . . I'm a part of it.

Just like that, I'm in.

• • •

Oliver makes Ainsley trade seats with Shaun for the ride home so I can hold her hair back if she pukes out the window. "That's a girl job," Shaun says from the front passenger seat.

"There are no such things," I tell him automatically.

Luckily for me (and the behemoth's paint job), Ainsley isn't pukey at all. In fact, she's rather the opposite. "I never knew you were so cool!" she coos into my ear, her arms flung around my torso. "I love you! Oliver, I *love* her!"

"Awesome." Oliver meets my eyes in the rearview mirror. He grins at me and shakes his head. I grin back before giving Ainsley a return hug.

"I love you, too," I assure her.

"We are going to be *such good friends.*"

I pat her arm. "Totally."

A part of me even means it.

PROM DAY

The behemoth takes off. I know it's pointless to try to catch it, but I try anyway, racing all the way down the driveway and into the street, waving my arms and screaming.

It's the only way I'm going to find out the truth.

I chase it for a couple houses' worth of road before slowing to a stop, my breath coming in short gasps. I'm not sure if it's sweat or tears covering my face. . . .

And miraculously, ahead of me, the behemoth also stops. I drop my hands to my knees, trying to catch my breath as the big car makes a slow U-turn and comes back for me.

It's coming back with answers. Answers that I already know will break my heart.

WINTER

Chapter 9

When the alarm on my phone chirps, I open my eyes to find Mom looming over my bed. I squeal, which startles her enough that she also squeals, and then it takes me a minute to sit up and rub the sleep from my eyes before I can figure out what's going on. Mom—already dressed to teach—is holding a plate of pancakes. They're adorned with fresh strawberries in the shape of the number seventeen, and there's a lit candle in the center.

"Thanks." I blow out the candle. "What are the chances you made coffee, too?"

"Pretty good," says Mom, and she hugs me.

• • •

"Wait, what?" says Oliver as he pulls out of my driveway. "How are you not eighteen?"

"You know I have to explain this to someone at least once a year, right?"

"Enlighten me."

"When Dad left for New York and Mom had to go back to work, everyone suddenly noticed that preschool costs money but kindergarten is free. I took some IQ tests and must have done okay, because they went ahead and started me early."

"So you were only *four* when we got married on the playground?"

I cringe. "You remember that?"

"God, I'm a pedophile!" he says dramatically, clapping a palm to his forehead. He's trying to be funny, but I'm embarrassed. As far as I'm concerned, our kindergarten marriage has always been this mildly shameful thing, a very tiny elephant in the room. I think it's because—technically speaking—it was my very first kiss, and I didn't have another one until eighth grade, when Will Michaels and I made out in the sports shed on a dare. It was sweet but sloppy and—although I have a nostalgic fondness for Will to this day—kissing wasn't something I felt like trying again for another year.

Whereas, if rumors are to be believed, Oliver was macking in fifth.

"Gross," I tell him, and then notice he is frowning. "Now what?"

"If your birthday is in November, why is your name June?"

"It's the month my parents met."

"Awwwww," he says.

"Stop it."

"Why? It's sweet."

"Seriously, shut up."

"I like it. Your name is cute and sweet and even *meaningful*."

"Blah blah blah!" I say loudly, covering my ears with my hands. "I can't hear you!"

Hey, I'm young for my grade and I'm smart. No one ever said I was mature.

Oliver pulls the wheel—

"What are you doing?" I squawk.

—and we bump off the road, startling a deer as we come to rest along the edge of a field. The deer takes off fast toward the woods, tail up and flashing white in alarm. Oliver puts the car into park and reaches toward me. I squeal (second squeal of the day) and yank backward, but of course his arms are longer, and he catches me by the wrists. Very gently, he pulls my hands away from my head and stares at me. It's the closest we have ever been, and something about it makes me stop wiggling and go silent. Oliver smiles that bright white smile right into my eyes. "Happy birthday, June."

And then he lets go of me and pulls back onto the road.

• • •

At first—as I'm walking down the hallway—I assume it must be someone else's locker. The one next to mine. After all, it's a big school; it's not impossible that someone would share a birthday with me. Lily and Darbs have never been into balloons and streamers, so clearly this isn't their work. . . .

Is that *lipstick*?

Someone slicked *Happy Birthday, June!!!* over my locker in scarlet lettering. Whoever did it also taped streamers all around and set helium balloons dancing against the ceiling. I open the metal door to discover they must have blown glitter dust in through the slanted vent, because my textbooks are covered in fine sparkles.

Because *that's* going to be fun to clean.

I stand looking at the craziness and trying to figure out how I feel about it. It's a tradition that other people participate in, but that my friends and I have always eschewed as ostentatious. However, now that I'm looking at it . . .

Maybe it's nice.

I take a photo and text it to both parents. It reassures them to see proof of my emotionally healthy social life. Mom's in class, but Dad returns a message immediately:

HBD baby girl!

I also send the picture—along with a message of gratitude—to the only person who can possibly be responsible for decorating my locker.

• • •

"I'm telling you, it wasn't me," Shaun whispers across the aisle in AP English.

"Was it Lily, then? Or Darbs?"

"Better not be. Neither of those bitches decorated for *my* birthday."

That leaves only one person. A surprisingly romantic act from someone who is not usually romantic.

The thought of it makes me smile.

• • •

"Nope." Itch slides his hands down my rib cage to my waist. "Not my style."

"What *is* your style?" Itch moved here in the middle of junior year, so I didn't meet him until after my last birthday.

He twists his fingers through the loops in my jeans and tugs me closer. "I'll show you on Saturday."

• • •

"Happy birthday!" Ainsley lilts as soon as I walk into physics class, and I make the connection.

"*You* decorated my locker?"

She springs up and flings her arms around me, and I am acutely aware that every straight boy in the room wishes he was in my position. I give Ainsley an awkward pat on the back. "Thank you." It's what you say when someone you hardly know spends an inordinate amount of time on your unrequested birthday celebration. This must be life when you're friends with the cheerleaders.

"You're welcome!" She beams. "Were you surprised? Come sit with us at lunch."

This is getting weirder by the minute.

"At the sundial?" Ainsley gives me a *duh* look. I shake my head. "I eat with Itch."

She doesn't even hesitate. "Bring him along!"

"And Lily?" I ask her. "And Darbs and Shaun?"

Ainsley's eyebrows dart down in the middle, just like they did at the bonfire when she was trying to wrap her head around my playlist song. "I don't think there are that many open seats."

Of course.

"I'll have lunch with you tomorrow," I tell her, wondering how I'm going to explain this to everyone else.

"Tomorrow." Ainsley gives me another fast hug before heading back to her lab table, where Oliver is already seated.

Watching us with interest.

Or something.

• • •

I wait for Mom out by the corner. As soon as I slide into the passenger seat, she hands me a vase of flowers. I stuff my backpack between my knees and the glove compartment so I can accept them. I'm about to thank Mom when—

"They're from your father," she says. "God forbid he call for our new house address."

"He has it," I tell her.

"Apparently he misplaced it, because he had these sent to my office."

The flowers—deep violet hydrangea mixed with white lilies and roses in a turquoise vase—smell wonderful. I breathe in their scent. "I love them."

"Your father has great taste," Mom says. "I'll give him that."

I find the tiny envelope buried within the buds and open it up. There's the message, called in by Dad and written in the florist's neat slanted handwriting:

> Baby girl—
> You are beautiful, brilliant, special.
> Hope your birthday is as wonderful
> as you deserve.
> Love you. Miss you.
> —Dad

My father's words bloom bright and warm inside me. Something I can hold on to. Something to remember.

When I send Dad a thank-you message, he again texts back right away.

UR welcome, luv U

When we get home, Cash is there. He's supervising a crew of plumbers and painters who are finishing up work on the downstairs bathroom. "Happy birthday." He grins, jerking a thumb toward my mom. "She told me."

Mom scurries into the kitchen and comes back with a foil-wrapped loaf of bread. "Rosemary," she tells Cash. "With flax seeds."

"Thanks." He slides a brown paper bag brimming with fabric scraps across the floor toward her. "Upholstery remnants for you."

I'm relieved that—this time—no one's around to witness the strange bartering world in which we live.

• • •

Itch takes me to a tapas restaurant downtown, where we share shrimp flatbread and mushrooms sautéed with garlic and a cheese plate. After, we stop by 7-Eleven for mints (because of the garlic), and I have yet another flash of guilt as I remember hooking up with Ethan Erickson behind the building. Once again, I wonder if I should tell Itch about it. Once again, I dismiss the thought.

After our stop for fresh breath, we get back in Itch's car and he heads us toward my house, except he drives past the turn. I shoot him a questioning look but he only strokes my leg. We pass several communities and finally come to a place where there's a break in the tree line and streetlights. Itch turns onto a bumpy dirt road, which we follow slowly until we reach a collection of bulldozers. He turns again and we drive even more slowly for a couple hundred feet. We finally park in the center of an empty clearing, where Itch kills the engine and flicks off the headlights.

"Where are we?" I ask him.

"It's a construction site. They're putting in one of those big douchebag communities, but for right now"—he gestures around at the darkness—"it's just us. We can stay as long as we want."

"Or until my curfew." We've never had tons of opportunities to do the Deed, but that's been okay with me. I'm still new to even *having* a sex life. It's fine if it's more of a once-in-a-while thing.

Itch, on the other hand, would much prefer if it happened more often.

He leans over the emergency brake to kiss me. I shift forward in my seat to meet him, because it's expected, because it's what we do. His kiss is warm and slow and familiar. I'm just starting to get into it when he pulls back. "Hold on. I almost forgot." He pops open the glove compartment and pulls out a small brown paper bag. He slides it onto my lap so I can crinkle open the top. Inside is a headset with a bow stuck to it. "Happy birthday."

"Thank you." I run my finger over the headset's surface. It's much bigger than the earbuds that came with my cell phone.

"Professional grade." Itch must see my confusion, because he explains further. "So you don't have to be subjected to

Oliver's crap on the way to school." He points to the tip of the cord. "It plugs into your phone just like a regular pair. Now you can ignore him and listen to whatever you want."

I feel my eyebrows come together and am briefly reminded of Ainsley. "That seems . . ."

"What?"

"Rude. To tune him out like that."

"He's the one who's rude," says Itch. "Not to mention cheesy. Didn't you tell me he put Air Supply on the playlist?"

That song doesn't even make sense; I'll give Itch that. Regardless—

"Oliver is still doing me a favor," I remind him. "It's not like he *has* to drive me to school."

"Please." Itch snorts. "He's not picking you up out of the goodness of his heart. His mom is forcing him to do it."

I mull that over, trying to figure out what to say to my boyfriend. Despite what Itch thinks of Oliver—a sentiment I used to echo—now I know that he's a decent person. Finally, I come up with this: "I already agreed to the system. We have this playlist thing going. Wearing a headset so I can listen to my own music would be cheating."

Cheating. Like what I did this summer.

I shake the thought away.

"It's not cheating if it's a stupid bet in the first place," Itch argues.

"It's not a bet. I told you that already." My voice rises and I don't try to stop it. We're at a freaking construction site. No one can hear us. "It's a competition. It's a game."

"It's bullshit."

"It's fun," I say even louder. With the words comes the knowledge: it's true.

Itch shakes his head. "You have a screwed-up definition of fun."

I sit back against the door, crossing my arms in front of my chest. "What's *your* definition? Because I honestly don't have any idea what you think is fun. You never seem to have any."

Itch is silent for a moment before leaning forward and turning the key. "It's getting late."

"I appreciate the present."

Neither one of us is telling the truth.

Chapter 10

"I've been thinking about something you said," Oliver tells me as his Air Supply song plays softly for the second time this morning.

"That we should be paying more attention to climate change?" I ask.

"No."

"That people should reconsider their feelings about insects as food because eating them instead of meat would be better for the environment?"

Oliver laughs. "No, but I would pay good money to watch you eat a grub worm."

"I said I'm reconsidering my feelings," I remind him. "Not that I'm ordering grub worm sandwiches."

"Poser."

"Baby steps," I tell him. "What have you been thinking about?"

"The senior prank." Oliver waits patiently while I perform a bunch of eye rolling and excessive sighing. "Is it out of your system?"

"One more." I heave a final deep groan. "Okay, I'm done. Go ahead."

"No more laxatives."

"Am I expected to cheer?"

"No." Oliver pokes me in the ribs.

"Hey!"

"But you are supposed to hush and listen."

I hush and listen.

"Theo says that Jimmy McKay says he can borrow a really tame cow from his uncle's farm."

" 'Borrow.' " I say it with a heavy dose of skepticism.

"We won't give it any laxatives and we'll be really nice to it."

"How?"

"What do you mean?"

"How are you going to be nice to Jimmy McKay's uncle's really tame cow?"

Oliver considers. "We'll bring it treats."

"Treats."

"Hay or alfalfa or . . . sugar lumps! Don't cows like sugar lumps?"

"*Horses* like sugar lumps." I purse my lips. "Go on."

"There's this scientific thing about how cows can go up stairs but not down them. So all we have to do is get the cow up to the third floor. It's way better than feeding it laxatives. It'll just be stuck up there, mooing around. I bet they'll cancel classes. At least in the morning."

"Hey, Oliver?"

"Yeah?"

"*Why* do you think cows won't go down stairs?"

Oliver's forehead scrunches up. "Evolution?"

I whap him across the biceps (God, that's hard!) and make a snort that sounds a lot like Itch. "It's because they're *scared*."

"We shouldn't scare the cow?"

"It's mean to scare cows," I tell him. "Even for tradition. Even for a *legacy*."

"It's mean to crush my hopes and dreams." Oliver slumps in an overdramatic way that makes me laugh.

We're both quiet for a while as the Violent Femmes (my one song, of course) play from the behemoth's speakers. "This music sucks," Oliver says mildly.

"You've mentioned."

I watch as the trees flashing by are replaced by storefronts. I would prefer to engage in our now traditional sport of song bashing, or even to continue discussion of the senior prank, but my mind keeps going back to my conversation with Itch. Or rather, my *lack* of conversation with Itch. "I have a question," I tell Oliver.

"Shoot."

"Hypothetically speaking, let's say that a person and her boyfriend made a decision to be free to date other people over a specific period of time. Say, a summer, for example."

"For example," says Oliver.

"Let's say that this hypothetical person didn't date anyone, exactly, but instead may have—one time only and with one person only—done some . . ." I pause, trying to figure out how to continue. "Done some *things*."

"*Things* that are physical? Like the *things* commonly done between two people who are dating?"

"Correct." I nod and then hasten to add, "But not *all* the things. Not even *most* of the things."

"How many things, exactly?"

"Like *one* thing. Maybe one and a *half*."

"Which particular things?" Oliver asks. "Be specific. Give details."

"You're heading toward Theo Land," I warn him. If Darbs or Lily or Shaun was the one asking, I would probably give more information. That would be normal. But the idea of telling those same things to Oliver doesn't seem fine or normal at all. It seems . . .

I can't figure out how it seems. Mostly, it just seems like I don't want to tell him.

"I'm an emotional detective," Oliver says. "A therapist. I'm basically like a priest. . . . Are you going to do that eye-rolling seizure thing again?"

"Probably." I stare at his handsome profile and decide just to go for it. I want a straight-male take on the Itch Sitch, and at the moment, the only qualified person in my life appears to be Oliver. "It was one time, one guy, and it was no big deal. A little making out, that's all."

"You did say maybe one and a half things."

"Fine, some over-the-shirt action. That's all you get."

"I can work with that," says Oliver. "Go on."

"I keep thinking about it," I admit. "Not about the guy, but about what I did. Even though it was technically within my rights, I feel . . ."

"Guilty." The word comes out of Oliver's mouth fast. And with authority.

He's right.

"Yeah, I guess that's it. I feel totally guilty. And I never told Itch, but now I'm wondering if I should have when it happened. Or if I still should. What would you do if Ainsley kissed another guy?"

Oliver's lips press together. "I don't know," he finally says. "Because I can't imagine okaying that in the first place. What's the point?"

Again, he's right—which silences me.

Oliver gives me a gentle tap on the knee. "You should tell him."

"I guess. Maybe. Probably."

"You're supposed to be honest with the person you're with. Y'know?"

"I know," I say, even though I don't know anything anymore.

When we reach school, I pause before opening my door. "Hey, Oliver?"

"Yeah?"

"Thanks for the ride."

"Anytime, Rafferty."

"And for the talk."

Oliver smiles at me. "You're welcome."

We're out of the car and almost to the front lobby doors when Oliver nudges me. "Oh, by the way . . ."

"By the way what?"

"By the way, studies show that high school popularity is a determining factor in later-life financial security. Look it up."

"What?" All that friendly conversation. Just Oliver lulling me into a false sense of complacency.

"Suck it, screamo," he says. But then he grins and nudges me again. "Have a good day."

He disappears into the crowd and—even though I'm mad about the song—I'm kind of bummed to see him go.

• • •

Itch and I are sitting on the swings at Cherry Hill Park, not far from my house. I asked if he would drive me home and he said yes, even though things have been a little tense since the weekend. We were quiet the whole way here. I was thinking about how to say it, and about what it would mean, and even about what I *wanted* it to mean. I kept going back to the thing Oliver had said, how things are supposed to be. How do I want things to be with Itch?

It sleeted this afternoon and now everything is gray and dank. The seat of the swing was spotted with water when I sat on it, but I already felt so damp that I didn't care. Now I'm regretting that decision as the temperature drops even more and I'm shivery everywhere.

"So what's up?" Itch says.

A nervous knot gathers in the pit of my stomach. Earlier, I thought of several ways to broach the topic but now I've forgotten all of them. "I have to tell you something."

"Go ahead." His voice is more even than usual.

I twist the swing to face him. "Remember how you said we should be open to dating other people this summer?"

"Yes."

I suddenly have an attack of the nerves so strong that I have to jerk out of my swing and stand up. I squeeze my thumbs inside my mittens, take a deep breath, and spit it out: "I kissed someone."

I wait. Itch digs his toes into the pebbles to bring his swing to stillness. He gazes up at me for a moment, a long moment during which I try to understand his expression, but I can't find anything in it. No anger or sadness or jealousy. Either I don't know how to read him, or those emotions really aren't there. I can't tell.

And then Itch's mouth tilts up into his lopsided grin. "Is that all?" I nod and he gets to his feet. He sets his hands on my shoulders. "Me too, June. It's okay."

I freeze—*what?*—before pulling back. I'm not jealous but I'm . . . I don't know what I am. I'm surprised. I'm *something*. "Who was she?"

A line deepens between Itch's eyebrows. "Just a couple Florida girls."

"A *couple*?"

"Maybe three. None of them meant anything."

"Did you have sex?" I ask, and he shakes his head violently.

"Not even close," he says. "I'm telling you, it was nothing."

And I have to believe him. I have to understand, because that's what it felt like with Ethan in the 7-Eleven parking lot. It felt like nothing, like it could have been anyone's mouth and anyone's hands. It was a time killer. A space filler. It wasn't fair and I'm not proud . . . but that's what it was.

Itch reaches out to me again, and this time I let him pull me in, let him wrap his arms around me and stroke my hair. "We weren't together," he murmurs in my ear. "Now we are. It's all good."

I nod against him, relieved.

And—somehow—also disappointed.

• • •

Oliver doesn't even turn on the playlist when I climb into the car. He just pulls out into the street before flipping a look at me. "Did you do it?"

"Yes."

"You told him?"

"Yes."

Silence for at least a full minute. I know Oliver is waiting for me to talk, but there's really nothing to say. Finally, he can't take it anymore. "How'd it go?"

"Fine." I scrunch down in my seat and stare out the window. "It went fine."

Chapter 11

Itch must have conned his way out of second period a few minutes early, because he's already waiting in the hallway when I exit environmental sciences. "My parents are going out of town this weekend," he says.

"For Thanksgiving?"

"No, right after. On Friday. Can you tell your mom you're staying at Lily's?"

I'm about to answer when an overgrown Saint Bernard bounds down the hallway and nearly barrels over us. It's Oliver, wearing an apron and carrying a bowl. "It worked! It didn't collapse!" He whips out a spoon and scoops a soft pile of brown onto it. "Chocolate soufflé. Here!"

I am hyperaware of Itch standing silently by my side, but I open my mouth so Oliver can feed me the bite and . . .

Sweet silky heaven.

"Wow," I say after I've swallowed. "That's incredible."

"I know, right?" Oliver turns to Itch—"Want a bite?"—but Itch shakes his head.

Oliver doesn't appear to be bothered. His eyes focus on

someone down the hall behind us and he calls out, "Lisa, Yana! Wait up!" He bounds away, waving his spoon.

"You're still wearing your apron!" I shout after him, but he doesn't hear me. That's Oliver in a nutshell. Exuberant and passionate and generous.

"Hey." Itch nudges me and I suddenly realize I have a goofy smile across my face. I wipe it away. "So can you tell your mom you're sleeping at Lily's?"

"Maybe," I say, my eyes still on Oliver.

• • •

Itch has to buy some things, so I let him take me to the mall after school. First we get smoothies, and then I end up holding his cup while he browses JCPenney's selection of boxers. I watch him, wondering when our relationship devolved to the point of purchasing undergarments together. Maybe it would be all right if I chose for him, if we were being sexy or romantic or if it was a joke or maybe if he was getting the kind stamped with little hearts or . . . or . . .

Or anything but this. This is just me acting as Itch's beverage stand while he tries to choose between large-patterned plaid or small-patterned plaid.

This is killing me.

I flash back to Mom's Deep Thought, about how sometimes things need to get messy before they can be good. Maybe that's what Itch and I need. Some messiness.

"That was nice of Oliver, don't you think?" I say it casually.

"What?" Itch drapes a pair of red-and-blue boxers (small-patterned) over his left arm and moves to a new rack.

114

"How he offered you some of that soufflé he made. It's not like you guys know each other that well or anything."

"Sure."

"It was really good."

"Cool."

"*Shockingly* good." Itch starts checking out the boxer briefs and I switch tactics. "You know what I appreciate about Oliver?"

"Nope."

"How he can just run up to anyone, to any group of people at school. Other jocks, artists, geeks, stoners, anyone. I don't ever see him being mean to anyone, you know?"

"Yup." Itch selects a four-pack of navy cotton undies.

I decide to bump things up, just a touch. "I like being friends with him."

"Great." Itch holds out his hand and it takes me a second to realize he's reaching for his smoothie. I give it to him and follow him toward the register, assessing the situation as we go.

My boyfriend isn't annoyed by my friendship with our school's hottest guy. He's not jealous. He's not worried.

That's the problem, I suddenly recognize. Itch doesn't *get* jealous or worried or passionate or . . .

Or anything.

He's a flat line.

I stand, watching him pay for his underwear, and I feel flat, too. No, worse than flat.

I feel nothing at all.

• • •

"Maybe he's gay."

It's four days later, and Shaun is hacking at a particularly sturdy buckthorn plant with a pair of red-handled clippers.

"Itch isn't gay," I tell him. "I have hard proof of that."

"Ha-ha, you said 'hard.'"

"You are a child. Here, give me those." I take the clippers and use them to grasp the buckthorn's woody base. "You have to grab and twist to pull the roots all the way out."

Shaun straightens with a groan. "I think the only thing I'm pulling out is my back." He rubs his hands together. "And my fingers might have frostbite."

"Don't be a baby. You're helping Mother Earth."

"I hate it."

"Hush," I tell him. "Find your Zen."

We're at the Ives Road Fen Preserve. Thirty miles south of Ann Arbor, it's a huge preserve with a wetlands area that is rare for this part of Michigan. I love it for its raw beauty and all the things that look like they've never been touched by people. Silver maples tower over acres of prairie dropseed grass. There are tree frogs and cricket frogs and shy, colorful birds. This is the real deal.

Ever since working at the nature center this summer, I've wanted to sign up for one of Ives Road's volunteer days, but this is the first time I've convinced someone to join me (and drive us there). To be fair, it's tough work. We've been at it for over three hours and my back hurts, too.

I tried to get Itch to come, but he declined even though his parents are out of town and it's not like he has anything important going on. He's probably pouting because I refused to lie to Mom.

Except I forgot: Itch doesn't pout. Itch doesn't do anything.

"It just seems like he doesn't care," I tell Shaun.

"About you?"

"About anything."

Shaun points at a small green patch. "That's not poison ivy, is it?"

"That's grass, Shaun."

He drops onto it with a sigh and falls backward, arms outstretched. "What's the worst thing that could happen if I fell asleep right here?"

"You could be eaten."

"By a wolverine?" He sounds almost hopeful.

"By mosquitoes." I twist another shiny buckthorn from the dirt before plopping beside him.

"It's too cold for mosquitoes," Shaun tells me. "Which means it's too cold for humans. Cuddle me."

He grabs the back of my jacket and pulls me down to rest against him. I place my head on his chest and wrap an arm around him.

"Just a like a real boy," he says.

"*You're* just like a real boy," I retort.

"So what are you going to do about Itch?"

"Nothing." Shaun doesn't say anything in return, so I elaborate. "I don't want to break up with him. I like being his girlfriend."

"Maybe you just like being *a* girlfriend."

The thing is, I *do* like being a girlfriend. I like belonging to someone in an official capacity. I like saying "my boyfriend." I like knowing that if I want a date, I have one.

Since none of those seem like really great things to admit, I change the subject. "How's Kirk?"

"Too far away."

"Chicago is drivable."

"My parents don't think so," says Shaun. "But even if they did, I don't know if I would go. Kirk isn't out to his dad yet. It would be weird."

"I'm sorry." My relationships are complicated enough without the extra baggage that Shaun has to deal with. "Are you going to break up with him?"

"I don't even know if I have to," says Shaun. "It doesn't feel like we're dating anymore."

"I know what you mean."

"Hey, lovebirds!" A deep voice with a strong New York accent startles us into sitting upright. It's an older man wearing gloves and work boots that mark him as a volunteer. "What do you think this is: Inspiration Point? Get the hell up and get to work!"

Shaun and I turn to look at each other, slow grins spreading over our faces. "I love you," Shaun says loudly so the man will definitely hear.

"I love you, too," I tell him. The man grumbles something under his breath and marches away. I stand and pull Shaun to his feet. "Just a few more buckthorns and then we can go home."

"Promise?"

"Promise."

Chapter 12

Itch finds me between Spanish III and calculus class. I lean up to kiss him, but he pulls away. "Where were you at lunch?" he asks. "Wait, let me guess. North Hall."

"It's warm there."

"The cafeteria is warm. And it's not riddled with cheerleaders."

Annoying.

"They're not cockroaches, Itch. They're people. When did you get so judgy?" He scowls at me and I hold up a finger before he can say anything else. "Besides, I texted you. I told you Ainsley wanted to hang." It wasn't 100 percent true, but it also wasn't a lie, since she *did* tell me I was always invited.

"Again," says Itch.

"You're invited, Itch! You're always invited."

"Lucky me."

Annoying *and* rude.

"How do you think it feels to have to make excuses for you every single time?" I ask him. "Just once, couldn't you make an effort to break out of your social circle and talk to someone new?"

"I *like* my social circle. *You're* in my social circle and get this: I actually like you."

"Really?" My voice scales up and a small pack of underclassmen turns to see what's going on. "You don't act that way."

"*I* don't act that way?" Itch shakes his head. "Priceless."

My heart speeds up and blood rushes to my cheeks. We've had little spats before—like the one in Rite Aid—but this time, it feels different. This time, *I* feel different.

Like I want to fight.

"You know what I have to say to my friends, Itch? 'Sorry. My boyfriend's not a joiner.' It's such an obvious lie. They all know it's code for 'he just doesn't like you.' "

"They're snotty," says Itch. "They're pretentious."

"Calling them pretentious is pretentious!" I snap, and remember that it was Oliver who first said that to me. "They're *fun,* Itch. They laugh and they have a good time."

"Yeah, I know all about their 'good times.' "

"What is that supposed to mean?" I'm furious now, revved up for a full-out battle. Itch folds his arms across his chest and glares. A split second before the bell rings, I realize the hall has cleared.

We're late for class.

"Shit," says Itch. He turns and stalks away. I watch him go all the way to the end of the hall and turn the corner.

He never looks back.

• • •

Lily has a three-hour violin practice, and Darbs had to take her youngest brother to Chuck E. Cheese's, and Shaun isn't answering my texts, so I have no one to call for a good Itch Bitch. Instead, I'm lying across my bed, listening to the Dead Kennedys and throwing paper clips into my metal wastebasket. I only make every third toss or so.

Suddenly, I pause. The tiny metal clicks aren't the only staccato sounds in the room. I wait and hear it again: a soft scatter shot against the window. I hop up and look outside to see that Itch is standing there, far below. As I watch, he tosses another handful of pebbles. I wave so he'll stop, and I point to the front of the house.

When I open the door, he's already standing on the welcome mat. "Let me in," he says. "It's freezing out here."

I step back so he can enter, and as I close the door, Mom calls from the kitchen. "Is someone here, June?"

"It's Itch," I call back. "He won't stay long."

"Hi, Itch!" calls my mom.

"Hi," he calls to her.

Now that all the calling back and forth is over, I put my hands on my hips and look up at him. "Pebbles against the window? Really?"

"It's a grand romantic gesture. I thought you would like it."

I'm pissed off and I don't want to give an inch. "You could have knocked at the door."

"That is neither grand nor romantic," he informs me, reaching for my hand. I pull away, so he sighs and takes a step backward, running his fingers through his hair. "June, I'm sorry."

I know it would be gracious to accept his apology, but I feel hard and angry and nowhere near forgiveness. "I don't know if sorry is enough. I don't know if anything is enough."

"I used to be a joiner," he says. "At my old school."

That's new information. "What kind of joiner?"

"The kind who did all the same things as Oliver and Ainsley and everyone else."

I blink. "Did you play sports?"

"No, but I hung out with the kids who did. The ones who were popular and partied a lot."

"Did you . . . party?" He knows I don't use that word as a verb.

"I had to. Back there, that was how you stayed on top. We didn't have any Shauns bouncing from group to group. We didn't even have any Olivers, who have an all-access pass by virtue of being at the top of the food chain. At my old school, you were either on the top or you were on the bottom. No middle ground."

I stare at him, trying to picture Itch joining things, playing along. "But you hate that."

"It used to be normal." He stops, biting his lip.

I've never seen him do that before and—although I don't know why—the hottest part of my anger melts away. "What happened?" I ask, because something had to have happened.

"It was my friend Xavier." Itch takes a deep breath. "We called him X. Really funny guy. Smart, too. Played guitar. All the girls loved him."

"He sounds like your worst nightmare." I say it to lighten the mood, but I only earn the smallest lip twitch from Itch.

"It was a party after a football game. One of those parties like all the other parties, except this time X snagged something from his aunt's medicine cabinet. I don't even know what it was, but June—" He looks into my eyes. "Any other night, I probably

122

would have taken some, too, because that's the way it worked. If X was offering, you took it. But I had to get up early the next morning to drive my parents to the airport. I didn't want to pass out and forget to show up or something, so I said no."

"What happened?" I ask in a small voice.

"The same thing that always happened," Itch says. "Everyone drank and got stupid and had a good time. Except in the middle of it all, X had a seizure and fell through a glass-topped coffee table."

A gasp comes out of me before I can stop it.

"Everyone screamed. There was a lot of blood and he kept seizing, but we were all drunk. And scared, I think. Scared of our parents and the cops and getting busted. I tried to help stop the bleeding, but I wasn't exactly sober, either, and someone finally called 911. It was—" He stops for a second, and I reach for his hands. I hold them between my own. "It was the worst night of my life."

I wait, my heart aching for this part of Itch he's never shared with me.

"X didn't die. He's back at school, but . . ." Itch swallows. "He doesn't play guitar anymore. He says it gives him a headache, but I think he doesn't remember how. I think it's gone." Itch removes his hands from between mine and cracks his knuckles. "I'm sure your friends are different. Ainsley seems nice. So does Oliver. It's just me. I don't want to hang with the kids at the top of the ladder because last time I did, I liked it." He sighs. "I liked it too much."

I had no idea that there was something more to Itch's scorn. Something more like *fear*. "I'm sorry," I tell him.

"I'm sorry, too." He lets me slide my arms around him, under his jacket so I can feel his rib cage. I squeeze, and after a few seconds, he reciprocates. "I'll try, okay? I'll try."

"All right." I listen to his heart beating beneath my ear. "I'll try, too."

• • •

Getting to North Hall sucks, because we have to walk down an outer corridor where the icy wind whips around us, but after we struggle to get the heavy double doors open, we're greeted with a gush of warm radiator heat. I choose an empty section of wall to settle my back against, and slide down it until I'm sitting on the floor with my tray on my lap. Ainsley beams at me from nearby. "Lucky us, two days in a row!"

Oliver nudges me with his foot. "Hi, you guys."

"Hey," I say to him.

"Hey," says Itch, sliding down the wall beside me.

We eat our lunches.

Chapter 13

There's a gift-wrapped cylinder on my seat when I open the passenger door. I start to hand it to Oliver, but he shakes his head. "Open it."

I'm startled . . . and also inexplicably embarrassed. The week before winter break is the traditional time for kids at our school to exchange gifts, but it didn't occur to me that Oliver would give me something. And it's certainly not like I have anything for him.

"Really?" I ask. "Because I didn't—"

Oliver grins at me. "Just open it."

I run a finger down the taped seam between the two edges of green-and-red paper and get a flash image of Oliver hunched over the gift, trying to line up the wrapping. It opens to reveal . . .

"A water bottle?"

"Metal," he says helpfully. "And it's not actually for you." I cock my head at him and he explains. "Lest you think otherwise, I am aware of your vast distaste for the plastic bottles all over my car."

As always, I'm amused—and, oddly, flattered—by the way

Oliver talks when he's with me. I know he doesn't use those words with Theo. And maybe not Ainsley, either.

"The bottle is for me," he continues. "But the peace of mind is for you."

"It's a symbol."

He bats his eyelashes at me. "A symbol of my desire both to A: contribute to environmental salvation, and B: lessen the number of times that you give me the stink-eye in the mornings."

Naturally, I give him the stink-eye.

But then I smile.

• • •

It's way too cold and snowy for the bleachers, so Itch and I are at a corner table in the cafeteria. We've slung our jackets over two chairs for Darbs and Lily and piled backpacks on a third just in case Shaun joins us today.

Itch picks at his lasagna. "Gross."

I hold up my cloth sack. "If you packed your own lunch, you wouldn't be subjected to the vile whims of the cafeteria demons."

"If I packed my own lunch, I'd lose approximately fifteen minutes of sleep." He starts chopping at the lasagna with his spork. "Since I'm leaving on Saturday, do you want to hang on—"

"Wait, what?" I freeze in the act of unwrapping my sandwich. "Where are you going?"

"Florida. Remember, my grandparents? Christmas and Serbian New Year?" he says with exaggerated patience, like he's explaining to a toddler. "I told you this."

"No, you didn't."

"No he didn't what?" asks Lily, plopping into the chair beside mine.

"Tell me he's going to be gone for winter break."

"I told her," Itch says, and goes back to the sporking.

Lily makes a face at his lasagna. "PMGO."

"What does that even *mean*?" I ask her.

"Puke my guts out," she says. "Darbs wants it to take off."

"Where is she?"

"In prayer."

"Oh, right." I always forget the God Squad kids have lunchtime prayer circle on Tuesdays.

"So are you a rainbow now or what?" Lily asks me. When I give her a blank stare, she elaborates. "It's like you have dual citizenship these days."

I still don't understand until Itch nudges me. "Because sometimes we eat lunch elsewhere, June."

Oh.

I have an urge to defend myself to Lily, even though what she said wasn't at all an attack. "Is that weird?" I ask her.

"For sure," she says. "I mean, it's *fine*. But it's weird." She shakes her head. "And now you go to football games."

"*Some* football games," I say, correcting her.

"Yeah, my girlfriend has school spirit now," Itch says. I know he's trying to be funny, but it irritates me.

"There are worse things," I inform him.

"Nope," says Lily. "That's the worst." Itch clinks his soda can against hers. I roll my eyes at both of them.

Itch turns to me. "Do you want to hang tonight? I can come to your house."

"I think Cash is going to be over, too."

I see Itch search his memory. "Cash the contractor guy?"

"Yeah." Another flash of irritation. Itch has met Cash half a dozen times, at least.

"What, is he dating your mom or something?"

"I think so."

"Ooh, juicy!" says Lily. "Is he hot?"

"Gross!" I swat at her. "He's with my *mom*."

"I'm just wondering," Lily says. "It would be nice to have adult eye candy in the house." I swat her again.

Itch—of course—doesn't say anything about Cash. "Cool. I'll come over after dinner. Maybe we can go for a drive."

Lily and I make eye contact. "Ah, euphemisms," she says.

● ● ●

I don't know what's wrong with me, but I am finding every excuse in the world *not* to be alone with my boyfriend. Mom and Cash have taken over the family room to watch a documentary about organic farming, so Itch and I are sipping hot apple cider in the kitchen. "How about the basement?" he suggests.

"It just got painted. There are fumes. Besides, the drop cloths are still all over. Nowhere to sit."

"We could drive to the park."

"I don't think Mom will let me go out late—"

"It's eight-thirty, June."

"—when it's this cold. She's worried about ice on the roads. In fact, do you think you should head home before it freezes even more?"

Itch shakes his head. "I'm fine. I just thought we would *do* something before I left."

"We're doing something right now. We're talking." Neither of us mentions that it's not exactly our strong suit as a couple.

We sip our ciders.

Later, after Mom and Cash finish the documentary, they go downstairs to look at the basement walls. "They don't mind the fumes," Itch says, getting up to stand behind the stool I'm sitting on. He places his hands on my shoulders and moves his thumbs in circles against the base of my neck. I know—I *know*—it's supposed to feel good. It has felt good a hundred times before, but tonight . . . it doesn't. Tonight, I hate it.

I suddenly spring up, nearly knocking my empty mug off the counter. "Let's go out on the porch."

"It's really cold."

"I know, but at least we'll be alone."

The word "alone" motivates him, because five minutes later, we're zipped and bundled and Itch has me pressed up against one of the wooden supports. My eyes are closed and my head is tilted back so his mouth can reach mine. I know his hands are roaming up and down my sides, but I can barely sense them. Everything is clumsy and muffled, wrapped as we are in all this winter wear.

And there's no more ignoring the truth: I hate this. I hate everything about it. I don't hate *Itch,* but I hate the way I'm feeling. Or rather, the way I'm *not* feeling what I'm *supposed* to be feeling.

In fact—and somewhat ironically—kissing Itch is making

me feel itchy. Itchy in my *soul*. Like I'm a little kid waiting for my mother to try on clothing at the mall and I just can't stand *being* there anymore. Like breaking out of Itch's arms and running screaming into the darkness, and then maybe hiding behind a tree or something, like that would be a totally reasonable thing to do.

This is not good.

It seems endless—the kissing—but I don't know a way to stop it without telling him the truth, without embarking on an interminable discussion that is going to be way more painful than his tongue in my mouth.

So I endure.

I go through the motions until finally—*finally*—Itch is driving away and I'm waving from the porch with a massive sense of relief washing over me. I know I need to savor it, live in this reprieve, because it's going to go away and only awful, tremendous, crushing guilt will remain.

But right now, right *this* second, I couldn't be happier that my boyfriend is gone.

Chapter 14

Mom is on campus, finishing up some paperwork. I have already showered, eaten breakfast (who am I kidding—brunch), and unloaded the dishwasher. I throw a load of laundry into the washing machine and look around for something else to do, but the house is clean, I have no schoolwork, and there's nothing I want to watch.

I text Lily to see if she wants to go to the mall, but she's rehearsing for her studio's winter recital. I try Shaun, but of course he doesn't text back. I call Darbs, but her mom is making her watch the twins while she goes Christmas shopping. She invites me over, and I politely decline. The last time I helped Darbs with the twins, we took our eyes off them for ten minutes and they pulled all the sheets off her parents' bed. By the time we realized what was going on, they had tied the bedding into a long rope and one twin was being lowered out the upstairs bedroom window. Those kids stress me out. And it's not like I have a way to get to their house, anyway.

Crap. The first day of break and I'm already bored.

I know I should take some time to figure out what I'm going to do about Itch, but I have a full two weeks until he's back.

Maybe I'll feel differently when we've been apart for a little while. Maybe I'll miss him.

My phone buzzes, and I'm basically a ninja, I grab it so fast. My brain reflexes, however, are a little slower. It takes me a moment of staring at it to realize who the text is from.

Oliver.

Apparently he was telling Marley—his mom—about our shared playlist, and there was something he didn't know how to explain.

what's the diff between punk & alt?

I flop down across my bed to message him back, but I'm not even halfway through when I realize it's complicated enough to warrant a phone call. Oliver picks up immediately. "You must miss me."

"Not even close," I tell him. "But I'm hardly going to type the history of music to you on a phone. It would devalue the importance of the lesson you so sorely require."

"You're impossible," he says, but his voice sounds like he's smiling. "What are you doing?"

"Not much," I admit, and the phone shivers in my hand.

"Click on the link." He hangs up.

"Wait," I say into empty air. "I still haven't educated you." And he calls *me* impossible.

I pull up the new message from Oliver. It's a link to . . .

A game?

Oliver has sent me an invite to play a game—a really geeky one—through our phones. When I accept the invitation, I find that it's a strategy game that is (loosely) based on Greek mythology. It's peopled by little animated figures who wear winged sandals or carry lyres or wield thunderbolts. They stand around on a battlefield and make moves that the players assign them. Oliver's opening gambit involves a long-haired demigoddess eating a "Pomegranate of Power" before leaping astride a Pegasus and galloping in the direction of my little huddle of figures.

Despite this possibly being the actual dorkiest thing I've ever done, I touch the screen to deploy an "Army of Angry Muses" toward Oliver's Pegasus. He responds with a "Whirlwind Gorgon Attack" followed by a "Trident to the Face" . . .

And the battle is on.

• • •

"Yes!" I shout with a fist pump. It startles my mother, who drops the scissors she's using to snip mint leaves. She leans down to pick them up off the floor.

"June," she says. "I could have taken off a toe."

"Sorry."

"What are you doing, anyway?"

"It's just this stupid game Oliver sent me. I finally beat him."

My mother shakes her head. "It can't be *that* stupid if you've been playing it since yesterday."

"Oh, you know," I tell her. "It's something to do."

• • •

It's a day after Christmas, a week before we go back to school. Our tree is still up in the family room and small white lights still outline the front windows. The ripped dark-dyed jeans my dad sent me from New York (all the rage among the stage actresses, he says) are folded carefully in a drawer, waiting for the perfect time to be worn. The array of books and sweaters and earrings my mother gave me are heaped on my dresser. The funky upcycled case Itch gave me is already wrapped around my phone.

Mom and I shoveled the driveway this morning. I thought it was pointless, since there's a snowstorm coming, but Mom said we should at least start with a clean slate. She's had the Weather Channel on the television since she woke up, and she keeps checking the generator in her studio.

The first fat snowflakes are falling when Cash's truck pulls up in front of the house. "Dammit, I told him not to come," Mom says before she bolts outside. I look out the front window and watch her run down the porch steps toward Cash's pickup. Despite her words, the minute he opens his door, she flies into his arms and kisses him on the mouth.

A minute later, they're stamping their feet on the rug in the entryway, setting bags of groceries on the floor. "You don't listen," Mom says to Cash.

"I listen to your wishes, not your words." He grins at me. "Hey, want to give us a hand with these?"

"Sure." I carry one of the bags to the kitchen.

"Stay here," I hear Mom tell Cash, and then she's in the kitchen with me. "I have to talk to you. Cash and I have known each other for a long time. We have several mutual friends and . . . He'll sleep downstairs."

"He doesn't have to do that."

"Thanks, but that's the best place for him to . . ." Mom wraps her arms around me. "Even though we have an evolved

134

and enlightened mother-daughter relationship, it doesn't mean you want my sex life in your face."

"You are really making it weird," I tell her.

"Sorry."

"Can I have a boy spend the night, too?"

"No way."

"It was worth a shot."

Mom pulls back and gazes at me. She pushes a strand of hair away from my face. "You are still the most important person in the whole world," she says. "He's just a guy with a bag of groceries."

"I'm not calling him Dad," I say, and she flicks me in the head.

"Now who's making it weird?"

• • •

It snowed hard—big, fluffy flakes—for hours. It was still coming down when I went to bed last night after an evening of games with Mom and Cash. If they get married, I wonder if Dad will be invited to their wedding.

Now that it's Wednesday afternoon and it stopped snowing hours ago, I'm well into the realm of stir-crazy. It's not only that I'm stuck in our house; it's that I'm stuck with a pair of love-birds. They're not all over each other or anything—in fact, I feel like they're going out of their way *not* to touch each other—but I can tell. There's an energy in the air.

My mom wants to be alone with her new boyfriend, and I'm the cock blocker.

Gross.

I'm on the couch, huddled under a blanket with my phone, and have just sent a "Fiery Chariot of Doom" at Oliver when a tiny star pops up in the corner of my screen: a notice of an in-game message. I click on it.

snowed in?

Oliver's obviously in the same boat as me . . . well, minus the thing where the two adults in his house are dying to get in each other's pants.

Or maybe they are; what do I know about the Flagg family?

I send Oliver a message in return:

y. sux.

A nanosecond later, my phone rings. I pick it up. "I think you're the one who misses me," I tell Oliver.

"All I'm saying is you've played a *lot* of Mythteries."

"Which you only know because *you've* been playing. Hold on." I squiggle out of the blanket and off the couch. "Going upstairs!" I call to Mom and Cash.

I get a muffled "Okay" in return and opt not to go see what they're doing. Once in my room, I leap onto my bed and set the phone against my ear again. "You still there?"

"I'm housebound. Where else would I be?"

"This snowstorm is *killing* me," I confide. "Cash stayed over last night—"

"*What?*"

"—and now he's stuck here. I'm the world's most awkward third wheel."

Oliver's amusement comes through the phone and makes me smile. "Are they actively doing it?" he asks through laughter.

"They *want* to and that's even worse!"

Silence. Just when I think maybe Oliver has hung up, I hear his voice again. "Do you want to come over here?"

I'm startled. No, more than startled. I'm shocked. And also . . . pleased.

I'm inordinately *pleased* that Oliver has extended an invitation to his house. Except: "I'm snowed in, remember? We're all snowed in."

"Hold on." I hear some bustling around and then Oliver's voice again. "The snowplow's been by. Walk over."

"Walk? Seriously?"

"It's less than a mile. I'll meet you in the middle."

I hesitate.

And then I assess my reason for hesitating.

It's not that I *don't* want to hang out with Oliver. It's that I *do* want to, which is exactly why I'm not sure if I should do it. We finally have this friendship thing down. It's easy. It's not awkward anymore. I get him and I think he gets me. Yes, his music and philosophy are still cheesy, but they're not unbearable.

All that being said, it's a friendship that lies squarely within a set of very specific parameters. We are friends in the car. We are friends in school hallways. Occasionally, we're friends at lunch. Yes, there was that one time Oliver had dinner at my house, but Mom and Cash were right there, which meant that it was safe.

"Hello? Did you hang up?" Oliver asks into my ear.

"No, I'm here. I'm just . . ." I stop, because I don't know what I'm doing. I'm inexplicably nervous about being alone with Oliver, which is silly, which is crazy, which is—

"My parents are here," he says, like he can hear my thoughts. It works, because I feel myself nodding even though he can't see me.

"Okay. I'll come over."

"Give me half an hour before you leave."

• • •

Exactly thirty minutes later, after trying on several combos of clothing and settling on faded jeans with a slouchy cable-knit sweater, I assure Mom I will be careful and step outside. I pause on the porch to look around, and I realize that maybe I didn't need *quite* as much bundling up as I thought. The day is cold, but not bitterly so. In fact, it feels refreshing after having been stuck in the house for so long (with lovebirds). The sky is bright blue, scattered with big, fluffy clouds, and sunlight bounces off the white ground.

Floundering down off the porch and across the driveway takes a while, because the snow comes up to my knees, but once I've struggled over the big drift to reach the road, it's smooth sailing. The plow has packed the snow hard and my boots have good treads, so walking is easy. I peer down Callaway Lane, trying to guess where I will meet up with Oliver.

But Oliver is already in sight. Only a few houses away, he's trudging in my direction, and when he sees me, he waves an arm in greeting. He's wearing a twill hooded jacket, plus dark cherry mittens and a scarf that stand out against the white of the road.

My heart swells in my chest and I cannot deny that I am happy to see him.

Really happy.

"How'd you get here so fast?" I ask him. "Did you run?"

He grins down at me, and his teeth are the same white as the snow. I want to touch them with the tip of my finger, to stroke their shiny surface, but of course that would be shockingly strange and I do not. "I left when we hung up."

"But you told me—"

"I may have bent the truth. I didn't think your mom would like it if you walked all that way alone."

There's my heart again.

"Besides," says Oliver, "if I waited, I wouldn't have the entire walk back to do this." He bends over and scoops up a handful of snow. It takes several seconds longer than it should for me to understand that he's packing a snowball.

"Don't even think about it."

"Or what?"

"Or . . . I'll be forced to retaliate."

Oliver gives me a look of wide-eyed terror. Or rather a look of *mock* wide-eyed terror. "I'm supposed to be scared of a person who thinks climbing into my car is a great and challenging task?"

"Your car is ridiculous." I reach down to grab my own handful of snow.

"You don't think so when it's transporting you to school."

"No, I think so then, too." I'm having trouble being intimidating, because I'm smiling so hard. My face feels like it's been taken over by one of those little wooden hoops that Mom's friends use to stretch canvas when they're embroidering.

Maybe it's the reprieve from classes and schoolwork. Maybe it's that I've been cooped up with Mom and Cash for too long. Maybe it's Itch's departure. Whatever the reason, being with Oliver today is filling me with radiant joy—

—even when his snowball whaps me in the abdomen. I squawk and Oliver throws his hands up over his head. "Retreat! Retreat!" he yells, springing backward. I wind up to throw my ball but of course I miss him by miles, so I take off running after him instead. Or at least what counts as running when I'm wearing all this clothing and heavy boots.

Oliver bolts away (or what counts as bolting) and starts climbing one of the drifts that the plow has kicked up by the side of the road. It's taller than Oliver and he's only halfway to the top when I finally reach the drift. I grab him by the ankle and pull. He fumbles forward and falls, sliding back down to catch me. I squeal and flail as we roll into the drift, but he's holding me down by the shoulders and my heels are on a slippery patch, so I can't get any traction to push back.

"Truce," he says firmly, his dark brown eyes on mine.

I stare back, and in that moment, there's a rip in the fabric of the universe. Everything I know—the laws of high school and hierarchies and history—they shimmer away into nothingness, and all I can register is that Oliver's body is settled over mine and his face is very, very close.

Abruptly, Oliver jerks himself to his feet. He reaches a hand down and I allow him to take mine, to pull me up. "Truce," he repeats. This time, he doesn't look at me.

"Truce," I tell him.

• • •

Oliver's mother, Marley, sets two mugs of hot cocoa on the table. When I thank her, she tells me, "Wait a second, honey," then flutters away and back. She drops a large marshmallow into each cup. "They didn't have the small ones."

Oliver bumps his mug gently into mine. "Cheers."

"Cheers."

After running and climbing and sliding and screaming our whole way to Oliver's house, we arrived sweaty and wet. Marley took one look and sent me off to change, then threw my clothes into the dryer. That's why I'm wearing Oliver's mother's yoga pants—more formfitting than I'm accustomed to—and her lavender thermal shirt embellished with white lace appliqués. My thumbs are poked through the holes at the edges of the sleeves, which I'm finding surprisingly comfortable. When I put it on, Marley winked at me. "It's like your thumbs are getting a day-long hug," she said.

Now I'm seated at the Flagg family breakfast table across from the younger Flagg family son, who is wearing a dry pair of jeans and a plain white T-shirt. Unlike me, he was able to choose his outfit on his own.

Oliver's mom has the same white-blond hair as he does, but hers falls long and straight down her back. Her blue eyes are big and round, and so are her boobs. Her fingernails are perfectly manicured and painted a bright red. My mom is pretty in an earthy, no-makeup kinda way, but you can totally see how a horny college senior would pick Marley first.

It's the same way a horny high school senior would pick Ainsley first.

"How are you?" Marley asks me. "You've gotten so tall." Oliver and I make eye contact and we both crack up, because she sounds exactly like my mom did when Oliver came over.

"Please don't mention changing her diaper," Oliver tells his mother.

"What? What did I say?" Marley asks, but we're both laughing too hard to explain. "You kids. So silly."

Oliver's father, Bryant, wanders in while we're still calming down. He greets me before swinging an arm around Marley's waist, pulling her in for a kiss. "Have you ever seen such a woman? Oliver, you should be so lucky."

"Dad," says Oliver.

"Stop it, Bryant." But Marley doesn't sound like she means it.

"Here, if you want to be more traditional about it." Bryant pulls her to the foyer archway and points to the mistletoe hanging overhead before sweeping her into an even lower, more prolonged kiss.

I wonder if it's generational, all this PDA.

When the moment of marital bliss is over, Bryant turns his attention back to Oliver. "I talked to Alex this morning."

"Cool," Oliver mumbles.

"He says he can push your application to the top of the pile." Oliver nods and Bryant claps him on the shoulder. "Family connections, right?"

"Sure." Oliver turns to me. "Let's go down to the basement. Bring your cocoa."

"We have chips and salsa," Marley calls after us as we head out.

Oliver's house is big and made out of bricks, and everything is new. There are no piles of unfinished projects lying around, no exposed beams. Every interior surface is painted a muted hue, and I've already seen two chandeliers and a built-in wine fridge. He leads me down a set of thickly carpeted stairs to something that I would never refer to as a basement. At the very least, it's a "lower level." The large room features a Ping-Pong table, a wet bar, and a seriously big-ass TV.

Oliver rummages around behind the wet bar and comes up with the chips and salsa his mom mentioned. "I'm going to make an executive decision that we don't need a bowl." He rips the bag open and sets it on the counter.

"I second. Hey, are your parents like that together all the time?"

"They act out for company."

"Lucky you."

"They do everything together. Finish each other's sentences, all that stuff that's cliché but really kind of amazing."

"And rare." I'm thinking of my own parents, separated since before my memories begin. I'm also thinking of Itch and me. "Most couples don't work like that."

"True." Oliver gestures to the barstools and I perch on one, reaching for a chip. I'm not sure what we're going to do for entertainment, but I know I couldn't take off even if I wanted to, because my clothes are still in the dryer.

"Do you want to watch TV?" Oliver asks.

"No." It comes out sharper than I intended. Watching TV is what I do with Itch. Or rather what I *don't* do with Itch. I soften my tone. "I mean . . . it's not like I don't have a television at home."

"Table tennis?"

"The mere fact that you call it table tennis instead of Ping-Pong kinda makes me think that you would clobber me."

"I'll play left-handed," says Oliver, and I groan. "Okay, what, then?"

I honestly don't know. This is new territory—this being alone outside a car—even for the already new territory that is my friendship with Oliver. I'm not sure how to navigate this version of us.

Not that we're an "us."

We're definitely not.

Oliver waits and there's an awkward silence that is reminiscent of our very first carpool mornings. I don't know what to do when I'm hanging out with a guy who isn't Itch or Shaun. Or maybe just when I'm hanging out with a guy who *is* Oliver Flagg.

"I got it," says Oliver. "Jump up."

"Pardon?"

"Off." He gestures to the high-backed barstool I'm perched on. I give him a perplexed look but do as he asks. He lifts the stool and turns it around so the back is against the bar, then does the same with the one next to it. He hops onto my stool and pats the other, to his right. "Here."

"You prefer the view of the Ping-Pong table?"

"Trust me," he says, and—because, oddly enough, I do—I clamber onto the stool beside him. "Now what?"

"Hold on." He pulls out his cell phone and stabs at the

144

screen. Before I can figure out what he's doing, some old-school Iggy Pop starts playing. *My* old-school Iggy.

Oliver sets the phone on the bar behind us and settles back on his stool, staring straight ahead. "Look." He points straight in front of us.

"At the Ping-Pong table?"

"At the road."

Oliver stretches out his hands to grip an imaginary steering wheel, and I get it. He's pretending we're in his car, listening to our playlist, driving to school. He understands what I'm feeling, that we're in uncharted friendship territory. Maybe he's even feeling the same way. He's trying to make me comfortable. It's really nice and also really . . .

"Cute," I say.

"I try."

We "drive" in silence, and I know I should be the one to start the conversation, since he came up with the idea and all. I go with what I think is a safe topic. "Did you apply early decision anywhere?"

"A couple places," Oliver says. "State. Central."

"Not U of M?" The second it's out of my mouth, I regret the question. University of Michigan is competitive. Even for me, it's not a definite slam dunk. Oliver mumbles something under his breath, and I tilt my head toward him. "What?"

"Yeah, U of M, too," he says. "I just got the early acceptance letter."

Again, he manages to surprise me.

"I only applied because it's Dad's alma mater and all," he

continues. "I didn't think they'd actually let me in, and I'm definitely not going there."

"Why?" It seems like a no-brainer. Prestige plus football. If you're Oliver, what's not to love? "It's a great school."

"All that pressure about being part of a legacy." Oliver shakes his head. "I don't even know what I want to do yet. Starting somewhere close by makes so much more sense. I could try things out. Experiment. But my dad—" He sighs. "He says if I don't go to Michigan, I should expand my horizons. He's got this list—Carnegie Mellon, USC, Chapel Hill—and I guess I should do what he says, because of his whole self-made-man thing. If anyone knows how to win at life, it's him. But going far away when I don't have it figured out yet . . ." I must have made a sound because Oliver glances at me. "What?"

"All I *want* is to go far away."

"Where?"

"New York. Maybe NYU or Columbia. I'm applying local in the next round, but only because Mom is making me." I watch Oliver slide his hands to the left, steering our mimed car. "Where are we?"

"Just turned onto Plymouth. I had to wait at the corner for a phalanx of Harley riders."

Once again, I am impressed and surprised by Oliver's vocabulary. "Hey, your dad was talking about the uncle at the bank?"

"Yeah, Uncle Alex. You may have seen his name in the main lobby's trophy case." I shake my head and Oliver laughs. "Let me guess. You've never looked at those trophies, have you?"

"Not even once."

"Star quarterback twenty years ago." Oliver's smile vanishes.

"Now he's a branch manager in Ypsilanti. Drinks a lot of beer. Two kids and a wife. I think he loves them, but he never looks happy. You can read it all over him, how he thinks he settled. I don't want that. I don't want to settle and I don't want to make someone *feel* like I settled for her. Dad's all over me about the bank internship. He wants me to wear a maroon tie during the interview because it's a 'power color.' He's got it all figured out for me and he's probably right, because he's right about *everything,* but . . ." His voice trails off. "Sorry, that was weird."

I don't think it was weird. I think it was *brave.*

"You're a good listener or something," Oliver says, mime-driving us toward our imaginary school.

Because it was a lot to say, because it *was* brave, I think carefully before I speak again. "In case you didn't know, you're pulling it off," I tell him. "You seem like nothing bothers you and everyone's your friend and the world is your oyster, so you're totally pulling it off."

"Thanks," says Oliver. "I don't know if I believe you, but thanks."

"Hey, I think being perceived as a rock of teenage solidity must be nice, especially considering my own personal angst is pretty much broadcast loud and freaking clear twenty-four/seven—"

"What are you talking about?"

"Life. College and whatever."

"No, I mean about your own personal angst." Oliver drops his hands and turns to face me.

"Careful," I tell him. "You're going to run us into a ditch."

"I parked by the side of the road."

"In the snow?"

"There was a conveniently located parking lot." He leans toward me. "June, for the record, you don't broadcast any of that. To all onlookers, you're stable. You're the most stable. . . . You're like . . . a *castle* of stability."

"You're a liar." I know damn well I'm much more like a crowd of rowdy peasants rioting in the streets *outside* a castle.

"I'm not." Oliver tilts his head, and now that we're this close and alone, I can again see the charcoal lines circling his brown irises, and the enlargement of his pupils as he peers at me, and the faintest scatter shot of freckles across his cheekbones. I know—I've known for years—that Oliver is gorgeous. I know because he's popular and all the girls want him, and because he has a fancy car and a letter jacket and muscles. But I never liked that kind of boy. I liked boys with messy hair, boys who played guitar or who refused to wear leather or who didn't believe in God. Boys who wouldn't *conform*. Oliver's particular brand of all-American never did anything for me.

Until now.

Now I'm struck by how good-looking he is—and not just objectively, but how good-looking he has become *to me*. And how nice and complicated and interesting. And I'm reminded that although Oliver hasn't defied society's expectations, he has defied *mine,* and maybe that's a thousand times more compelling.

And a million times more dangerous.

Because I'm already there, and because this moment is fleeting and fragile, I take a tiny step further into the danger. "You know my castle of supposed stability?" I ask him. "It's surrounded by a moat."

"What's in your moat?" Oliver asks.

Insecurity. Self-doubt. Fear.

But I've already said too much. I look at my wrist like I'm checking a watch and then gesture toward the Ping-Pong table. "We're going to be late for school."

Oliver gazes at me, his eyes roving over my face, before he pulls away and turns forward. "Let's get moving," he says, and swings our imaginary car back onto our imaginary road.

• • •

We're in the kitchen again, completing the re-bundling so Oliver can walk me home. "Ready?" he asks.

"Almost." I pull my jacket sleeves over the cuffs of my mittens.

We're heading toward the foyer when we hear Marley calling for us to hold on. She scurries into the kitchen and sees us stopped under the arch. "Oh, good. You're still here. June, I have something for your mom. Wait just a second, okay?" She darts off before I can answer.

I look up at Oliver. "It's not going to be a sewing machine or a pair of heavy bookends or something, is it?"

"If so, I will carry your burden," he says in a (bad) British accent and then he bows, which I think is intended to be gallant. I laugh, and when I do, I catch sight of what's hanging above us.

Mistletoe.

Oliver sees two things: my glance and also the way my laughter cuts off abruptly. I start to step backward, out of the minefield, but he takes hold of my upper arms and I allow it. I let him

149

keep me there, under the mistletoe, looking down into my eyes while my boyfriend is in Florida and Oliver's girlfriend is . . .

Actually, I have no idea where Ainsley is.

Oliver must see the turmoil on my face, because he gives me the gentlest of smiles. "It's okay, June." He leans over and grazes my cheek with his lips. They're softer than I would have guessed. Warmer. Sweeter.

I suddenly realize I've closed my eyes, and I pop them back open. Oliver's smile morphs into a grin. "Nailed it." My eyebrows rise in a question, which he answers. "Tradition."

He's turned it into our playlist. Lightened the mood. Changed the meaning of the moment.

It's the right thing to do.

"Mistletoe is an American cultural tradition," I inform him, playing along. "Not a high school one."

"Still," he says, and I relent.

"Fine. You can have a song."

"Cutting Crew or Heart?" Oliver taps his chin in mock consideration, and I give an overly dramatic sigh. "I'm torn. What do you think?"

"I found it!" Marley rushes back in, waving a paper at me. "It's the gift certificate for a massage that I traded your mom."

I tuck it into a pocket. Apparently Oliver's mother also dabbles in the gypsy ways. "Thank you for having me over," I tell her, and then I follow Oliver away from the mistletoe and out into the snow.

Chapter 15

I thought about talking to Mom about this whole Itch dilemma, but she's so flushed and cuddly about Cash, it makes me not want to drag her back down to earth with my problems. That's why I'm sitting in the passenger seat of Shaun's hatchback, riding straight into the mouth of Saint Nicholas. Luckily for Shaun, a warm front came in this week after the snowstorm, so he was actually able to convince his parents that he should be allowed to visit his favorite place in the whole world: Frankenmuth.

Frankenmuth is a little over an hour north of us and is self-heralded as the "Little Bavaria" of Michigan. The tiny town is riddled with covered bridges and wooden cottages and inns decorated with towers and clocks and balconies. During the winter holidays, it looks like Christmas vomited on it.

Shaun and I coast up Main Street under the blinking white star lights hanging overhead. On all sides of us are shops selling ornaments, breweries selling wheat beer, and restaurants selling sausage.

"We should have left earlier," Shaun grumbles. "We could have taken the pretzel-rolling class." He slides into a parking spot between a Buick and a horse-drawn carriage (currently missing the horse). He's out of the car and opening my door before I've even unfastened my seat belt. He grabs my hand and pulls me onto the sidewalk. "First up: the world's biggest Christmas store!"

Minutes later, we're browsing a row of plastic candy canes. I point up at the two-story ceramic Santa Claus looming over us. "If that fell, we would be dead."

"But at least we'd go out happy."

"Speak for yourself." We watch a lady in a red apron wind up a tiny reindeer and place it in front of a customer's toddler. The reindeer clatters over the floor toward the kid, who claps and giggles before stomping on it. The kid's mother gasps and I burst out laughing. Shaun drags me around a corner, out of sight.

"Rude!" he tells me.

"Come on, that was funny."

His lips twitch. "Fine. It was funny. So you know you have to dump him, right?"

"Non sequitur much?"

I talked to Shaun about my problems with Itch on the drive up here, but he stayed mostly quiet, only asking a question here and there before turning on music (*decent* music!) and humming along for the rest of the drive. Now I find out he's actually been thinking about what I said.

"You can't keep dating someone you don't like anymore," Shaun tells me. "That's a recipe for tragedy."

"It's not that I don't *like* him. It's that I don't like him the way I used to like him. Or maybe I don't like him the same way he likes me. Or as much. Or . . ." I trail off, because I know Shaun is right. "I need to break up with him, don't I?"

Shaun nods. "Yeah."

"Yeah." I pick up a red glass ornament and see myself, looking small and lost and confused, reflected in its shiny surface.

"Hey, June?" Shaun is looking right at me. "Is there someone else?"

Of course Oliver flashes into my mind, because—duh—I just hung out with him a couple days ago, and there was that whole thing with the mistletoe and the imaginary car and the hot cocoa. It's only because he's the one boy I spend time with besides Shaun and Itch. It's only because we carpool together and listen to music together and argue philosophy together. It's only because, objectively speaking, he's an attractive guy. That's all. That's it.

"Nope," I tell Shaun. "No one else."

He regards me before picking up a Mrs. Claus puppet and sliding it over his hand. Mrs. Claus tilts her head at me and bobs up and down. "That's what I thought," she says in a funny voice that sounds very much like Shaun's.

• • •

Two days later, I end it.

"Why?" Itch asks.

We're back at Cherry Hill Park, but this time I'm the only one sitting on a swing, my bare hands wrapped around the metal chains and my boots sliding across the patch of ice beneath me. Itch stands facing me with his arms folded across his chest. His eyes are hard and angry.

"I'm sorry," I say from my seat. "It's not about someone else, and it's not really even about you."

"Thanks for that."

"Maybe it's because we're halfway through the year and real life is on the horizon, I don't know. Whatever it is, we're not working anymore." I wait but he doesn't respond, so I pull myself up from the swing. My fingers are cramped, frozen from the cold of the chain and the tension in my body. I shake my hands and rub them together, then step closer to Itch. I look up into his hazel eyes, and I remember how I used to think he looked like he was daydreaming, and how touching his flop of almost-curly hair used to make me warm inside.

Used to.

"Do *you* think we're working?" I ask him. He looks down and scuffs at the hard ground with the toe of his sneaker. "Adam. Are you actually happy when you're with me?"

Maybe it's his first name, or maybe it's the question itself that elicits a reaction. Itch shakes his head and steps backward. He puts space between us, looks at me from across a distance that might as well be acres and acres of land. "You know what's crap?"

"My timing. I know, I'm sorry." And I truly am. "I didn't want to have this conversation at school tomorrow. I thought we could—"

"No, June. Your timing is fine. Perfect, in fact. Couldn't be better." His eyes narrow. "What's crap is you making me drive all the way the hell out here and pick you up at your house and say hello to your mom and drive you to a park just so you could have the pleasure of choosing the location of our breakup. That is some epic crap."

I blink at him, shocked. "I'm sorry," I finally manage to get out. "You're hurt, I get it. I'm—"

"I'm not hurt, June. I'm *pissed.* Your timing doesn't suck. It's *you* that sucks. You need to grow some already, learn to freaking drive and . . ." He stops, shaking his head again. He runs his fingers through his hair, that messy hair that is no longer mine to touch, and I suddenly wonder if there's a chance this is all a horrible mistake, merely a flash of stupid teenage insecurity or desire for drama. I reach a hand toward Itch but he pulls back.

"Never mind," he says. "It's done."

This morning when I was working out what I'd say to end my relationship with my boyfriend, it didn't occur to me that I might be the one to cry, that it would be me dissolving into tears before him.

And yet now here I am.

"I'll call my mom," I say through sobs. "You don't have to drive me home."

Itch glares at me. "I'm not leaving you alone outside in the winter. I'm not an asshole." He points to where he parked when we arrived at Cherry Hill, when he thought we were coming here for a make-out reunion, before he knew I was dumping him. "Get in the car, June."

So I do.

Chapter 16

I hear Oliver's horn outside as I'm shoving my feet into boots. "Hold on!" I yell in his direction, even though he can't hear me through the door.

When I make it out to the porch, I find him standing right there, waiting for me. "Hello?" I say it like a question and am shocked when the answer comes in the form of a giant hug that lifts me off the ground. "What are you doing?" I squeal as he sets me down and then bounds toward the behemoth.

"Picking you up!" he yells back. "Get it? *Picking you up.*"

"That's terrible." I follow him across the driveway, not acknowledging the way something inside me lit up when he held me. "It's not a pun. It's not even a joke." I reach the car and climb inside. "I can't believe you get this excited about school."

"I am a man of high emotion."

"You are a boy of great ridiculousness," I tell him as we pull onto Callaway Lane.

The thing I'm dreading doesn't come up until we're halfway to school.

"How was the rest of break?" Oliver asks me. "Did you see Itch?"

"Fine. We got together yesterday."

I can't put my finger on exactly why I'm not ready to tell Oliver about breaking up with Itch, although I know it's at least partially because I'm ashamed. I feel bad that I made Itch angry, and I hate how he shined a giant glaring light on the ugliest parts of me.

But that's not all of it.

The idea of talking to Oliver about Itch—of letting him know I'm single—something about it makes me feel . . . nervous. It's too intimate. It exposes me. Leaves me raw and open. It makes me available.

It makes me an option.

So instead, I change the subject. "Do you guys have a new terrible plan for the stupid senior prank?"

"Well, since you asked so sweetly, yes we do," says Oliver. "The day before spring break starts, we're going to cover the teachers' cars with birdseed."

"No."

"Perhaps you don't understand." Oliver switches to a slower, more pronounced method of speaking. "We'll put the seed out in the morning, and by the time the last bell rings, all their cars will be covered in poo."

"Oh, I understood fine," I assure him. "It's still awful."

"Theo thinks it's genius," Oliver argues.

"We've already established what I think of Theo." I point a finger at him. "That amount of bird poo will wreak havoc with the paint on the cars. Do you comprehend how little teachers make?"

"I can't win with you." Oliver gives a rueful laugh. "You know that, right, Rafferty?"

• • •

I come out of the environmental sciences classroom and automatically turn in the direction of the stairwell, but I take only a couple steps before I remember that I don't go there anymore.

It's weird and also a little sad.

I know Oliver is probably still in family sciences and I could say hello or hang with him during the break, but instead, I walk past Mrs. Alhambra's room quickly, with my head down.

I could go to physics early, but then I'd be sitting in my seat when Oliver and Ainsley came in, and the thought of trying to make conversation while avoiding any mention of Itch makes me feel tired. So this time I *do* go to the stairwell, because I figure that's the last place my ex-boyfriend will be. There I edge my back into a corner and I ignore all the students bustling past me in an effort to get upstairs or downstairs. I don't want to see Itch and I don't want to see Oliver. I don't even want to see Shaun, because he'll ask how it went, and then I'll have to relive the breakup by telling the story of it. There's only one guy I want to talk to right now, but he's on a very different schedule from me. I send a text anyway, just in case—

hey, are you there?

—and he answers right away.

yep, on way to work. what's up?

itch & i broke up.

u ok?

158

I pause before writing back but decide to go with the truth.

    i'm sad

There's a pause before his message appears on my screen:

    sorry, hon. he's a fool if he can't see how beautiful
    you are. best girl in the world. hands down.

I could clarify. I could explain that I'm the one who did the breaking up, that I'm only sad because it's the end of something, because change is hard, because change is scary. My heart doesn't have to be broken to ache.

But all that is too complicated, so I just type back two words:

    thx, dad

• • •

I eat lunch in the library. We're not supposed to have food in here, because they think we'll drop a pizza in the books or something, but I huddle in a study desk and hide my sandwich behind a magazine.

No one bothers me.

• • •

When Darbs enters Spanish class, she makes a beeline for my chair and pokes me in the shoulder. "First day back and you're already sitting with the pom-poms?"

"No," I tell her. "I ate in the library."

"We're not allowed to eat in the library."

"Since when do you follow the rules?"

"I don't," Darbs says. "But you do. What's up?" She slides into the chair beside me, ignoring the huff of annoyance from Zoe Smith, who had been about to sit down.

"Itch and I broke up."

Darbs nods in a way that I think is supposed to imply infinite wisdom. "Now it all makes sense."

"Why? Did he say something at lunch?"

"He didn't show, either. Why'd you do it?"

"Why do you assume I was the dumper and not the dumpee?"

"Come on, June." Darbs tilts her head at me. "For a one-note guy like Itch, all that poser crap—eating lunch with the jocks and listening to you talk about football games—it was a lot. He was bending over backward to try to make you happy." I blink at her and she gives me a compassionate smile. "But you checked out a while ago." I nod and she reaches across the aisle to hug me. "It's okay, Junie. Having a change of heart doesn't make you a bad person."

I feel a lump rise in my throat and I swallow it back. "How are things with you?" I ask so we can stop talking about Itch. "Any news on the Yana front?"

"Nope," says Darbs. "But I made out with Ethan Erickson over winter break." I almost choke on my gum. Darbs whacks me on the back, and after a second, my coughing morphs into laughter. "What's so funny?" she asks when it's clear I'm not about to die.

"I made out with Ethan Erickson over *summer* break."

She stares at me and then she's cracking up, too. When the bell rings, we're still laughing so much that Señora Fairchild gives us a stern stare from the front of the room and refuses to start class until we calm down.

• • •

"How was your weekend?" Oliver asks once I'm strapped in and we're heading onto the road.

"Great. I caught this punk band at a warehouse in Ypsilanti. The cover charge included a free download, so fear not: you'll be hearing them multiple times just as soon as I prove to you yet once again that I am right and you are wrong."

"Are they loud and screamy?"

"The loudest and the screamiest."

"Awesome. Who'd you go with? Itch?"

Oh, right. This.

It's been a full week—one in which Itch has avoided me like the prom, and in which I still haven't told Oliver that Itch and I broke up. It just doesn't seem relevant anymore. Or at least, it doesn't until Oliver mentions him and I remember he still thinks we're together.

Crap.

"No," I tell Oliver. "It was a girls' night. Just Lily and Darbs and me."

He raises an eyebrow. "Lily likes punk?"

"Lily tolerates punk," I tell him. "But she loves punk *boys.*"

"I would not have guessed that," Oliver says, shaking his head. "People are so interesting."

"Totally."

• • •

The next day, I decide to take action. At least in one area of my life.

I sprint out of world history when the bell rings, and I somehow make it into the adjoining building and to the second floor just as Itch is coming out of Ms. Jackson's class.

"Hey," I say to him.

"Hey." He doesn't break his stride. I have to whip around and jog to catch up to him.

"Slow down," I say. "Please." Itch does, but not very much, so I grab his sleeve. "Actually, can you stop walking? I just raced here from the main building and I kinda need a second to catch my breath."

He stops, shaking free from my hold. "What do you want, June?"

"It doesn't have to be like this," I tell him. "This thing where we avoid each other and make it weird for everyone else."

"Everyone else is fine."

"I'm not fine. I miss you." Itch's expression doesn't change, but his shoulders tense and the rest of him goes still. "I miss you as a friend," I clarify.

A puff of air escapes his mouth and he presses his lips together hard. "The thing is, I already have friends."

"Really? Because I thought we had the same friends, and apparently they don't see you, either. All I'm saying is come have lunch with us again. We are all evolved people. We aren't cretins who can't handle a shift in our interpersonal dynamics." I nudge his arm. "Besides, I think maybe they miss you, too."

Itch looks down at me for a long moment. "Were you lying? The part where you said there's no one else. Was that a lie?"

"No," I say immediately. "Not a lie. I am one hundred percent single and I don't see that changing anytime in the foreseeable future."

"All right." Itch starts walking down the hall away from me.

I watch him go for a second before calling after him. "Wait! Itch, hold on." He doesn't stop, so yet again, I find myself chasing him down. This time, I fall into stride alongside, although I use the word "stride" loosely, as I'm taking two steps for every one of his. "Where are you going?"

"To the cafeteria. Our friends are probably already there."

I stop in mid-step and then have to run to catch up with him again. "You're right. They probably are."

We walk there together.

Chapter 17

"Okay, check this." Oliver merges onto the highway. "Rock salt."

"Rock salt," I repeat.

"We'll use it to write our class year in huge numbers on the football field." He holds up a hand toward my face. "Hear me out before you start squawking." Since I am, in fact, poised to squawk, the only thing I can do is clamp my mouth shut. "No one will be able to tell at first. The field will look exactly the same as it always has, but then the salt will slowly kill the grass and the numbers will gradually appear. Like magic."

"Magic."

"Magic!" Oliver does a sparkle thing with his hands, as if he's revealing a card trick. "Best of all, no animals!"

I smile because he's so goofy, but of course I still don't approve. However, I pretend to consider it. "It *does* seem like a reasonable prank, because you're not really harming anything."

"Exactly! Just the grass!"

"And grass will grow back sometime, right? It's not like it needs to be on the field permanently or anything."

Oliver grins, triumphant. "Finally, something the relentless June Rafferty will approve!"

"Yeah." I nod, still pretending. "I mean, it's just a football field. Only the *stage* upon which plays a myriad of high school dramas that will fade into obscurity the minute we all disappear . . . much like the grass under your salt."

Oliver deflates. "You don't actually approve, do you?"

"Nope."

"And you're taking a new song."

"Yep."

"You're the worst," he tells me.

"You're going to be hearing a lot more of the Clash."

"Fine," Oliver says. "Back to the drawing board."

• • •

I'm almost done with my sandwich when I ask it. "Where's Itch?" It's a reasonable question, since he's been sitting with us for the past few weeks.

Darbs's soda pauses halfway between the table and her mouth. "I don't know." Her gaze slides to Lily.

"What?" I ask. "Lily, I saw that. What was that? *What?*"

"Calm down," Darbs says. "You weren't here yesterday. You were off with the pom-poms again. Itch can do the same thing. He can have lunch elsewhere."

I look around the cafeteria. No Itch at any table that I can see. "Where else would he be?"

Lily's the one who tells me. "He's eating in the art room."

"The art room? Itch doesn't do art. Is he being weird about

me again? I thought we were over that. We've been fine. Haven't we *seemed* fine? . . . *What?*"

"I don't think it has anything to do with you," Darbs says in an overly gentle tone.

"Of course it does. Why else would he be in the art room?"

"Because that's where Zoe eats," Lily tells me.

"Zoe Smith? What does Zoe Smith have to do with . . . oh." The synapses suddenly connect. "Itch likes Zoe."

"Zoe likes him back," Darbs says helpfully, and Lily elbows her. "What?"

"It's cool," I tell them. "Really, it's totally fine."

And it is. Or at least it should be. Just like I told Oliver, none of this really matters anyway. In the grand scheme of life, Itch is just some guy I dated for a little while in high school. A bump in the road.

Still, it's inordinately annoying when your bump is with another bump so soon after the road got paved.

Or something like that.

• • •

"What are you doing for Valentine's Day?" Oliver asks me.

"Nothing," I say on autopilot, because I'm busy trying to add my latest win to our shared playlist. (Thanks, blog post about teenage conformity contributing to limitations in success!)

"Aren't you going to at least bake him cookies or something?"

Oh hell. He's talking about Itch. I still haven't told Oliver that we broke up, and the longer it takes, the weirder it'll be to mention it.

"Uh, yeah. I guess so. Cookies. That's great." *Hell hell hell.* "What are you guys doing?"

"I was hoping you'd have a brilliant idea. Maybe something a little unique."

"Flowers?"

"Call me crazy," says Oliver, "but I sort of thought that you, with your genius brain, might come up with something slightly more original than flowers."

"Cookies shaped like flowers?"

"You suck," says Oliver, but he laughs.

I don't laugh. I'm bugged. Seriously bugged. Worst of all, it's not just that I'm continuing this stupid lie-by-omission. It's that I don't want to come up with a cutesy gift for cutesy Oliver to give to cutesy Ainsley on Valentine's Day.

Jeez.

Get a life.

• • •

I bring it up to Darbs later in the day. "Are you doing anything for Valentine's Day? Like with Ethan or something?"

"Gross, no." She picks through the wads of paper crammed in her locker.

"Hey, I don't know. You think stupid *prom* is so romantic."

"Yeah, because you can smuggle in beer. Make a *date* out of it. Valentine's Day isn't even a real holiday. It's made up by people who sell cards."

She's got a point.

Suddenly, Theo is between us, leaning against the lockers

and looking down at Darbs. "I got a fake ID," he tells her. "I can hook you up with beer for Valentine's Day."

Darbs gives him the once-over. "In exchange for what?"

"A blow job."

Seriously, a nuclear bomb is more subtle than Theo.

"I'd rather be boiled in hot oil," Darbs tells him. "Or die from a thousand salted paper cuts."

"Why not?" He points at me. "She gives road head every day."

"I do not!" I explode, furious and mortified. "And do you have any idea what an epic douche you are?"

"Whatever." Theo stays focused on Darbs. "Come on, you'll do anyone. Boys. Girls. Everyone's your type. I don't see what the big deal is."

Darbs and I both glare at him. "Actually, I only have one type," Darbs says. "Human. And you don't qualify."

She slams her locker door shut and starts down the hall. I'm about to follow when Theo grabs me by the shoulder. "Hafferty."

I yank away. "What do you want?"

"Stop cock blocking me, already."

I laugh out loud. "I could roll a red carpet out for you, and Darbs still wouldn't be into it."

"Not *her*," says Theo. "Oliver."

I momentarily wonder if Theo has lost his mind. "What are you talking about?"

"It's just grass." Theo frowns down at me. "But of course you say no, because you're a loser killjoy, and he *listens*. Back off already. No one's buying the 'now I'm cool' act. Let us have some fun." He glowers at me before stomping away.

Maybe I should be upset about the slam, but instead, I zero

in on the part that seemed like a compliment. Like a good thing. It was a reminder: Oliver listens to me.

• • •

The next day, I'm in physics. Class started ten minutes ago and Oliver still hasn't shown up. I wouldn't think twice about it except he drove me to school this morning and never said anything about missing class. Also, Ainsley stopped by my desk on her way in to ask if I've seen him.

No idea.

I'm taking notes on rotational inertia when a hesitant underclassman opens the door. As he walks to the teacher's desk, I realize why he's familiar. It's because he's the smallest sophomore on the football team, the one who once—very temporarily— sported the silhouette of a penis and balls on his head, thanks to Theo Nizzola.

He says something quietly to Mrs. Nelson and they both look at me. Mrs. Nelson crooks her finger for me to approach her desk and I comply, knowing the rest of the class is wondering what I did wrong. "Go down to the office," she says.

"Why?"

The sophomore shrugs. "They said they needed your information. I think some files got corrupted in the school computer or something."

"Thanks," I tell him, and he nods before padding from the room.

"Should I take my stuff?" I ask Mrs. Nelson, but she's already at the board, writing about triple integrals in her big, loopy scrawl, so I make an executive decision and pack everything up. Better safe than sorry. I head out, taking care to pull the physics door closed behind me, and turn to go down the hallway. . . .

Oliver is standing right in front of me.

I jump. "What the hell!" I say out loud, and then remember we're right outside a classroom. I bring my voice down to a stage whisper. "What are you doing here?" Oliver opens his mouth but I cut off whatever he's about to say. "Actually, tell me later. I got called to the office."

"No you didn't."

"Yes, I did. Someone came in and—"

"That was me. He did that for me. The office doesn't need you."

I gape at Oliver. "You really are the King of Everything."

But Oliver doesn't seem amused. In fact, he looks pissed. "I just did something that may surprise you," he tells me. "Three guesses. Go."

This is the weirdest thing ever, Oliver busting me out of class to angry-quiz me in the hall. Since I don't have the faintest clue what he might have done, I toss out something facetious. "Got an A on a new recipe in family sciences class?"

"Wrong," says Oliver. "And whatever your next two guesses are, they will also be wrong, so I'll go ahead and tell you. I punched Itch in the mouth."

"What?" My backpack hits the floor. "Why?"

"It's kind of a funny story."

"I sincerely doubt that." Now I'm pissed, too. What kind of Neanderthal goes around hitting people?

"I was heading to my locker to get my physics book, minding my own business, when guess what I saw in the stairwell?"

"I think we already established that you're not interested in my guesses," I tell him, setting my fists on my hips.

"Good point," says Oliver. "I saw Adam 'Itch' Markovich rounding first base with Zoe Smith."

It takes me a second to put the pieces together. My ex-boyfriend making out in our ex-make-out place with his new girlfriend. Utterly rude. But why did Oliver . . .

Oh.

Oh, *shit*.

Of their own accord, my hands have flown to my face to cover my mouth. "Oliver, I—"

"I was furious," Oliver continues. "Furious on behalf of my very good friend June Rafferty, one of my best friends, the one with whom I made a solemn fist-bump promise to always speak the truth, the one whom I don't want to see get hurt. That is why I followed Itch to study hall, and why I punched him in the mouth. Because he was cheating on my very good, very *honest* friend."

"Oliver . . ." I try again, except I don't know how to follow up after I've said his name. Words have completely escaped me.

"Itch was a little confused about why I was hitting him," says Oliver. "He didn't try to punch me back or even defend himself."

"What happened?" I whisper from behind my fingers.

"He said, 'Dude, what the hell?' and then he wiped the blood from his mouth and looked at it like he was shocked. And I realized that he *was,* in fact, shocked. So I explained to him why I had felt the need to defend your honor."

"I'm so sorry." There's nothing else to say.

"And then I find out there *is* no honor to defend, that you and Itch are broken up, that you broke up *weeks* ago and never happened to mention it to me even though we spend every morning together. Even though only yesterday—*yesterday*—I asked what you and Itch were doing for Valentine's Day, and instead of telling me the truth, you pretended you were still a couple."

"Oliver." I take a step toward him, but he pulls back.

"Don't," he says. "You can't make this better with big words or flowery speeches. Maybe you think I'm this big, stupid jock who always runs around punching people—"

"I don't think that, I swear!"

"—but just for the record, I've never hit someone unless it was during a football play. Now, because of you, I'm a guy who punches people." He glares at me and I'm scared by what I've done to him, by his anger. "Thanks for that, June. Thanks a lot."

Oliver whirls and stalks away down the hall. I watch him go, the fear blossoming, expanding inside me. It's not that I'm afraid he'll hurt me. I'm terrified that I have hurt him in some way that can never be healed.

• • •

I don't go back to physics. Instead, I wait by study hall until the bell rings and students pour out of the classroom. When Itch sees me, he turns and walks in the opposite direction, so I have to run to catch up with him.

"Itch, please." I'm practically jogging beside him. "I'm sorry Oliver hit you."

He jerks to a halt and narrows his eyes at me. "Oliver is already sorry that Oliver hit me. Oliver told me so about a hundred times,

172

and then Oliver insisted on buying me several cold sodas to hold against the place where Oliver's fist connected with my mouth."

I zero in on Itch's lower lip. It's swollen but not too bad. I feel a tiny bit better. After all, I've seen Oliver throw a football. He has a hell of an arm. There's no way he put full effort into that swing.

"Why didn't you tell him?" Itch demanded. "Why pretend we were still dating? You're the one who broke up with me, so what the hell is your problem?"

The only thing I can say is 100 percent true: "I don't know."

For a while, Itch stares down at me without speaking. He finally says, "Actually, I don't really care what your problem is. Your problem is not my problem. Not anymore."

And for the second time in one day, I'm left standing in a hallway while a boy walks away from me.

Chapter 18

The next morning, I gear up for the day by spending some quality time with the sweet note Dad sent with my birthday flowers. I try to convince myself that I am a decent person. That's why I keep the note on my bedroom bulletin board: for just such emergencies.

It doesn't really help.

However, since *Oliver* is a decent person, he shows up in front of my house, just like every other weekday morning.

"I didn't know if you were going to come," I say as soon as I climb aboard the behemoth.

"I honor my promises," Oliver says, backing out into the street. I appreciate that he didn't add the words "unlike you." Still, he doesn't look at me.

"I'm sorry," I tell him.

"I know."

"What can I do?"

Oliver is quiet for a while. He finally says, "You can explain why."

"It's high school, remember? People just know when you're dating; people just know when you break up."

"Friends know *before* the random people know," he says. "Friends tell each other when big life events happen. I thought . . ."

He stops and I fill in the rest of the sentence for him. "You thought we were supposed to be friends." Oliver nods. "We are," I say.

Snowy fields go by in silence. The highway happens in silence. Main Street is nothing but painful, empty silence. I can't think of the right way to break it, to make this okay. All the sentences I write in my head seem flat and cliché. All apologies, all excuses. They don't make any sense, because . . .

Because I don't make any sense.

That's what I realize as we drive onto campus: I, myself, June Rafferty, don't make any sense. So that's what I tell Oliver.

My friend Oliver.

As he pulls into a spot, I set my hand on his arm. "Wait."

Oliver puts the car into park but doesn't turn off the engine. He keeps his eyes pointing straight ahead through the windshield and does what I ask. He waits.

"There was no *reason*. Itch didn't do anything wrong. He was exactly the same as he always was. I just . . ." I stop as guilt washes up and over and through me again. "I just didn't like him anymore. Not like that. It all went away and was gone, and no matter what I did, it wouldn't come back." My words tumble out faster now that I'm giving voice to my confusion. "I hate that I did that to Itch, but it would have been worse if I'd continued on with it, if I'd kept putting one foot in front of the other, moving in the same direction when all I wanted to do was jump to a different path and—"

"What path?" Oliver turns to look at me. The morning sun is brilliant behind him, blazing his white-blond hair into a halo, and just like that, I'm speechless again. Oliver leans closer. He stares directly into my eyes. "What different path did you want to jump to?"

I swallow. "I didn't . . . I just knew this one was wrong."

Oliver gazes at me for a long, long moment. I go warm inside and he finally pulls away, settling back against the window. "You did the right thing."

"I did?"

"Not the part where you didn't tell me. That sucked. I mean breaking up with Itch." He pulls his keys out of the ignition and twists in his seat so he can retrieve his backpack from the floor behind him. "It would be worse to stay with someone because of convenience or because senior year is halfway over or something. That would be worse."

Before I can answer, he opens his door and swings out of it. "So you're forgiven," he says. "But from now on—"

"No secrets." I cut him off. "Promise."

"Good," Oliver says, and slams the door.

• • •

Ainsley is standing in front of my locker when I arrive to switch out one science book for another. Her eyes are extra sparkly against her light brown skin. "Dude!" she says, wrapping an arm around me. "You are at the center of some very epic drama. What happened with you and Itch? Did he cheat on you with Zoe?"

Oh, good. Now I get to deal with this.

176

"Did someone tell you that?" I ask to buy time, twirling the combination dial.

"*Several* someones."

"Well, they're wrong." I pull away from her so I can open the door and toss my environmental science textbook inside. "Itch didn't cheat on me. I broke up with him and then he started dating Zoe. Completely legit and no big deal. It was all a misunderstanding. Oliver shouldn't have punched him."

I turn to find that Ainsley has a startled look on her face. Her eyes lock on mine and her brows slowly move toward each other. "What?"

Whoops.

I didn't tell Oliver I had broken up with Itch, and Oliver didn't tell Ainsley he had punched him. She heard about the breakup from someone else (or, rather, *several* someones), but it hadn't gotten back to her yet that her boyfriend had roughed up my ex-boyfriend, probably because how do you tell someone that?

Suddenly, it's really awkward up in here.

"Oliver *hit* Itch?"

"Uh, yeah?" It comes out of my mouth like a question. "Oliver saw him kissing Zoe and thought he was cheating on me. From what you're saying, it sounds like he wasn't the only one who thought that, but I guess Oliver got a little . . . overly zealous."

Ainsley doesn't say anything. She studies me, like she's trying to figure something out. If she succeeds, I hope she'll let me in on it. "Why didn't Oliver know you broke up with him? You're with him every single morning."

177

Ah, the million-dollar question.

"Oliver and I don't get personal."

It's not exactly the truth, but it's not completely a lie, either. How are you *supposed* to tell someone you've pledged a friendship of honesty with her boyfriend? It's on the up-and-up . . . but somehow, it doesn't sound like it.

How did this get so complicated?

Ainsley keeps staring at me, and I can't tell what she's thinking. There's a long pause, during which I can't help wondering if she has any inclination toward violence. After all, her boyfriend did just throw a punch. Maybe they were brought together by their shared love of physical savagery?

Ainsley makes a move toward me and I flinch backward, but she's fast. In a second, her arms are around me. "You poor thing," she whispers into my ear. "It's so embarrassing."

Embarrassing? I think other words are more appropriate, but I'm not about to quibble over semantics. I just go with it. "*So* embarrassing."

"I mean, Zoe Smith." Ainsley says it with a shudder. "You know she only passed chem last year because she let Mr. Welch look at her tits."

I try to imagine Zoe doing such a thing. She's artsy and quirky, but an exhibitionist? I don't know.

"Don't worry," says Ainsley. "You're way prettier than her."

Where I fall on the beauty scale in relation to Zoe is actually the least of my worries, but given the weirdness of this whole situation, I'm willing to let Ainsley think that's where my concerns lie. "Really? You think so?"

"Totally," Ainsley assures me.

"Awesome," I say, even though this conversation is anything but awesome.

• • •

I manage to catch Oliver alone as he's going into the cafeteria for lunch. "Heads up. Ainsley was a little surprised to find out about the whole Itch debacle. You might want to tell her that you have a thing about cheaters or something. . . . What?"

Oliver is grinning at me. "It's all good, Rafferty. Ainsley is into knights in shining armor or something. She thinks it was chivalrous." He sees my look. "Don't worry. I'm not about to make it a thing, where I go around hitting people. I'm just saying that in this one scenario, this one time . . . it ended up just fine."

"Except for the part where Itch got a fat lip for no reason."

At least Oliver has the good sense to look uncomfortable. "Right, except for that," he says.

God, I can't wait to get out of here.

Chapter 19

I meet Shaun at his locker after homeroom. He gives me a dead rose and I give him a burnt heart-shaped cookie, and then we hold hands on the way to AP English. No one even looks at us funny. "Are you sure you can't just be straight?" I ask him. "It would make everything easier."

"It would." Shaun's tone is more earnest than usual, making me wonder what's going on with him.

"How's Kirk?"

"Fine, I guess." Shaun heaves a long, deep sigh. "But I wish he was here and we didn't have to be long-distance. We could go to a movie or do our homework together or make out on the bleachers or whatever people do when they live in the same place."

"Making out on the bleachers isn't all it's cracked up to be. You're either too hot or too cold, and someone is always at an uncomfortable angle."

"It's got to be better than this." Shaun pulls me to a halt. He reaches for my other hand, and as kids flow around us in the hallway, he closes his eyes. "Nope." He shakes his head. "Not good."

"What are you doing?"

"Close your eyes."

I oblige, because it's Shaun. "Now what?"

"Pick someone. Someone like Itch, from your past. Or someone else. Whoever, just as long as it's someone you know. Try to picture him."

I imagine Shaun. "You look cute today. Nice shirt."

Shaun squeezes my hands. "Come on, someone who makes your heart go *whammo*."

Oliver rises behind my lids. He's grinning so I can see the top row of his teeth. His eyes are crinkling straight at me and he's happy—so happy it makes the corners of my mouth tug upward in response.

"Got someone?"

"Yes."

"Good," says Shaun. "Can you see the person? Like *really* see him?"

My imagined Oliver's grin widens. He leans toward me and suddenly I can do more than picture the way he looks. I can smell the clean, soapy scent of him; I can hear his laugh the way it sounds when it rings out in the behemoth. "Yes," I whisper. Shaun doesn't answer, so I open my eyes.

He's looking at me with sadness written all over his face. He gives me a smile that is rueful and agonized and heartbreaking all at once. "When I close my eyes, I can't see Kirk anymore," Shaun says. "I used to be able to picture him so clearly. There was this hallway downstairs in the main building where we met at Rutgers. The first time we kissed, it was in a corner down there, under one of those crappy fluorescent lights that make everyone look terrible. Everyone except Kirk. Even under that flickering, greenish light, he still looked like a Greek god. That's what I could always picture, what he looked like under those lights."

"But technology," I say. Because it's Shaun, he understands.

"It makes it worse. We talk on our phones or our computers and it's supposed to be better, it's supposed to connect us, except now when I close my eyes, all I can see is the tech version of Kirk. He's pixelated or blurry or frozen because the connection has died." Shaun sighs again and my heart hurts for him. "Maybe that's it. Maybe our connection has died."

"You're such a poet," I tell him, and his eyes snap to mine. Then he grins really big, because he gets it—that I'm defusing, I'm softening, I'm making it better the only way I know how.

"You're such an asshole," he tells me.

"I love you," I say, and hug him hard.

"I love you, too."

"Happy Valentine's Day, Shaun."

"Happy Valentine's Day, June."

• • •

After lunch, I'm trudging toward Spanish III when everything goes dark red. Someone has covered my eyes with their hands. I spin, which puts me right in the circle of Oliver's arms, and I'm looking up at him. We both immediately break apart, stepping backward. "What are you doing?" My tone sounds belligerent, which is the opposite of how I feel.

"I have a present for you."

Color rises up my chest and past my collarbones, making me feel the unholy triumvirate of flushed, pissed (at myself), and embarrassed. "Oh, really?" It's supposed to come out nonchalant, but . . .

But it doesn't.

Oliver reaches under his jacket and I see that his left side is bulky because he's got something hidden there. "I made it myself."

My blush deepens, and I try to distract from it with a glare. "Why?"

He laughs. "You're so dependable." He pulls out the thing that's been in his jacket, and presents it to me with a flourish. I accept it and . . . stare.

"It's a pillow," I say.

Oliver laughs again. "Your powers of perception are overwhelming."

"Thank you?" I am honestly not sure what I am supposed to do with a pillow that might be made out of felt and is definitely turquoise on one side and hot pink on the other. Also, one corner is truncated, like someone lopped it off and sewed it back together.

"It's for the mornings," Oliver explains. "Because you think my car is too big and you're never quite comfortable. You can sit on it."

What Oliver has just given me is—by a long shot—the most awkward gift I have ever been given, but that's not why I feel awkward. I feel awkward because it is a gift. All I

can manage to do is accept the pillow and mumble some gratitude. "Thanks."

"Happy Valentine's Day!" Oliver says, and he doesn't look
at all awkward. He just looks happy.

Damn it all to hell, Oliver is more than good-looking.

He's beautiful.

Chapter 20

Mom and I are getting ready to start a game of Scrabble. It was her idea, I suspect because she's feeling guilty about forbidding me to move in with Dad next year. I got turned down for financial aid at all of my New York college choices, but I thought we could still swing it if I lived with him. But Mom says his apartment is small and the neighborhood is sketchy. When I talked to Dad about it, he said he would love to have me, but he wouldn't do it against Mom's wishes. Thus—since Mom has been putting money into Michigan's prepaid tuition program for a while now—it looks like I'm heading to U of M next year.

It's not my first choice, but I guess it won't be terrible. Darbs is going to Eastern, so I'll still be able to hang with her, and Shaun will be only three hours away at Ohio State. He claims that we will be locked in a heated football rivalry that may break our friendship.

Oliver hasn't made a final decision yet, and I'm kind of glad about that. Ever since Valentine's Day, I've found myself being just a little more *careful* around him, taking extra caution not to cross any lines.

And caring what he does with himself next year—that kind of feels like crossing a line.

For Mother-Daughter Bonding Night, Mom is making hot apple cider. She adds spices to the steaming pot while I set a bag of popcorn in the microwave. I've just pressed the start button when the home phone rings. "I got it," says Mom, so I assume she's expecting a call from Cash.

As she heads into the living room, I watch the digital numbers on the microwave count down and I wonder if Shaun is talking to Kirk yet. Shaun said he wanted to discuss the "quality of the relationship" tonight, whatever that means. As I'm rewarded with the first pops from the bag, Mom answers the phone in the other room. "Hello?" she says in that questioning way that you do when you honestly don't know who is on the other end.

Landlines.

I still assume it's Cash until Mom says, *"What?"* and I hear something heavy slam down, like maybe she dropped a book. My stomach dips and I have a sudden terrible image of my father dead in New York, either run over by a taxi or shot with a wayward bullet. If it happened, this is absolutely the way I'd find out.

I step away from the microwave so I can hear better. Mom's voice has scaled up an octave and she's saying things like "Are you freaking kidding me?" and "Calm down, I'll be right there!" . . . so at least it doesn't sound like it has anything to do with Dad.

The microwave beeps as Mom rushes back into the kitchen. She turns off the burner under the apple cider and looks at me. "Honey, I'm so sorry but I have to cancel on our game."

186

"Is everything okay?"

"Friend drama." She comes close and gives me a hard kiss on the forehead before scooping her keys off the counter. "Back soon," she says, and flies out.

I hear the front door open and close and then the sound of her car driving away into the night.

So that's weird.

I clean up the kitchen and head upstairs. After I shower, I huddle in my bed, lights off and phone on. I've just finished a turn against Oliver with my "Marauding Medusa" when I hear faint sounds from outside. I jump up and go to my bedroom window. I can see my mother's car in the snowy driveway. She's getting out of the driver's side as someone else exits from the other door. It takes me a moment to realize it's Marley.

Oliver's mother.

I hurry back to bed and listen to the sounds below. The front door opens and closes. There are whispers as two sets of feet plod up the wooden stairs. They go past my room to my mother's, and then one turns back. A second later, the knob twists and my door opens a crack. Mom's face appears. "Honey?"

I raise my head as if I'm not completely awake. "Hi," I say in my sleepiest voice.

"Just wanted to tell you good night. I love you."

"I love you, too," I murmur, and settle back into my pillows long enough for Mom to close the door. The second she's gone, I hop up and crack it so I can eavesdrop.

Down the hallway, Marley is weeping. Mom is saying she's going to be okay and she's going to sleep here tonight. "I didn't win after all," Marley says between sobs. "I got the *booby* prize. It's worse than *losing.*"

"Shhh," my mother says. "It's going to be okay."

And then Mom's door closes, so I can't hear anything else.

• • •

I'm perched on a kitchen stool, eating an orange-rhubarb muffin, when Marley shuffles in. She's wearing my mom's robe and her messy topknot is secured with the tortoise-shell clip I gave Mom for Christmas a few years ago. Her shadowed, bloodshot eyes meet mine and immediately water up. "Hannah said I could hide upstairs until you left, too, but I need coffee." I point to the coffeemaker—which Mom thoughtfully left on—and Marley pours some into the mug waiting for her on the counter.

"Your mom is the best."

"She's not bad," I agree.

"I need a favor." I know what it will be before she says it. "Don't tell Oliver I'm here."

It rubs me the wrong way. Oliver and I made that honesty pledge, and especially given the Itch-pocalypse, I don't want to betray it. "He might notice that you're not at home," I tell his mom.

"I've already worked that out with Bryant," she says. "This isn't Oliver's business—"

But it's mine?

"—and I don't want to worry him."

Okay, that actually makes sense. I can imagine Oliver's freakout if he knew his mom had a weeping sleepover—a weepover, if you will—with my mom. Besides, she's a parent, which means she outranks me in a significant way.

"I won't tell him."

"Thanks," says Marley.

• • •

Oliver has just taken a bite of toast when I clamber aboard, so he only waves at me with the crust before cranking up our playlist and pulling onto the road. The Ramones beat harsh and fast, and it's the perfect thing to propel us toward school, toward Regular Life, to let the triviality of here and now fade away, trampled by the drums.

When Oliver finishes eating, he turns down the music so we can hear each other. It's the way things are these days. The music means less, and talking to Oliver means more.

"In case you're wondering, my mom has a headache," he tells me. I have a flash of panic—does he know she's at my house?— before making the connection. It helps that he's brandishing his crumpled napkin at me. "She didn't come down to make breakfast, so I had to fend for myself."

"You have the worst life."

"I know, champagne problems. That's what my dad would say. Speaking of which, guess what."

"What?" I say on autopilot.

"I talked to my dad. He at least *acted* like it was okay."

Wait. Oliver *does* know what's going on with his parents?

Oliver stuffs his napkin between his seat and the center console. "Although he says it's squandering my legacy, to not take the internship."

I don't even realize I'm holding my breath until I let it out in a whoosh of air. "Oh yeah?" My attempt to speak casually is laughable. "He's not trying to make you do it?"

"Not yet," says Oliver. "But he might be pretending now so he can spring his disapproval on me later."

"Lovely." So Oliver's dad is lying to him: about Marley's whereabouts, about his own feelings, about everything.

Kinda like me, except my lie is by omission. Again.

Dammit.

• • •

I'm pretty sure Mom specifically told Cash *not* to come over, because usually he'd be hanging around, but right now it's just the two of us with TV trays in the living room. Normally we're a little more civilized, but tonight we're having what Mom calls "retro dinner." It means we have a layered salad with mayonnaise dressing, and chicken casserole with crackers baked into the top. For dessert, there will be blue Jell-O with Goldfish crackers "swimming" in it.

Apparently this is the food of my mother's youth.

A few bites into the cracker chicken (shockingly delicious, BTW), Mom says she appreciates my discretion. I knew this would be coming, but still, it's nice to hear. "Oliver's parents are having some problems," she tells me. (Duh.) "You should stay out of it."

I've been turning this over and over in my head all day and I've come to a decision. Yes, Oliver and I made a pact about honesty, but telling him this truth would only hurt and confuse him, and I don't want to do that. I know it's risking our friendship and the rare trust we've somehow found between us, but this is one of those times when I'm going to choose what's good for another person instead of what offers the most safety for me.

Besides, it's not my story to tell.

"Okay," I say to my mom. "I'll stay out of it."

Chapter 21

General cacophony abounds as we trundle along the highway behind the other yellow bus. People throw wads of paper and bounce in their seats. Someone starts the school fight song and most of our bus joins in with great exuberance. It's like they've all turned into a bunch of children.

I am squeezed between Darbs and Lily on one of the narrow vinyl seats. Darbs sings along but Lily is looking out the window and talking to me. "Ice-skating," she says loudly so I can hear her. "Isn't there a rink out this way?"

"They did that last year. Cal Turman broke his ankle."

"Oh, that's right. Maybe apple picking?"

"Wrong time of year."

Lily is trying to guess where we're going for Senior Off-Campus Day. It's (yet again) one of our high school's traditions, but this is one I can get behind, because it means no classes for a day. In fact, that's apparently the reason it was invented a decade or so ago: to combat the previous tradition of Senior Skip Day. The only unfortunate part is that we have zero say in where we go. The administration plans it all and then we're surprised when we get there.

No one ever claimed that high school is a democracy.

As we find out when we arrive, this year's senior class of Robin High is going bowling. Wolverine Lanes has been rented out so we can bond over balls. I came here once as a kid, maybe for someone's birthday party, and it doesn't look like the decor has changed since then. Still the same spatter-printed carpet and lime-green walls and ancient arcade games. Still the lingering scent of greasy food and feet.

A teacher tells us to line up for shoes and explains that during our three hours of knocking pins down, we also get free sodas and hot dogs and hamburgers. Predictably, Darbs pitches a fit about the lack of vegan options and ends up with an extra bag of chips.

We accidentally get in line behind Theo, who hefts two bowling balls in front of his crotch. "Just like the real ones," he tells me.

"Just like your brain," I say. It's not a great comeback, but it's the first one I think of.

"I hate him so much," Darbs says to me, and Theo swings his head (and his balls) in her direction.

"I can hear you."

"Good." She gives him the finger.

"Next!" says the woman at the counter, and Theo finally turns away from us.

"I hate him, too," I tell Darbs.

Once we're all wearing red-and-blue shoes, we head to a lane, where Shaun is typing our names on the sticky keyboard attached to the ball return. "Do you want Darbs or Darby?" he asks as we arrive.

"Darbs, dumb-ass." She flicks him in the head.

"Hey, this is a sporting event. Maybe you're formal at sporting events."

"Speaking of formal, are any of you going to the prom?" Lily asks.

"A: it's like four months away," I tell her. "And B: I wouldn't be caught dead."

"I bought a dress," Darbs says, then sees my look. "What? It's a big deal."

"Whatever, I'm not going."

"I'm with June," says Lily.

Shaun taps a final key. "Darbs is first."

We play our first ten frames, taking turns flinging a heavy ball down the lane. Shaun gets two strikes and a whole bunch of spares, so of course we tease him mercilessly. "This is terrible," he moans. "I'm good at bowling!"

"You're going to get one of those shirts," I tell him. "The ones with the collar and the embroidered name on the pocket."

Oliver arrives at our lane and hears that last bit. "Ooh, what's Shaun's bowling name?"

"King of the Pins," I tell him.

"The Strikemaster," Oliver says.

"Holy Roller," I shoot back.

"Ball Buster."

"Gutter Guru."

"Spare me," Darbs groans.

"Good one!" Oliver tells her, and she rolls her eyes.

"No, I actually meant please spare me having to listen to

the two of you play this game. Do you ever stop competing with each other?"

"We weren't competing," I say. "We were—"

"Having fun," Oliver says, and grins at me.

"Whatever," says Darbs. "Are we going again?"

"I'm out." Lily grabs her bag. "There's an arcade."

"I will kick your ass in Pac-Man," says Darbs.

"Bring it," Lily tells her, and they take off.

Shaun looks back and forth between Oliver and me. "You guys play. I'm going to see if they'll give me an extra hot dog."

Oliver and I almost knock each other down trying to get to the joke first. "That's what she said," Oliver tells him.

At the same time, I say, "Kirk's not going to like that."

Shaun shakes his head—"You two are predictable"—and walks away.

Oliver nudges me, motioning in the direction Shaun went. "Are he and Kirk still a thing?"

"Yes and no. I think they're in the Awkward Conversation section of the relationship, where things either get better or go downhill."

Oliver nods and we both stand there for our very own Awkward Moment. Then he lifts his chin toward the pins. "Should we?"

I glance at the far lane, where I know Ainsley landed when we all came in. Sure enough, she's looking at us. At *me,* standing here with her boyfriend. I raise my hand toward her and flap it around a little, because maybe that'll make it less weird. She immediately flashes me a brilliant smile, waving in return . . . and then Theo leans over and whispers something to her. They both crack up—and look at me again before laughing even more.

I turn back to Oliver, who doesn't seem like he's noticed any of it. He has blinders on where Theo is concerned.

Well, screw Theo.

And screw my stupid caution where Oliver is concerned. There's a strong chance his perfect family life is going to explode around him any minute, and if I can give him a little fun before that happens, I'm doing it. I choose a glittery pink ball. "I'm warning you," I tell Oliver. "I'm small but I'm feisty."

"Just how I like 'em," Oliver says, and then looks uncomfortable. "That came out weird."

"It came out right." I immediately feel the same way Oliver looks, and I shake it off by giving instructions. "Make yourself useful. Type in our names."

He gets busy at the keyboard and I get busy looking anywhere besides at him. I know—I *know*—what's trying to happen in my heart, but I refuse it. I'm not going there. Oliver Flagg and I are just friends, and that is how it's going to stay. He has a wonderful girlfriend and I have a wonderfully uncomplicated life.

Even if I feel my insides tighten when he flashes a grin at me from behind the keyboard. He points up to the screen, at the names he's assigned us for everyone to see: Roller Rafferty and One-Ball Ollie.

I burst out laughing and Oliver looks confused. "What?" he asks. "They're our bowling names."

"Some people might take yours wrong," I manage to say before being overtaken by another gale of laughter.

Oliver squints at the screen and I see the look of comic horror wash over him. "Oh crap!" he says, and plops back down in front of the keyboard. "I meant the pins! I can knock down all the pins with one ball!" He taps at the keys. "How do I change this?"

"Too late," I inform him, and sprint to the lane. Before he can figure out how to get back to the name screen, I chuck my glittery pink ball and watch it knock over two pins on the right side. "Already started!"

I look back at Oliver, who is shaking his head. "You're killing my rep, Rafferty." But he has a big goofy grin plastered on his face.

Oliver and I end up playing only one game together (he wins, but not by much) before Shaun and Lily return to join us. The four of us play, and of course Shaun clobbers everyone again, and then Ainsley arrives to retrieve Oliver. She says she wants to get a picture with him in the photo booth. I try not to look at the curtained area where they're definitely *not* getting pictures, because they're in there way too long and Ainsley's feet are facing his.

Instead, I head to the arcade to beat Darbs at Dance Dance Revolution. We play Skee-Ball and Ms. Pac-Man, and then take turns trying to balance on the railing surrounding the snack area until we get yelled at by a food worker. At some point, the bowling people remember they have a sound system and start pumping really loud disco music, so Darbs and I find Lily and pull her onto the spatter-patterned carpet to dance. Ainsley pops out of the photo booth to see us leaping about and decides to join in with one of the cheerleaders. In a flash minute, a whole bunch of them are there and everyone is dancing and the teachers are trying to make us stop but they're not trying very hard. The day is silly and fun and crazy, and on the way home in the bus, someone starts up the Robin High fight song again.

This time, I sing along.

Chapter 22

"Hey, what's going on with the Flaggs?" I ask Mom. We're out on the porch, using brooms to sweep the cobwebs from the rafters above us. "Marley hasn't been over this week, has she?"

"No." Mom pokes at a particularly dirty corner of the ceiling. "She and Bryant are going to counseling, so I think things are getting better."

"Did he cheat on her?"

"I can't . . . That's not a question I should answer."

"So that's a yes?"

"It's not a no," she tells me.

"Oliver doesn't know, right?"

"I don't think so," she says. "Marley says he hero-worships his dad. She doesn't want to jerk the rug out from under him. Besides, it doesn't really have anything to do with him."

I personally think it *does* have something to do with Oliver, but I guess it's not my business. Besides, if Marley and Bryant are working it out, then hopefully this will blow over and Oliver will never hear about it. I know how Oliver idolizes his father. This would kill him.

"You and I really shouldn't be talking about it," my mom says.

"I know."

I'm curious, but promises have been made.

It would be better if I didn't know anything at all.

But I do, and I said I'd keep my mouth shut.

• • •

I'm weaving through the crowded hall on my way to calculus when Zoe Smith grabs my elbow and pulls me to the wall by the lockers. "I need you. Save me."

I look around but don't see any dragons or people with guns. "From what?"

Inexplicably, Zoe bursts into a gale of laughter that goes on way too long. She beams at me. "You are totally right!" she says in a super-loud voice. "He *does* do that with his tongue!"

"What?" It comes out as a horrified hiss, under my breath. It doesn't quiet Zoe at all. Her laughter scales up in volume.

"That's so funny!" she screams.

Maybe Zoe has gone crazy.

"I didn't say anything funny," I tell her, but she's stopped laughing. In fact, her smile is gone completely and she's gazing at something beyond me. I turn to see that Itch is down the hall, walking away from us. He's holding hands with . . .

"Liesel Glassman," Zoe tells me. "They're dating now."

Wait.

"Weren't you guys together at bowling like a week ago?"

"Yep," Zoe says. "I thought everything was fine, but apparently it wasn't. He broke up with me on Saturday and here it is, five days later, and he's already dating Liesel." Her hands fly to her hips. "Do you think he was cheating on me?"

"I have no—"

"Did he ever cheat on you?"

"No!" I am completely out of my element in this conversation. "Well . . . not really. It's murky."

"I knew it!" says Zoe. "God, I hate men."

"Me too," I tell her, although it's not true.

"Thanks for helping. You've been screwed over by him, too, so I knew you'd do it."

"But he didn't—"

"Catch you later."

And she's gone.

High school is ridiculous.

• • •

Shaun completely disagrees with me about Oliver's parents. "You should tell him." We're huddling together, alone on the bleachers. "If someone knew a secret about my family, I'd be really pissed if they didn't tell me. It's not fair that Oliver doesn't know if you do."

"But my mom thinks—"

"Of course your mom wants to make your decisions for you. She's a parent. It's her job to control everything you do."

I narrow my eyes at him. Shaun's lips are pressed together in a thin line and his shoulders are hunched. "Are you okay?"

"No." Shaun slumps. "My parents won't let me visit Kirk over spring break."

"What? Why?"

"They're saying they don't know his parents, so I can't go."

"Can't you set up a phone call between them or something?"

"I tried that." Shaun heaves a deep sigh. "Dad says it would force him and Mom into deception. Kirk still isn't out to his parents, so any conference call or whatever would mean Dad and Mom pretending that Kirk and I are just friends, when they know we're more than that. Dad says they're not going to lie to other parents about their own kid."

"That sucks."

"I get it," says Shaun. "It's not fair. None of this is fair. The thing is, the only reason lying is even on the table is because of Kirk. He could end this right now by just telling his parents he's gay."

"You're mad at Kirk."

"Yeah." Shaun sighs again. "But only because I'm crazy about him."

"Sorry," I say, and tilt my head against his shoulder.

• • •

The base of the school flagpole is a warm line up the center of my back. I'm leaning against it while I wait for Mom. Even though Shaun is still pouting about Kirk, and even though I just found out I got a mediocre grade on a physics test, and even though I miss talking to Oliver, today is glorious, because it finally feels like spring is coming. The sky is the clearest of blues and crocuses are coming up along the edge of the sidewalk. I'm wearing a black scoop-neck ballerina top over a dark gray wrap skirt, and for the first time in months, I don't need a sweater.

Mom is already on spring break, so she's driven me every morning this week. I see Oliver at school, of course, but it's not the same as having that alone time with him every day. Yesterday, I overheard Theo ask him if we'd ended our little exchange—transportation for me, sexual favors for Oliver—and Oliver told him to shut it.

When Mom pulls up, I lope over to her car and slide inside. She's scribbling on a piece of paper held against her knee. "Green apples," she mutters. "Candied pecans."

"What are you doing?"

"Marley's coming over for dinner and I didn't get to the store this afternoon . . . got a little lost in painting."

"I can tell. Your right eyebrow is pink." Mom hands me the paper and pulls into the street, absently rubbing at her face. "Is Marley coming by herself?" I say as casually as I can.

"Yes. Bryant's at a conference in Atlanta."

Just to be clear, Bryant isn't who I was asking about . . . but of course Mom doesn't know that.

I glance over the shopping list. "What else is on the menu?" It's a reasonable question, given that all I see are salad ingredients and feminine hygiene products.

"Cash is grilling steaks and corn on the . . . Oh heck, can you write down aluminum foil, too?"

Good thing I asked.

Mom and I do a mad dash through the closest grocery store and manage to find everything except for the foil. Mom makes a solemn vow never to shop here again, because what kind of store runs out of something so basic? Then she sends Cash a text message to pick up some on his way over. "You know what's great about Cash?" Mom says as we're walking out to the car with our bags. "He's stable. If he says he's going to pick up an item from the store, I know he'll do it."

I'm not sure if it's merely an observation or if it's intended as a veiled slam against Dad, so I don't answer. Mom and I have a much better relationship than most of my friends do with their mothers, but I sometimes think she's jealous of the connection I have with Dad. He *gets* me in a way that she can't quite understand, that she's not really a part of. Like the note he sent with the flowers on my birthday. Sweet, but also specific.

Mom, with the way she bounces from thought to thought, and with wares from friend to friend . . . nothing about her is direct. Nothing is specific.

But we have a life together that works anyway, so I can't complain.

• • •

Cash arrives right on time with steaks and corn and aluminum foil. Marley shows up half an hour late with three bottles of wine and a slow cooker full of zucchini soup. "I thought you were bringing dessert," Mom says.

Marley sets the bottles on the kitchen counter. "This *is* dessert."

"I'll make brownies," I tell them, and Marley gives me an approving smile.

"You raised her right," she says to Mom. "Where's your wine opener?"

Mom eyes the bottles. "I don't think we need all three of those."

"Probably not," Marley agrees. "However, they're the three best bottles in Bryant's collection, so we're going to at least taste them all."

Mom laughs. "You're terrible."

• • •

By the time dinner is over and I'm pulling brownies out of the oven, all three of the bottles are open . . . and one is empty. Cash only had a glass and I was given a tiny sip of each flavor (although I couldn't tell the difference between them). The rest was all Mom and Marley. Now they're taking turns between the other two bottles while huddled over one of their phones, looking through photos on some sort of social media site and occasionally cackling.

Cash gestures to my pan of brownies. "I'll take one to go. This is feeling more and more like a ladies' night."

"You can stay!" Mom calls out, and blows him a kiss.

"I know." Cash winks at me. "But I'm still going to go."

I can't exactly blame him, especially when Marley leaps off her stool, knocking it over. "Indigo Girls!" she calls out. "Let's listen to the Indigo Girls."

As the moms start comparing playlists (apparently this isn't something one grows out of), Cash swings around the counter and picks up the stool. He sets it in its place and looks at me. "My advice is go up to your room, close the door, and put on some decent music."

"You got a suggestion?"

"Something loud," Cash says. "I'd go with Petty, myself. Tom."

"You and Mom belong together," I tell him, and watch as his face cracks wide open into the happiest of grins.

"Thanks, June."

"Have a good night, Cash."

Cash kisses my mom and says good-bye to Marley. He's

almost to the front door—which I know because he's a stompy walker—when he turns around and comes back into the kitchen. "Hey, June."

"Yeah?"

"Don't let them drive anywhere."

"Closer to Fine" blares to life from the living room and I nod. "Good call."

And it *is* a good call, because an hour later, while I'm up in my room listening to the Pogues, there's a knock on my door. I open it to find my mother standing there, waiting to deliver a world of justification to me. "You should know that, yes, Marley and I are drinking, but it's okay because it's rare and because we are adults." All her words are very clear and she almost wouldn't seem drunk, except she points at me when she says "rare," and her right elbow clonks into the doorjamb. "Ow."

I've seen my mother buzzed a couple times before, so I smile at her, because I know that's what she wants. "It's fine, Mom."

She counts on her fingers. "One: we would never get behind the wheel of a car in this condition. Two: we would never make sexual decisions while inebriated. Three . . . dammit. I had three a minute ago."

"I got it, Mom. You're in your house and you're over twenty-one, drinking with your best friend. Seriously. It's fine."

"I love you," she tells me.

"I love you, too."

"And I have to tell you something," she says. "You gotta learn to drive, baby."

My insides twist. "What?"

"Marley wants to go home."

206

• • •

By the time Oliver arrives, Mom and Marley have moved on to The Jesus and Mary Chain. When we walk into the kitchen, the moms are wild dancing to "Between Planets." They have their eyes closed and they're waving their arms in the air while they bounce around. Oliver shakes his head and goes to Marley, catching her arm in mid-gyration. "Hey, Mom."

"Ollie!" She beams up at him and then immediately gets super serious, like she's just gotten busted. "I understand you might have some questions about why your mother needs to be chauffeured. . . ."

Except she says "needsh."

My mom elbows her in the ribs. "Marley, chill. Our kids are cool."

Marley looks at her and then back at Oliver. He nods. "We are, Mom. We're really, really cool."

He glances at me and I hurry to back him up. "*So* cool, Mrs. Flagg."

"Let's go, Mom," Oliver says.

"I'll walk you out!" my mom singsongs, and we all start toward the door together.

We're almost there when I remember Marley's slow cooker. "Your mom left something," I tell Oliver. "I'll be right back."

The big pot is in the sink, right where my mom put it. It's mostly scrubbed out, so I make the executive decision that in this case, half-assed is better than no-assed. I shove it into a grocery bag before trotting back through the house and out the front door onto the porch.

Oliver stands patiently by his car while Mom and Marley—their arms linked together—sway toward him, singing a Prince song. I'm pretty sure it's the dirty one. Oliver and I trade amused glances and I head to the rear of his car. I set the grocery bag on the ground so I can figure out how to open the behemoth's trunk. I've just found the button under the handle and yanked up when I hear Oliver shout.

"Don't! Stop!"

I look up, startled. "Stop or don't stop?" I ask him, but he doesn't answer, because he has run over to me and is now looking all big-eyed and blinky. I follow his gaze into the behemoth's trunk.

Aluminum foil.

His trunk is *packed* with boxes of aluminum foil. Completely full. All different brands.

The first thing I say is "No wonder the store was out!"

The second thing is "What the hell?"

Oliver shakes his head. "Don't worry about it."

And the thing is I might *not* have worried about it if he hadn't said that. As it is, my hands fly to my hips and I glare at him. "What's going on, Oliver?"

At least he has the grace to look chagrined. "It's for the prank."

"The *senior* prank?"

"Is there another one?"

My glare intensifies and he withers under it. "What is this?" I say.

"Don't get mad."

"That's what people say to someone with a legitimate reason to be mad."

"It's tonight. The prank is happening tonight."

"What?" Indignation blazes up inside me. "Why don't I know about this?"

"Why would you *want* to know?"

"Because I'm a senior!"

"But you've dismissed it since the beginning of the year," he reminds me. "You *hate* it. Why would anyone think you'd want to be involved? Why would we think you wouldn't narc us out?"

We.

That's all I hear. If there's a "we," it means there is an "us" and a "you," and I'm the "you." I'm separate. I'm not one of us.

I stare at him, my mouth open but nothing coming out, because I'm so offended. No, I'm not offended. I'm angry.

I'm *sad.*

I'm about to say something—I don't know what, but *something*—when a loud blast of the behemoth's horn makes us both jump. "Our mothers are out of control," Oliver says as we hear a gale of giggles from the front of the car.

Oliver slams the trunk and heads to the passenger side. I follow and watch him settle Marley into the seat. Once she's buckled, he looks at me. "I'm taking her home and then I'm driving to school. I'll come right past your house, so if you change your mind and actually want to be a part of it, call my cell."

"I'm not calling you."

"Well, you should." He says it quietly, but it lands hard.

"If you really thought that, you would have told me about the prank in the first place." Hurt threatens to close my throat. "I'm not part of this. I'm not a part of anything."

Oliver stares at me for a long moment. "Don't move," he finally says. He closes Marley's door and then nods to my mother, who is standing nearby, looking super happy and super buzzed. "I need to talk to your daughter."

"Go ahead," says Mom. "I might not remember it tomorrow anyway."

"Cool," says Oliver.

"Cool," says Mom, shambling off toward the house.

I feel like I should say something, too, but "cool" doesn't seem appropriate.

Oliver walks over and stares down at me. Even by moonlight, those eyes are lethal. "Here's the thing: once we're out of here, we won't come back. Most of the time, we won't even *remember* who we used to be."

"I'll remember."

"No," he says. "You won't. Trust me on this one. I've seen it."

This time, I don't answer, because I don't know what to say.

"When we get those few chances to remember, *this* will be the time we come back to," Oliver tells me. "It'll be *now,* tonight. Do you know why?"

I wish I had a smart-ass comment, but I only shake my head.

"Because we're young enough to break the rules. This is one of our last moments of freedom, and guess what."

"What?" It comes out in a whisper. Oliver leans down to me. He's close—so close that even though we're in the moonlight, even though I can hear his mother singing from inside his car and my mother tromping around on the porch, I am viscerally aware of the warm, minty smell of his breath and the hard angles of his jaw.

"You get to taste it," he tells me, also whispering. "You get to *live* it."

I stare at him, and all I can see is his *goodness*. Because Oliver Flagg is good and real and true. . . .

"Get in the car," he tells me. "You know you want to."

He's right.

And still I can't.

• • •

I'm standing in the front hallway, looking out the window, when Oliver drives back past my house. I see the behemoth cruise down Callaway. It slows down, almost coming to a halt, and then finally speeds up. It keeps moving and disappears down the road.

Pain rises inside me. I can't explain it, can't define it. It's something that makes no sense whatsoever. It's *loneliness*. I miss something I've never had.

Crap.

I lean my forehead against the glass, aching for Oliver's brake lights, which have receded into the distance, when I hear my mother's voice. "You should go."

I turn to look at her. "You're encouraging vandalism?"

Mom leans against the wooden storage bench, smiling at me. "It's not like you're going to kill someone. It's a prank."

"I don't even know what it is," I tell her.

"I do," she says, and I stare at her, not sure if I'm pissed or upset or amused. My freaking *mother* gets to know about the prank, and I don't? But then Mom shakes her head. "Not the details. I have no idea what you kids are up to, but I *do* know it's okay to be involved in something bigger than yourself, even if it's just a goofy joke with a bunch of teenagers you might never see again after graduation."

"But *why*?" I say. "Why should I do it?"

Mom walks over to me and I can tell she's moving slowly so she won't wobble. She reaches out to stroke my hair. "June," she says in a voice that is all kinds of loving and gentle. "I think the real question is, why *not*?"

Yet again, I don't know how to answer. Mom smiles at me. "I'm going to bed," she tells me. "Do what you want but just know that, tonight only, you have no curfew."

I watch her walk up the stairs before I turn to look out the window again, and what I realize as I stare into the blackness is that I wish I could still see Oliver's headlights approaching, because if I could, I would run out into the night and flag him down.

But unfortunately, there are no headlights.

There are no lights at all.

Chapter 23

It's midnight when Shaun finds a spot two blocks from campus, far away from any streetlights. When we're both out of the car, he grabs my hand and pulls me toward the school. "We're already late," he reminds me.

"Thank you again," I tell him as we head down the darkened sidewalk. "I didn't know if you'd come get me. Most of the time, you don't even answer your phone."

"Most of the time, you don't have anything important to say." He grins at me and I grin back.

"Did you text Lily and Darbs?"

"Yep, but I don't think they're coming."

We circle the flagpole and go down the east side of the school, away from the main entrance. A couple of "guards"—Danny Hollander and Sara Francis—are stationed outside the art suite. They beckon us over and explain that we're going in through a window several yards down, behind a pair of spruce bushes. "Don't turn on any lights," Sara tells me. "Feel your way through the room and close the door behind you. Things are happening on the second floor."

Getting through the window is easy. Getting through the

pitch-black art room—slightly less so. Edging our way down the hallway toward the staircase is downright terrifying, but by the time we reach the steps, we can hear laughter from upstairs and it starts to feel more like a fun caper and less like a low-budget horror movie.

We arrive on the second floor to find lanterns placed all around and students *everywhere*. There are tons of senior athletes and—surprisingly—tons of nonathletes, too. Ainsley is there (natch). She is at a table piled high with combination locks and is handing them out to a line of perky cheerleaders. She waves me over. "Bo Reeves scored the universal key. We took the locks off every single locker in the school and now we're mixing them up and putting them back."

I stare at her—"That is genius."—and she beams in return.

"I know, right? Everyone will have to try all the lockers in the school just to find their own lock. We could use some more hands, but before you jump in, go check out the third floor. It's seriously magical."

"Go on," Shaun tells me. "I'll help with the lockers."

I hesitate only a second before running off.

• • •

Apparently I've been kept in the dark for a long time, because a lot of work has been done. A *lot*. It looks like our seniors have enjoyed some major crafternoons, because there are *zillions* of snowflakes stuck to the walls and dangling from the ceiling. Shaun will love it. Students are going in and out of several open classroom doors, so I peer inside one of them.

It just keeps getting better.

The first thing I see is a glittery silver disco ball that I'm sure was once a globe of the world. It sits beside several glittery silver pens and what appears to be a stack of individually wrapped glittery silver documents. All of those are perched atop a glittery silver desk, which is beside a glittery silver trash can.

Suddenly, I understand why Cash had to make a special trip to his local market on the way to our house for dinner. *This* is why there was no aluminum foil at the store near school. Everything in this room—like, *everything*—has been individually encased in foil. Desks, whiteboard, wall hangings, dry-erase markers. Everything.

I walk all the way inside and stare around. Not only is it pretty—in a strange, spacey kind of way—but absolutely nothing was hurt in the creation of this prank. No property—school or personal—and definitely no animals.

There's a noise at the doorway and I look over. It's Itch. "Oh, sorry," he says, and turns to leave.

"Wait!" I say really fast and a little too loudly. Itch stops moving but he doesn't come any closer. He slumps against the doorframe and waits. "I haven't seen you around," I tell him.

"Really? Because we go to the same school."

I try again. "I'm surprised you're here."

He folds his arms. "Oh, you can suddenly be a joiner, but I can't?"

"Itch."

"Let me guess," he says. "You want forgiveness. You want us to be all friendy."

"I broke up with you," I remind him. "I didn't *stab* you."

Itch lets out a short bark of pissed-off laughter. "Right. No stabbing, no big deal." He shakes his head. "Forget it, June."

This time when he turns to go, I let him.

• • •

I finally find Oliver after Theo points me in his direction. ("You know his girlfriend's here, right?" "Bite me, Theo.")

There are orange traffic cones placed at the entrances to North Hall. Oliver is there alone, in the lobby, threading yellow caution tape around the entire area. He smiles really big when he sees me. "How'd you get here?"

"Shaun." I watch Oliver loop the tape around the radiator twice and tie it so it stays in place. "Do you need help?"

"No. I'm almost done."

"Oh. Okay." I'm disappointed but I can't complain. After all, I'm the one who showed up late. "I'll see if they need anything on the third—"

"Don't go," Oliver says, so I don't. "How do you like it?"

I duck under the caution tape and join him in the center of the North Hall lobby. There are snowflakes taped to the walls here, too. "It's pretty."

"Pretty? That's all I get?"

"Someone spent a lot of time with paper and scissors."

"For sure." He stretches his right hand toward me and points to his index knuckle. Because he seems to expect it, I run my fingertip over the small hard spot. It's polished smooth. "I cut roughly a million snowflakes while waiting for you to take your turn in Mythteries."

I get a sudden flash image of Oliver on one of the stools

216

in his basement, hunched over the bar with a pair of scissors, and I go clenchy inside. I realize that I'm still sliding my finger gently against him and I start to pull away, but Oliver catches my hand before I can. I look up into his eyes and the clenchiness increases.

"You could have called," he says. "I would have come back for you."

And that's when it happens.

In that moment, the world turns and everything around us dims. Oliver's eyes are focused right on mine and his shock of angel-blond hair is the only light in the room. It's not just about how he looks; it's about who he *is* and my heart cracks wide open. I am slammed with the absolute, painful knowledge that somehow, accidentally, this boy has squeezed in. Against all my plans and denials, I missed a spot when I was setting up barriers around myself. There was an opening somewhere, and then there was Oliver.

I gasp with the realization, and this time when I pull back, he lets me. "Aren't you going to say anything?" he asks.

It's like he can actually *see* my mind spinning, or maybe it's that he can hear my heart flinging itself against the wall of my chest. I shake my head, because Oliver has a girlfriend, one who is pretty and popular and *nice,* and I am the one who is at fault here; I am the one whose feelings changed, and—

"No animals." Oliver spreads his arms wide. "No vandalism. No destruction of property."

He's talking about the prank.

Just the prank.

Not us.

Because there *is* no "us."

I'm just the charity case he drives to school.

So I nod. I force a smile. "Great job. Really, really great job."

"Good news." Oliver beams huge. "You're here for the coup de grâce."

"Amazing. You're even bilingual when Theo's not around." Since I'm clearly not going with honesty, I guess I'll rely on my old friend Glib. I want to leave, run, escape, but there's no way to do it without Oliver's wondering why.

Oliver jogs to a duffel bag by the far wall. I watch him, finally admitting to myself that I *like* the way his body moves, that I am the same as any other girl watching his muscles and his hair and his . . . *Oliver-ness.*

If I could punch myself in the soul, I would do it right now.

Oliver hefts a gallon jug from the bag and carries it back to me. I squint at it. "Vegetable oil?"

"Don't freak out." He turns it upside down and thick oil *glunks* onto the floor.

I jump out of the way. "What are you doing?"

The oil oozes, spreading out into a big, slick circle, and Oliver tosses the empty jug to the edge of the room, where it clunks against the wall. "Come on, you're more observant than that."

Apparently not observant enough to notice I was falling hard for the school jock.

"It's a winter wonderland," Oliver explains. "Hence the snowflakes."

I point to the widening circle. "And you've made a wintery, wondrous oil spill?"

"This is the ice-skating rink." I think he mistakes my

avoidance of his eyes for recrimination. "It's not *hurting* anything. Easily cleaned up with soap, and there's caution tape around so no one will be surprised by it. It's what you wanted, right?"

Except that everything I thought I wanted has suddenly been turned on its head. "Sure," I say with what I'm pretty sure is a sickly grin. "It's great."

Oliver grabs my right hand and pulls me into the slick circle of ooze. I skid toward him, nearly falling, and he catches me against his body. For the briefest of seconds, I'm circled by his arms, my entire length against him, and I know every other girl has had it right this whole time, because even my *shins* are tingling from the nearness of him. My left hand is against his chest and—totally acting on their own—my fingers flare out, feeling the muscles beneath them, feeling Oliver's hand slide over mine.

And surely—*surely*—this time he has to hear my breath catching in my throat, but he doesn't mention it. He only pushes me backward, holding both my hands in his own. "We're skating," he says, and pulls me into a spin. I squeal and he laughs, but his laugh is cut off, because now *he* almost falls . . . and then I'm laughing, too, because even though none of this is real and even though it's going to end in pain . . . for this moment only, I'm holding hands with Oliver Flagg and we're skating together in a winter wonderland.

PROM NIGHT

The lights cut off and the glare is replaced with darkness. I can't see him, but I can hear his voice.

"June, what are you doing?"

I know I need to say something important and epic and romantic, because this is a moment that requires an important, epically romantic gesture, but the words aren't there. Instead, all I have is the overwhelming fear that I've already lost the one person I want the most to find.

So I blurt something out—something that hasn't always come naturally to me.

The truth.

SPRING

Chapter 24

My cocoon is soft around me. Protective. Warm. I'm nestled inside, happy and comfortable, and when a muffled sound edges against my consciousness, I shake my head in irritation. I bury myself deeper in my own shell, no reason to become a butterfly, no need to change. . . .

But it's not a cocoon; it's a quilt. And the sound is coming from somewhere outside.

A horn.

The behemoth's horn.

Ack!

I fly out of bed, and now that I see my phone on the nightstand, I have a fuzzy recollection of turning off its alarm. I grab the skirt from last night, the one I dropped on the floor before crawling under the covers a couple hours ago, but it's greasy with vegetable oil, so I rush to my dresser. I find a pair of jeans and am yanking them on when my door opens. I squeal and whip around, thinking it's Oliver, but it's only Mom. Her hair is stringy against her face and she has mascara smudges under her eyes. We stare at each other. "You don't look good," I finally tell her.

"Speak for yourself," she says, and I remember that I didn't even wash my face or brush my teeth before falling asleep last night. And by "last night," I mean "earlier this morning," since that's when Oliver dropped me off. "I told Oliver to go," Mom says. "I'll drive you."

In the car on the way to school, Mom says she's proud of me. "But FYI, you still have a curfew."

"That's fair."

"By the way, don't drink too much at Michigan," she says. "This type of headache . . . it really sucks."

• • •

I miss homeroom, but I rush through the snowflake-strewn halls and into English just as the bell is ringing. I slide into my seat, my hair twisted into a still-damp knot atop my head. I had time to take a quick shower, but not enough to use a blow-dryer.

Everyone is laughing and chattering, and no one has their books with them. "We can't," Lily tells me. "They changed the locks on all the lockers."

"She knows." Shaun plops down next to us. "June helped."

Lily stares at me. "Who *are* you?"

I don't answer, because I'm still trying to figure that out for myself. Apparently I'm the awful cliché mess who has it bad for the boy everyone wants. I'm not sure if I'm more terrified of running into Oliver today and having to make small talk or of not seeing him at all.

Ms. Jackson doesn't even try to have class. "I'm grading papers. Keep it to a dull roar."

She sounds amused, which is why Shaun asks the question. "You're actually not mad at us about the prank, are you?"

The corners of Ms. Jackson's peach-slicked lips twitch upward. "Let's just say I'm relieved my car isn't covered in pigeon shit."

The room bursts into uproarious laughter and she waves us toward the door. "Go."

Every hallway is lined with students spinning dials and yanking against shackles before stepping to the next locker and trying again. After forty-five minutes, I finally find my combination lock on a locker by the math rooms. "Winner!" I shout, which is apparently what we're supposed to do. Just like everyone else's, my victory yell is met with cheering and applause.

It attracts the attention of Ainsley, because suddenly she's right there with her arms around me. "We did it! We're rock stars!"

I pat her on the back as Oliver arrives, brandishing a lock. My heart jolts when I see him. "Mine was on third," he says. It appears that he is unaffected by exhaustion, because his eyes and hair and everything are as bright and perfect as always.

Ainsley gazes up at him with adoration. "Isn't he a genius? Most epic prank ever and all because of him." She rises on tiptoes to kiss Oliver, and it lands on me like a piano.

"I gotta go—" I start, but Ainsley suddenly grabs my arm.

"Oh my God, what are you doing for spring break? Kaylie flunked algebra, so her mom won't let her go, and now we have an extra bed in the cabin. It's in Cheboygan. Want to come?"

"June's going to New York," Oliver says quickly.

Actually, I'm not, because Dad got cast in a new play, so he's going to be in rehearsals, but this is definitely not how or when I wish to share the information that the Grand Plans for my senior spring break involve me at my house with my mom. "Sorry," I tell Ainsley. She hugs me again.

When I return her hug, my gaze accidentally floats up to Oliver's face. We make eye contact and he smiles at me.

I look away.

Chapter 25

Luckily for me—but unluckily for them—neither Darbs nor Lily has big spring break plans. That's why we decide to schedule a Girl Day, when we go out to lunch before splurging on manicures and shopping. When we all have pretty fingernails, we hit a bookstore (my choice), then go kiosk-hopping in the mall (Lily's), and then make our way to a craft store (Darbs's).

"I like the soy wax," Darbs tells us as we browse the candle-making aisle. "It's better for carrying the essential oils."

"How about this color?" Lily holds up a tube of light blue candle dye. "Look, it matches."

She flutters a periwinkle-tipped hand at us and I look down at my own fingernails, painted a bright red. Halfway through the manicure, I realized I was channeling Marley Flagg with the color, but it was already too far gone to switch. Now I can see that I've already chipped my ring finger.

Figures.

"Are you hanging with any of your rah-rahs over spring break?" Darbs asks me. When she sees my quizzical look, she clarifies. "Cheerleaders. Jocks. Assholes."

"Some of those assholes are my friends," I tell her.

"Seriously, June. *Theo.*"

"Gross," says Lily.

"Not Theo," I tell them. "Definitely not Theo." I look at Darbs. "Are you hanging with Ethan?"

"Unclear."

"If you're not, Lily should go make out with him," I say, and then Darbs and I crack up. Lily only blinks at us, so I explain. "Because I did it over summer break and Darbs did it over winter break, so spring break—your turn."

"Actually, hold off on that," Darbs says. We turn to her, surprised.

"You actually like him!" Lily accuses her.

"Maybe," she says. "I don't know. I just don't want anyone else putting their tongue in his mouth yet."

"That's fair," says Lily.

We reach the end of the aisle and round the corner to find Zoe Smith carrying a plastic store basket. After we all exchange hellos and commiserations about a lame spring break, she shows us what she's buying. "They're candy melts," Zoe says. "All you have to do is cook them down and pour it into molds. They harden into chocolate candy, like magic."

Lily looks down at the bags in her basket. "But they're already chocolate candy," she says. "They're shaped like little hearts."

"I know," says Zoe. "But after I'm done melting and pouring, they'll be shaped like little teddy bears. Way cuter."

"Are they a present for someone?" Darbs asks, and Zoe shakes her head.

"I wish. They're for home ec, which is bullshit. It's supposed

228

to be an easy class, but somehow I'm failing it. My GPA is all screwed up, so I have to cook for extra credit over spring break—how shitty is that?" We all agree it's shitty, and Zoe continues. "Even Oliver Flagg—who only took it because of that bet with Theo—even *he's* getting a better grade than me. When a jockstrap like that is schooling you in flambé, you know you suck."

Anxiety tickles my insides. I forgot about the bet, and I never found out what it was about. Suddenly, I feel like I really, really would be better off in blissful ignorance.

Darbs is the one who asks, "What bet?"

"Oh, you don't know this?" Zoe sets her basket on the floor at her feet. "So Oliver started dating Ainsley sometime last year, right?"

I hearken back to eleventh grade, when Itch moved to town. When I was the girl who got the new guy. Back then, I wasn't exactly paying attention to Oliver, but now that I think about it, Zoe's time line seems right.

"It was around this same time," Zoe says. "Spring break adjacent. Oliver bet Theo that he could get into Ainsley's pants by the Fourth of July."

"No." I don't realize I said it out loud until everyone looks at me. "Oliver's not like that," I say as an explanation.

"Please." Zoe snorts. "They're *all* like that. My brother's on the track team. He's the one who told me."

I turn into a statue. Cold. Hard. So still that I can't turn my head to look at Lily or Darbs.

"All the letter jacket guys knew about it," Zoe says. "Oliver didn't make the deadline, so he had to sign up for home ec. And yet he's still killing it while I'm flunking the class."

The waves of horror wash up and over my statue self. I've been feeling jealous of Ainsley when really I should have felt *sorry* for her. And Theo—thinking he's the devil incarnate, but now it turns out Oliver is just as terrible. Or even worse. Because Ainsley is *his* girlfriend. He's supposed to cherish her, protect her, be *kind* to her. Not treat her like an *object.*

Oliver.

I am so disappointed in him I could cry.

Zoe is still talking. Something about how she also needs to do an extra-credit sewing project and do we think latch-hook counts. I don't answer and neither do Darbs and Lily, because they're both looking at me.

Looking at me with pity.

Chapter 26

I'm already on my porch when the behemoth rumbles down Callaway. I've been preparing for this all week, and now that it's here, I'm ready. In fact, I'm more than ready. I'm *ecstatic*. I no longer have to wrestle with some moronic crush on Oliver, with my stupid *feelings* for him. All that has vanished in one heartsickening moment, with the knowledge that he is exactly the person I thought he was the very first time I climbed into his giant gas-guzzling monster of a car. I have been reminded that Oliver Flagg is a dick boy making dick bets, and that means it was just an attraction. That's all. Stupid chemistry. Nothing else.

This is a *relief*.

Oliver pulls into the driveway and I'm there before he unlocks my door. I fling it open, launch myself inside, and slam it. Then I turn to look at him, and I give myself full permission to notice his man-beauty, all the muscles and angles and everything. All of it nothing but a mask for his true self: a misogynist, woman-using prick. Everything that I loathe.

He flashes a glance at me before backing out onto the road. "You okay, Rafferty?"

It barely computes that he's back to calling me by my last name.

"Fine," I snap, folding my arms across my chest.

Oliver drives. He doesn't start the playlist. Neither do I. He doesn't speak. Neither do I. Finally, I realize that his jaw is set and his eyes are narrowed. He looks every bit as furious as I feel.

Well, screw him, then.

We get all the way to Main Street before we come to a red light and Oliver finally turns to me. "What is your problem?" he asks in a voice that is rough and angry.

I glare at him. "I thought you were different." I spit the words out between gritted teeth. "I would be *so* pissed if I found out that Itch had made bets about our private life."

Color rises up Oliver's cheekbones, docking in the tips of his ears. Those dark circles within his eyes deepen, and his muscles tense in his neck. We stare at each other, and for a second, I'm almost afraid of him, because he looks so, so livid.

But then he turns back to the road. He steps on the gas. His fingers tighten on the steering wheel and his knuckles go white. He doesn't say a word for the rest of the drive.

• • •

I manage to avoid Ainsley by arriving late to physics class and scooting out early. Later, I catch sight of her in the cafeteria, but I make a fast turn and head in the other direction. I can't explain to her why I'm not going to sit with her and her friends at lunch today. Or tomorrow. Or ever.

The guilt over not telling her the truth—it's too much.

I run into Oliver in the main lobby between afternoon

classes, but he pointedly looks away from me—which makes no sense at all, because *I'm* the nice one here. *I'm* on the side of the angels. *I'm* not a bet-placing, girl-exploiting asshole.

What. The. Hell.

• • •

Shaun grabs me at my locker after school. "Lily and Darbs told me what's going on," he says. "Are you okay?"

"I'm fine. Why wouldn't I be fine?" He only looks at me, so I spell it out for him. "He drives me to school, whatever. It's not like we're really *friends.*"

A few days ago, it would have been a lie.

Now it's not.

• • •

Third day of the Silent Treatment. Oliver showed up late (for him) and now we've sat in stony, awful silence for the last twenty minutes. As we pull into Robin High's parking lot, I steal a look at him.

Still staring straight ahead.

Still gripping the wheel.

I shake my head and don't even care when Oliver notices.

Two hours on a bus doesn't sound that bad anymore.

Chapter 27

A week later Oliver apparently has had enough. "It's none of your damn business," he says as soon as I climb into the behemoth. He's staring straight at me, not putting the car into reverse, not heading toward school, nothing. "Yes, taking that bet was a dick move, but I can't explain it to you. I don't *want* to explain it to you. It's not something you can understand."

I find my voice. "Being on the receiving end of a jerk is universal. It's a global experience."

"You and I live in two different worlds," Oliver snaps. He leans across the seat, so I know he means business. "And my world might seem stupid to you, it might seem basic and dumb and boring—"

"I didn't say that—"

"But you don't know that world." Oliver glares at me. "And apparently you don't know *me,* either."

But I thought that by now I *did* know him.

"You could have told me," I say. "Back at the very beginning, before we were friends. At least then I . . ."

I wouldn't have cared. I wouldn't have gotten hurt.

"You what?" he asks. "What would have been different?"

I stare into his brown eyes, ringed in gray and outrage, and it hits me: nothing would have been different. It's all one big cruel trick of fate. I could have taken any other road—the one where I stayed with Itch, the one where I took the bus, the one where I didn't help with the prank—and it wouldn't have mattered. All those other roads, they still would have led to the same place. I was always going to fall for this boy.

And he was always going to break my heart.

"Fine," I tell him, because the truth isn't an option.

"Fine?"

"Fine-I'll-make-a-concerted-effort-to-stop-judging-you-for-the-bet." I spit it out all as one word, retreating into the corner of my seat. Trying to put as much distance between us as possible.

"Fine." Oliver frowns at me. "Besides, there's something else we need to talk about."

His voice is still hard and the sound of it jolts my sadness into panic. He's been mad at me all this time—this whole week—and I haven't known why. Maybe it was more than a reaction to *my* anger. Maybe it was something else.

His parents.

Oliver could know about his parents, which would mean he knows I know about his parents, and now he might hate me, and—

"Oliver," I say, but he doesn't seem to hear me. He has taken out his phone and is sliding a finger over the screen.

"Here's the deal," he says. "It's not a big thing, so don't freak out or make a huge fuss, and I definitely don't want to have a whole conversation about it, but for today—just today—we are going to listen to my music and my music only." He starts a song—I think it's Warrant but it's not one from our playlist—and finally looks at me. "Ainsley and I broke up."

The news sends my heart racing. Oliver sees me open my mouth—although I'm not sure what I'm going to say—and he hastens to add: "No, I don't want to talk about it."

So *that's* why he's been such a mess ever since getting back from spring break.

Oliver backs out of my driveway and heads toward Plymouth. He stares straight ahead, but I'm gawking right at him. He shakes his head. "I knew you'd be like this." He glances at me and sighs. "Don't, June. Just . . . don't. The only reason I'm even telling you is because I don't want to repeat your bullshit when you and Itch broke up."

I turn away and look out my window. Yep, Oliver definitely has the ability to hurt my feelings. Beside me, I hear him shift in his seat, and I wonder if he's going to say something, but instead, his stupid music blares louder. He's only turning up the volume.

As I watch the fields blur by, I realize I'm not unhappy only because Oliver's acting like a douche. It's because the rules just changed again and I'm surprised by that. No, worse. I'm rattled.

I don't know how to *do* this whole friendship/not-friendship with Oliver if he's single.

• • •

I'm waiting for physics to start when a pink notebook plops onto the lab table. I look up to see Ainsley standing beside me. She gives me a wry smile. "Can I sit here?"

"Sure." Part of me is painfully curious about what happened between her and Oliver. The smarter—but smaller—part of me thinks I should stay blissfully unaware. Besides, the less we talk, the less guilty I feel about not telling her about the bet.

She sits down and sets her elbow on the table, leaning her head against her hand so she's gazing up at me. "You've been avoiding me."

"I didn't want to get in the middle of it." She keeps looking at me, so I elaborate. "It felt awkward." At least that part was true.

"How is he?"

I'm not sure what the right answer is, so I reply truthfully. "I don't know. He didn't say much."

Ainsley nods. "But he told you we broke up."

This time I can't keep myself from asking: "What happened?"

She presses her lips together before answering. "I just didn't want to do it anymore. Being his girlfriend stopped being *fun.*"

Wow. It wasn't a mutual breakup; it was a dumping. Which means Oliver is heartbroken. It sure explains his behavior when we got back from spring break.

"How did he take it?" I ask Ainsley.

"He was quiet. I couldn't tell if he was upset or angry or what. How was Itch when you broke up with him?"

At least that's an easy question to answer. "He was really mad."

As the bell rings for class to start, a last group of kids hurdles through the door, Oliver among them. He stalks right past my (our) lab table without a look.

Ainsley sighs. "I think Oliver is mad, too."

• • •

"Here." Oliver juts his phone at me as I strap myself in. "Add a song."

"Why?" I look at him warily. "Did I prove something that I somehow missed?"

"No, but you will. You are amazingly competitive, so as soon as you think it's been long enough, you're going to use my breakup as a reason that high school doesn't matter. Since I won't really feel like fighting about it or taking it up with Shaun, you'll win, so here." He shoves his phone into my hands. "Go ahead. Add your song."

He cranks the car into reverse and I look down at the phone in my hands. The opening screen used to feature a photo of him and Ainsley smiling at the camera, but now it's blank.

"I need a second," I tell him, and pick up my own phone.

A few minutes of purchasing and texting and sending later, our "Sunrise Songs" playlist has one new addition. I touch a final screen and the opening drumbeats reverberate out of the speakers, followed by an acoustic guitar and piano. A moment later, a melodic voice floats over us both.

Oliver frowns. "This doesn't sound like your usual screamo."

"It's not."

He glances at me. "Then what gives? Who is this?"

"Carly Simon. Seems appropriate."

I sit back in my seat and cross my arms over my chest just as the chorus of "You're So Vain" hits the air. Oliver takes the turn onto Plymouth with a little more vehemence than usual. "Cute, Rafferty. Really cute."

• • •

238

It's the fourth day of nothing but music on the way to school. I want to have an actual conversation with Oliver, to see how he's doing, friend to friend. To try to get past this crap about the bet and the breakup. I want to comfort him, to talk it out, to slide my arms around his waist and hug him hard, to feel his breath in my—

No, wait! Not that. Never that.

I just want us to be normal again.

But we're not.

"Hey, Oliver," I say over the music as we pull into the parking lot. "I was wondering—"

I stop, because of course Oliver is waving to someone, and of course that someone is Theo, who is strutting across the asphalt toward us. So much for any last hope of reasonable discourse today.

Theo is there by the time we get out. He gives me a very obvious and obnoxious once-over before head-bobbing at Oliver. "You check out that link I sent you?" He cuts his eyes toward me and drops his voice. "The one about *literature*."

Yeah, right.

Oliver nods. "The literature was very . . . well *rounded*."

Then some high-fiving and fist-bumping occur, after which Theo makes hand motions that leave nothing to the imagination in terms of what this website link was actually about. It's definitely—*definitely*—not literature.

"Bye, guys." I head toward the school. Unfortunately, Oliver and Theo follow right behind me. They don't even bother to lower their voices.

"I'd like to try some of that," Theo tells Oliver, apparently still talking about their gross website. "Wouldn't you?"

"Who says I haven't?" Oliver asks, and a sour taste crawls up the back of my throat. My attraction to him shrivels up, turns to dust, and blows away in the spring wind. I know some girls are inexplicably into guys who are pricks, but I am 100 percent *not*.

Which means, now that I think about it, maybe it's a good thing Oliver has reverted to his jock-hole ways.

Chapter 28

Ainsley grabs my arm as we stand up from our lab table at the end of physics class. "There's a party at Kaylie's next Saturday. You should come."

"Kaylie and I don't really hang out." It's true, since I've spoken maybe twelve words to Kaylie in my life, and some have been things like "Excuse me" and "That's my pencil."

"Everyone can come. The whole senior class."

"I'll wait for my invitation," I say, and she bonks her purse into me.

"This *is* your invitation." She's smiling, but then it drops from her face. "Can I ask you something?"

Not-about-Oliver-not-about-Oliver.

"Sure."

"It's about Oliver." Natch. "How's he doing?"

"I honestly have no idea."

"You just listen to music when you drive to school?"

I nod. "You might want to ask Theo."

Ainsley's arched eyebrows jut together in the middle. "Theo?"

"From what I can tell, that's the only person who Oliver's hanging out with."

Ainsley shakes her head. "That's not good."

"Tell me about it."

• • •

It's spring, which means it's sunny and lovely but not yet too hot. It also means that all kinds of people eat on the bleachers. Lily and Darbs and Shaun and I are at our regular spot, but now there are tons of others dotted all around in little clusters like ours. We've just finished an entire conversation about the end of spring break and Yana and the final book report for the year when Lily asks the question I've been hoping to avoid. "Are you guys definitely going to prom?"

Shaun and Darbs both nod, which I was not expecting. Shaun, yes. Darbs . . . I kinda figured she'd flake.

"I'm deejaying," Shaun says. "I can't escape it."

"I don't *want* to escape it," Darbs tells us. "It's going to be hilarious."

"Will you go with someone?" I ask her.

"I'm debating."

"Between what?" Lily asks.

"Taking a risk on asking Yana or saying yes to Ethan."

"Ethan asked you to prom? He never even texted me." I gawk at her. "You must be an awesome kisser."

Darbs waggles her tongue in my direction. "Oh, I've got moves."

"Gross," I tell her.

"Are you going?" Shaun asks Lily.

"Maybe if my new boyfriend's into it." She smiles when she

says it, all smug and amused because we react exactly the way she knew we would: by squealing and hammering her with questions. Apparently Lily has been hooking up with a twenty-year-old dude she met in Saline at an underground concert. His name is Gordy, his hair is dyed shiny black, and he wears eyeliner. "He's so hot," Lily tells us.

Later, I'm walking back into the main building with Shaun when he nudges me. "Are you still anti-prom?"

"One hundred percent."

"Just because it's an antiquated tradition from a patriarchal era that disenfranchises females by placing them in the subordinate position of waiting to be asked by a male?"

"Pretty much."

"Change your mind," says Shaun. "Be my date."

"What about Kirk?"

"I can't ask him. He'll say no and I'll be destroyed. It's better if I just let him drift away. You be my date instead."

"That's crazy," I tell him. "And no. You'll be deejaying."

"You could keep me company."

"No offense, but no thanks," I tell him. What I *don't* tell him is that the idea of hanging in the deejay booth with my gay best friend during the most sacred of high school traditions makes me feel like a pathetic loser. Like the girl who can't find a *real* date. And yes, I know plenty of my fellow seniors are planning to go in big groups with each other and that it's totally fine to fly solo . . . but I don't want to. I don't want to because—

"Oliver," says Shaun, and I feel my body twitch in response.

"What about him?" I say in the most casual tone I can scrape up.

"He's single. You're single." Shaun shrugs. "It kinda seems like a *duh*."

"I thought you would be on the Oliver hatred train with Darbs and Lily."

"No, I've done stupid things because I was trying to fit in." Shaun shakes his head. "Granted, not since middle school, but *still*. Most of the time, Oliver's a really good guy. He should get credit for that."

"I guess." We walk in silence until we're almost to the building. "But we're friends, or something like friends. Going to prom—that would make it a different story."

"Maybe you need a different story." Shaun gives me side-eye and I shove him.

"Maybe shut your trap-hole."

• • •

"Are you going to Kaylie's on Saturday?" My question is a desperate attempt to make conversation with Oliver as we approach campus.

"Nope." And then, for the first time in a week, he actually asks me a question in return. "Are you?"

"I'm thinking about it."

"You should. Kaylie throws a good party."

"Then why aren't you going?"

"I've been to a lot of Kaylie's parties."

I eye him, debating asking a different question. We seem

to be making progress—at least in this moment—but I don't want to piss him off and possibly send him back to the Land of Jerkdom, even though there's a certain peace in that land, because when he lives there, I have no fear of the attraction coming back.

"Is it because Ainsley will be there?"

Oliver glances at me, and I see him weighing how to answer. "No."

"Then why?"

"I promised my mom I'd help her with some stuff at home, that's all."

We're silent as Oliver finds a parking spot, but when we're walking toward school, he suddenly turns to me. "Do you think I should go?"

"Yes." I say it reflexively, which is why I don't have an answer when Oliver asks the inevitable next question.

"Why?"

Because I want you there.

It comes into my head as a simple fact over which I have no control. Like gravity. "Because . . . because it'll be fun."

"But don't you think there will be other fun parties?"

I'm not sure what Oliver is getting at. "Maybe. Or maybe not. We don't have that much school left."

Oliver nods. "So it's one of the last times I'll get to hang out with all my friends."

"Yes. It might even be the last big party of the whole year."

"Except for prom."

Ugh.

"Right. Except for prom."

Oliver's face gets very serious. "So you're saying that it's important."

"Exactly," I tell him, and then realize my mistake as the first bell rings and Oliver grins really big. "Dammit!"

"Oh, June," Oliver says, and all my attraction to him comes flooding back, because his smile is so wide and his eyes are so brown, and something about the way he says my name makes my abdomen tighten. "Another song for our playlist. When will you ever learn?"

Apparently the answer is "never," because here we are again: me falling hopelessly; him unaware and unattainable.

Of course, the only thing I say is "Shut up."

It makes him laugh out loud.

Chapter 29

When Shaun arrives at my house, he insists on playing dress-up. At least, that's what I call his desire to pick out my clothing for the party. "It's not that you look *bad*," he says, scanning me. "But it's hardly party attire."

"My dad says these are the hottest jeans in New York," I protest, pointing to the elaborately ripped hole along my upper thigh.

"Those are sexy," Shaun assures me. "But you could wear that shirt to teach Sunday school. What else do you have?"

After half an hour in my closet (and several jokes about coming out of it), Shaun has exchanged my T-shirt for a long-sleeved crop top screen-printed with tiny zebras: a present from Dad two summers ago. I tug at the bottom of it, which barely skims my navel. "I think this might be too small."

"There's no such thing as a shirt that's too small." Shaun assesses my outfit. "Shoes."

I want flip-flops and he wants stilettos. Since I don't own the latter and he refuses to sign off on the former, we settle on a pair of jewel-studded platform wedges that I've worn only a couple times.

"If I break an ankle, I'm blaming you," I tell him.

Shaun only points to my hair, which is pulled back in a pony-tail. "Down."

"It gets out of control when it's down."

"You could stand to be a little out of control," he tells me. *"Down."*

A few minutes later, my hair frames my face in already tangled waves. Shaun gives me a double thumbs-up. "This is fun. We should always do this."

"Or not," I tell him. But my reflection in the mirror is smiling.

• • •

Since I don't usually go to these house parties, I'm a little disappointed to discover that people aren't jumping off the roof into a pool and no one is playing a game of Suck and Blow and there hasn't been even one fistfight. Looks like Hollywood got it wrong.

What they got right, however, is the loud music and the beer keg and the revealing clothes. When we walk in to see a pack of girls with a lot of skin showing, I have a flash of gratitude for Shaun's pushiness.

We find Kaylie in the kitchen, in the center of a crowd. She's leaning against the counter and giggling through a slice of lime between her teeth. As we watch, Bo Reeves shakes salt onto her chest, right above the line of her halter top. He licks it off, then tosses back a shot glass. As the crowd cheers, he slurps the lime wedge out of Kaylie's mouth and sucks on it for a second before spitting it into the sink. He turns back to Kaylie and presses his mouth down on hers, which she allows for a scant moment before pulling back with a loud "Woohoo!"

The crowd echoes her response and I exchange glances with Shaun. "Romantic."

Kaylie squeals again, and I realize she's looking at us. "June! Shaun! Come do body shots!"

Shaun grins at me. "I'm driving."

"What the hell," I say, which makes Kaylie squeal again. She sloshes some tequila into the shot glass and hands it to me. "Have you ever done one?"

I glance around at my audience of what I assume are body shot veterans. "Nope."

"You're supposed to put it in your cleavage," Kaylie says in a confidential tone that everyone within twenty feet can hear. "But I didn't want Bo's face in my boobs."

"Generally speaking, I have a face-free boob zone myself."

"PMGO," Kaylie says, and I laugh because Darbs's thing has finally caught on. Kaylie gestures to the crowd. "Who's it going to be?" I know most of the faces but don't see anyone I'm particularly dying to lick, so I point at Shaun. Apparently it's a good choice, because cheering and laughter erupts.

"Make him straight!" says Danny Hollander, and Shaun gives him the finger.

I take the proffered lime wedge from Kaylie and slide it over the back of Shaun's hand. "I'm pretty sure this won't make you straight," I tell him as Kaylie sprinkles salt over the area.

"You're welcome to try." Shaun opens his mouth so I can set the wedge between his teeth.

I lick the sour salt from his hand and drink the tequila. It's way stronger than I imagined, and my face involuntarily squinches up tight, which makes people laugh. I shake my head and lean into Shaun so I can take the lime from his mouth. "Yuck," I say once the taste is gone from my tongue and people have stopped clapping for my amazing feat.

"Congratulations on losing your body shot virginity," Shaun says.

"Thanks. Are you straight now?"

"I actually think you might have made me gayer." Yet another squeal from Kaylie heralds a new group of guests, so with the attention off us, Shaun and I head for the keg. "We can share," he tells me.

It's a good call, especially because the tequila is still burning in my throat. As Shaun fills up a plastic cup, the door to the backyard bangs open and a girl totters in backward. It's obviously Ainsley, because that's Ainsley's thick, curly beach-sand hair hanging almost to her waist, and yet it can't *possibly* be her, because visible at her waist is a pair of very big, very male hands. They're groping her quite extensively, and they belong to Theo Nizzola.

I want to think it's a party game—one I don't know, like another version of body shots, maybe—but Theo and Ainsley aren't carrying any alcohol that I can see. Also, they're so into each other that they can't even separate their mouths long enough to walk into the house. They're murmuring between kisses, and as Shaun and I stare, Ainsley takes Theo's hands away from her waist so she can entwine her fingers with his. She steps into the kitchen, pulling him after her.

Because he's facing forward—and because Shaun and I are just standing there with our mouths wide open—Theo addresses us first. "What are you looking at?"

We're saved from answering by Ainsley's gasp of surprise. "June! You're here!"

"You invited me." I hear the chill in my voice. Suddenly, I understand what might have made Oliver punch Itch in the face.

"You said you weren't coming." She waves her hands in front of her body, distressed, and her eyes are bigger and greener than usual.

"Shaun convinced me otherwise." I eye Theo. "I guess I should have alerted you that I changed my mind."

"No." Ainsley shakes her head. "Of course you didn't have to tell me. I'm sorry. I'm surprised, that's all."

"I see that." I turn to Shaun. "Let's go anywhere else."

"Wait," says Ainsley. "Can I talk to you?"

I don't especially want to listen to Ainsley explain why it's okay to make out with Oliver's best friend, so I look at Shaun. I'm hoping he'll save me, but he only nods and pushes the cup of beer into my hands. "Go ahead."

I follow Ainsley through the kitchen and the crowded living room and out onto the front porch. It's not as big as ours, but there's a porch swing in the corner. I sit on one end and Ainsley plops onto the other. "Theo was going to tell him tonight," she says. "That was the plan, but then Oliver decided not to come."

I gesture to the house. "Do you really think everyone here is going to keep it a secret? You're all over each other." I don't add what's really going through my mind: *grossgrossgross*.

"We didn't think it through," says Ainsley. "We were just going to come to the party like friends, but then we were holding hands and suddenly it seemed silly to keep trying to hide it, you know?"

"I actually *don't* know. You could have any boy you want, and you choose the one who's besticles with Oliver?"

"That's not *why* I'm with Theo. I just like him."

I don't say anything, because although I cannot remotely understand liking Theo Nizzola, what I *do* understand is not getting to choose how emotions work.

"I know it's breaking the bro code. Theo knows it, too. That's why he's going to talk to him." Ainsley leans forward, training her eyes on my face. "Please don't be mad, June."

I turn it over in my mind. I don't know why Ainsley cares if I'm mad at her, which I'm not. Not exactly. It's more that I don't want anyone to get hurt and this seems like it has big potential for hurting everyone involved, Ainsley included.

"I have to tell you something," I finally say, and watch Ainsley's smile vanish. "In the name of sisterhood, I think you need to know."

"Go on." This time her voice is sharp. Cold.

"When you and Oliver started dating, Theo made a stupid bet with him about how fast Oliver could"—I pause and Ainsley waits, tapping her foot against the porch floor—"have sex with you." It sounds so awful when I say it out loud, and suddenly I hate myself for being the one to inflict this knowledge on her. "Theo bet Oliver he couldn't do it by the Fourth of July. That's why Oliver took that family sciences class, because he lost the bet." Ainsley stays quiet and I can't tell if she's furious or if she's going to burst into tears or what, so I keep talking to get it over with, the words coming out faster and faster. "Yeah, it was crappy of Oliver to take the bet, but maybe it was worse of Theo to make it in the first place. He brought it up in the locker room or something, so everyone was listening and all the athletes know about it. I'm so sorry, Ainsley. . . . What?"

Ainsley has burst all right, but not into tears. She's laughing, the sound of it ringing hard and clear through the night air. It's not joyful. It's *scornful*. "God, June. You're just so *earnest*. It's kind of adorable."

I don't know what's going on here, but I'm pretty sure she's not giving me a compliment.

"I already know about their stupid bet," she tells me. "I've known forever. It's not a big deal."

"Not a big deal?" Indignation rises in me and spills out. "Are you kidding? A whole locker room of asshole boys speculating about how fast you'll put out? It's awful! It's *gross*! It's—"

"It's a lie," Ainsley says.

"The bet? The bet was a lie?"

"No. Oliver *taking* the bet was a lie. When Theo brought it up in front of everyone, it was a done deal. Oliver and I had already had sex, but Oliver didn't want all those guys to know it. He thought it would make me look bad."

I shove back the part of me that cares about Oliver having sex.

"He told everyone he lost the bet to save . . . like your *honor* or something?"

"I know." Ainsley shakes her head. "Stupid, isn't it?"

It's not stupid to me. It's revelatory. Oliver let me think he was an asshole jock so he could protect Ainsley's privacy. Oliver might be the best person I've ever known. Oliver is a *prince*.

Ainsley hops up. "I need another drink. We're cool?"

"Sure." Because what else would I say?

She beams at me. "Awesome. See you in there." She traipses back into the house. I look down at the plastic cup I'm holding and reflexively take a gulp. It's not very good. I don't love the taste of beer and this particular cup is already getting warm, so I stand and dump the contents over the porch railing. I have an urge to throw my cup into the darkness beyond, but that would be littering, so I don't.

I stay there for a while, wondering how to approach Oliver on Monday. Sure, I'm not thrilled about the way he's been behaving, but I was supposed to be his friend and I accused him of something he didn't do. I accused him of the exact *opposite* of what he did. I started off the school year by believing the worst of him, and then I believed it *again* after he'd already proven me wrong.

Maybe I'm the jock-hole.

I wait for clarity that never comes. Finally, I'm tired of being alone and tired of slapping at mosquitoes, so I decide to see if Shaun is ready to leave. I'm starting toward the front door when I hear the sound of an engine and see headlights approaching fast as a car rumbles up the long driveway from the road. There's a spray of gravel as the behemoth grinds to a stop, nestling in a grove of trees beyond the other cars, at the edge of the darkness.

I stand on the porch, frozen, as the door slams and Oliver appears, stalking toward me, winding his way through the other cars. I don't need to see his face to know he's pissed. I can tell by the way his body is moving, by the fact that he slammed the behemoth's door. Someone must have texted, or called, or posted a photo of the party online.

Oliver knows about Ainsley and Theo.

I rush to the top of the porch stairs just as Oliver storms up them. He stops when he reaches me. "Hey," he says, but there's no true greeting in his voice. I'm a blip on the radar, a fork in the road. An obstacle to get through.

"I thought you weren't coming." It's an attempt to stall him, an accidental echo of what Ainsley said when I arrived.

"Yeah, I thought so, too." Oliver's whole body is vibrating, angry, tense. "But I got some information that made me think I should be social after all."

He shoulders past me into the house and it's a full thirty seconds before the commands make their way from my brain to my feet so I can chase after him. More people have come in from the backyard, and now the living room is full and loud. Someone cranked up the music and it's finally starting to look more like a house party in a movie: dancing and drinking and groping. I don't see Oliver, but Shaun is by one of the coffee tables, bopping around with a guy from the theater department. I grab him mid-bounce. "Quick, where's Ainsley?"

Shaun shrugs. "You had her last."

I shake him—"Oliver's here!"—and see the *Oh, shit* blossom across Shaun's face. He knows what I know: if something starts between Oliver and Theo, it's not going to end well for Oliver. Sure, he's strong and muscly, but he doesn't know how to *fight*. We all saw Itch's face after Oliver hit him and—let's be honest— there wasn't much damage done.

"They might be upstairs," Shaun tells me. "I'll check."

"I'll look outside. Meet me back here." I race down the hallway, careening between pockets of acquaintances who are kissing or smoking or doing something that I think is supposed

255

to be dancing. Unfortunately (or maybe fortunately, depending on what path Oliver took), none of them are Ainsley and Theo. I round the corner into the kitchen and see that the body shot thing is still happening and that Oliver is here, waiting his turn to take one. As I arrive, Mark Silver leans over to take a shot glass out of Jeana Katz's cleavage with his teeth. He kicks it back and goes for the lime in her mouth. Major tongue action ensues, leading me to believe that we've passed the sobriety point of the evening.

I rush up to Oliver and grab him by the arm. I ask, "What are you doing?" which is the first thing that comes to my mind.

"Getting a drink."

"Here?"

He gives me a funny look, which I actually take as a good thing, because at least it's cutting through all the anger and tension he's currently sending out. "Yeah, this is the kitchen."

I spot a full bottle of tequila on the counter and I snag it. "Gotcha covered," I tell him in an extra-cheery voice, holding the bottle in front of his eyes. I grab him by the wrist. "Come on, let's go."

I tug him into the hallway and Oliver goes along with it for a dozen steps before pulling me to a stop. "Wait, what are we doing?"

"You said you wanted a drink. I am in possession of a drink. Thus, we're going to go have a drink." I wave the tequila. "*This* drink, to be specific."

Oliver frowns. "I told you I came here to be social." But then he looks down at my fingers, clasped around his arm, and his expression softens. "What's going on, June? Are you okay?"

"No." It's not entirely a lie. "Look, can we go hang out somewhere private?" My whisking Oliver away will give Shaun enough time to warn Ainsley and Theo to knock off the PDA. I don't know what I'll say to him once we're alone, but I'm sure I can come up with something about school or our playlist or anything besides "Your ex is hooking up with your besticle."

There's a pause, during which Oliver scans my face and I suddenly realize we're standing very close together in a place of heat and humidity and hormones. What had been urgency morphs into . . . awareness. All I can see are Oliver's eyes and all I can hear is my heartbeat in my ears. Oliver's pupils dilate and something swells in my chest. I open my mouth to talk but words don't come out, because he's taking my hand—the one on his wrist—in his own. "June," he says, but I'll never know what the rest of that sentence would have been, because Theo's voice drowns it out.

"Got your sloppy seconds right out in public?" And there's Theo, hulking from a door that I think leads to the basement.

"Shut up," I tell Theo, because for God's sake, that's not even what "sloppy seconds" *means,* but then two manicured hands are sliding around his waist from behind, and Ainsley's face emerges from the darkness below. When she sees us, she gasps and jerks away from Theo, but it's too late. It doesn't take a genius to figure out what's going on. What's *been* going on.

"Oliver!" she says, coming all the way up into the hallway and closing the door behind her. "Theo and I had to get some beer from the—"

"You weren't getting beer," says Oliver.

"Are you calling her a liar?" asks Theo.

Oliver turns to face him, and since I'm so close, I can see his jaw tightening. I grab his arm but he shakes me off. "You said it," he informs Theo. "And by the way, what are you doing with my ex-girlfriend?"

"Same thing you're doing with *her*, I guess." Theo makes a suggestive gesture in my direction and Oliver grabs him by the shirt and slams him into the wall. It's fast, it's violent, and it makes someone scream. A second later, I realize it was me.

In the living room, the music stops and, from the kitchen, we hear Kaylie's voice. "No fighting! No fighting in the house!"

"Stop!" No one listens to Ainsley's command.

Oliver and Theo are glaring full fury at each other, their faces an inch apart. People pour into the hallway, and since apparently everyone is drunk, no one does a damn thing to stop them, so I grab Oliver's arm while Ainsley grabs Theo's.

"Oliver, don't!" My tone is pleading. "Please stop."

There's a beat, during which they keep staring at each other, and then Oliver's muscles relax under my fingers. He takes a step backward and slowly lowers his fist. Theo does the same.

"Thank you," I whisper as Ainsley tugs Theo toward the kitchen. She and I make eye contact, and a flash of something— understanding, clarity, grace—goes between us, and then they're gone and I'm pulling Oliver out of the party and into the night air on the porch. "Come on." I lead him down the steps as music blares back to life behind us.

"Where?" Oliver asks, and I don't know how to answer. I only know I need to get him away from this house, away from Theo, away from everything dangerous. It's only when we've arrived that I realize I've taken him to the behemoth. Oliver realizes it at the same time as me and digs in his heels. "I'm not leaving."

"We don't have to leave. We'll just . . . be here."

There's a long pause and then Oliver sighs. "I'm only saying yes because you're the reason I didn't hit Theo."

"Thanks for that." I reach for the passenger door handle, but Oliver blocks me.

"We've spent too much time inside this car already."

"Then where?"

He places his hands on my waist and lifts me onto the hood like I weigh nothing at all. He swings up—because apparently that's the easiest thing in the world to do if you're Oliver—and looks at me. "Is that yours?"

I realize what's been in my hand the entire time: the bottle of tequila. "No," I tell him, and he laughs.

"At least we got something out of this party."

But he doesn't take the tequila. Instead, he clasps his hands beneath his head and leans back against the windshield, looking up at the night sky. He's as beautiful as always, because it's not like starlight makes people *less* attractive, for crying out loud. I scoot over and recline against the windshield beside him.

"I know Theo deserved it, but I'm glad you didn't punch him. It wouldn't make you feel any better about Ainsley."

There's a rustle beside me. Oliver has propped himself up on his elbow and is facing me. "Wait, you think I wanted to hit Theo . . . why?"

"Because he's . . . whatever he is . . . with Ainsley?"

I think it's a *duh,* but Oliver looks bewildered. "June, what the hell." He shakes his head. "It was because of what he did to *you*. That thing he did. The gesture."

I stare at him, because of course that doesn't make any sense whatsoever. "Theo always does stuff like that to me."

"I know. I've tried to get him to stop. I'm sick of it."

"Wait." I peel off the windshield and sit cross-legged on the hood of the behemoth. "Isn't that why you came here? Because you found out about Theo and Ainsley?"

"No." Oliver sits up also. He faces me on the hood of his car. "I needed to get out."

"Why?" The second it comes out of my mouth, I realize I already know the answer.

"It's been weird at my house. Like all the air has been sucked out and the three of us are rattling around in this big, empty vacuum, but I haven't known *why*." I nod, dreading what he's going to say next. "Tonight, I found out. My dad is cheating on my mom."

"He *is*?" Like, he's still doing it?

"Is, was, I don't know. He definitely did it—more than once—and he admits to it. I guess he and Mom are trying to work it out, but today they had a big fight. I came downstairs as he was driving away and she was pouring his most expensive bottle of scotch down the kitchen sink."

Sounds about right.

"Then what happened?" I ask him.

"Mom told me about the cheating." Oliver shoots me a wry look. "I think she was drinking some of the scotch before she dumped it."

I swallow hard. "Did she say anything else?"

"Just highlights from the divorce chapter of the parent handbook. It's not my fault and everything will be okay." He shakes his head. "Dad always seemed so in love with her. I can't believe he did it. I thought . . ."

His voice trails off and I finish the sentence for him. "You thought he was better than that."

Oliver nods. Our knees are touching and I want to slide my hand over to hold his, but I don't. I can't.

I'm scared.

Oliver's gaze slides to the bottle leaning against the windshield. He picks it up and scans the label. "You stole Kaylie's tequila."

"I don't know about *stole,*" I tell him. "Borrowed, maybe. I borrowed Kaylie's tequila."

"There are people in there who are going to be really mad if they don't get to do their body shots," Oliver says. "You're disappointing the masses."

"The masses already saw me do one." I immediately wish I hadn't said that, as something passes over his face—something I can't quite pinpoint.

"Who did you do it with?" His voice is careful, deliberately casual.

"Shaun," I tell him, and watch his body relax.

"I didn't get a chance to do one." The way Oliver says it makes the night air hang hot and thick and still around us. My eyes go to the tequila bottle in his hands, then back up to his face.

"Really?"

"Really."

It's only one word, but it carries all kinds of meaning. A question. A wish. A promise. I stare at Oliver's shadowed eyes, and the smooth heat of the car beneath me increases, radiating up through my thighs and into my abdomen. Something between us has changed, become charged. He lifts the bottle and his posture shifts so his knees bump against mine. My normal reaction would be to scoot backward, to give him space, to put a barrier between us.

Instead, I lean forward just a little. My knees press into his.

Oliver smiles.

I smile back.

"We don't have a lime." It's a last feeble effort at self-protection, at preventing what I know is about to happen. What I *want* to happen.

"Remember when we were in my basement?" Oliver asks me. "When we pretended we were in the car?"

"Yes." It comes out in a whisper.

He cocks his head, just a little, and I realize that even though I haven't made a conscious decision to do it, I'm tilting my head in the opposite direction. I'm lining myself up for him.

"Where should I put the salt?" His gaze dances down my face, skims over my torso.

I raise my hand, because that's what I did with Shaun, but then it's moving of its own accord and my index finger is pointing to a spot on my collarbone.

"Good choice," Oliver says, not in his usual joking manner. He slides his own finger over the place where I touched. "Lime." He lifts the imaginary slice, lightly touching the corners of my mouth when he places it there. I part my lips to accept what doesn't exist. Then Oliver shakes his hand over that spot at the base of my neck. "Salt."

He moves even closer and now he's looking straight into my eyes.

"Yes," I say again, answering what he hasn't asked out loud. He dips his head. I feel the tip of his tongue touch my collarbone and trace an inch along it. Even though his mouth is warm, even though it's hot outside, I shiver.

Oliver lifts his head. "Still okay?" This time I don't have the voice to answer him, so I only nod. He tips the tequila up to his mouth, pretending to drink from the unopened bottle, then sets it back on the hood of the behemoth. He looks at my mouth. "I'm supposed to have the lime now."

Slowly, I reach up and take the pretend lime out of my mouth and wave it at him. "It's right here." I mime setting it back where it was.

Oliver smiles and I lean forward. He tilts and then his mouth is against mine, warm and soft and tasting not at all like tequila and limes, but instead like mint toothpaste and cherry ChapStick. All on their own, my lips part under his. All on their own, my arms wrap around him and my hands slide up his back, feeling the ripples of his muscles beneath his shirt. It's so different from kissing Itch, from kissing Ethan, from kissing any other boy, because this boy is *Oliver,* and even though he's completely familiar, I'm discovering him with every tiny movement we make.

He leans back against the windshield once more, but this time he takes me with him, pulling my entire body on top of his, and we kiss for a thousand years or maybe only five minutes.

I can't tell, because the whole world has turned into Oliver. It confirms what I already knew, what I've shoved away and buried over and over again.

Oliver means everything to me.

Oliver *is* everything.

Chapter 30

Warm sunlight stripes my face and I roll over in my bed. The clock on my nightstand tells me it's morning but not so late that I *have* to get up. I can sleep some more, because it's the weekend and weekends mean sleeping in.

So the first thought that goes through my head is this: *More sleep, please.*

The second thought jolts me upright. It brings my shoulders to my ears and my hands to my mouth. That second thought is this: *Oliver kissed me.*

My third thought of the morning comes almost immediately. It is abrupt and shocking and loud inside my head. It is this: *OH, SHIT.*

• • •

It's almost noon when Oliver calls. I'm sitting alone at the kitchen counter, trying to force some cheese and crackers past the knot in my chest, when my phone shivers. I see his name on the tiny screen, and I don't even hesitate before touching the button to silence it, silence him.

I can't talk to him.

Not yet.

What I *can* bring myself to do is listen to his voice mail.

"Hey, June. It's Oliver. Flagg." He lets out a self-deprecating chuckle. "Which you already know, because I'm calling on your cell phone and cell phones broadcast the caller's name, so basically everything I've said up until this point is completely worthless. I should hang up and start over, except that then I'd be calling twice in a row and that's super weird and creepy, so . . . June Rafferty"—he takes a deep breath—"I would never dream of asking you to prom. It would be an insult to your intelligence. That is why . . ."

This pause is the longest of all.

"That is why I want to let you know that if a certain strong-willed, brilliant feminist intellectual just so happened to take it upon herself to invite a certain behemoth-driving jock to prom . . . that jock would say yes. He would say it very, very happily."

The knuckle on my right ring finger hurts, and I realize it's because I'm clutching the phone so tightly. I loosen my grip and listen to the end of Oliver's message.

"So I hope she asks him. I also hope she calls him back, because Saturday was . . ."

A mistake, a mistake, a mistake.

". . . the best." I can hear his smile through the phone. "Call me."

And then he's gone. I'm alone with the knowledge that I've opened a door that can never be closed—one that leads to a place holding my greatest vulnerabilities, my biggest weaknesses, and everything that terrifies me the most.

No.

• • •

Early Monday morning, Mom parks in one of the employee lots on the U of M campus and we get out into the cold morning air. I trudge behind her, sending Oliver a text as I walk.

> came in w/Mom today so no need 2 pick me up.
> srry hvnt called yet. super busy

He writes back immediately.

> no problem! see you at school.

Mom has office hours, so she lets me into one of the galleries, where I sit on a bench and stare at a wall of turquoise canvases. I decide that both the bench and my life are hard, and that both the art and my heart are inscrutable. I sit there, feeling self-congratulatory about those poetic thoughts, until it's time to walk to school.

• • •

It starts in homeroom when Lily plops down next to me. "How was your weekend?"

"Fine." It's not completely a lie.

"Was the *fine* part when Oliver almost punched Theo, or was it *fine* when you rolled around the back of a pickup truck with him?"

"It wasn't a pickup truck. It was the hood of Oliver's car." I drop my head into my hands.

When homeroom is over, Shaun finds us in the hall as we're all on the way to English. "How was that tequila?"

"We didn't drink it."

"They were too busy," Lily tells him.

"I know," says Shaun.

"*Everyone* knows," says Lily.

"I think I have a migraine," I tell them, and bolt.

● ● ●

After lying around the nurse's office for a couple hours, unable to produce either a fever or some vomit, I get sent back to class. I consider ditching—just walking off campus and away from school, my senior year, graduation, life—but can't bring myself to do it. After all, true escape is so close on the horizon, and then I'll never have to see any of these people again. Only a few more weeks.

I just have to get through them.

Everyone would have stared at me anyway, because it's natural to stare when a student walks into class totally late and drops a note on the teacher's desk, but today—as Mrs. Nelson glances at the slip from the office and dismisses me with a nod—I feel all those eyes like they're heavy objects dropping on every inch of my skin, turning it hot, pressing against my body.

Judging.

Even though I don't look toward the back of the classroom, I know that two of the eyes belong to Oliver and they are the heaviest and the hottest of all. I can't meet them with my own.

Because there's nothing else to do, I sit by Ainsley, slinging my backpack onto the floor beside my chair. Given that even people who *didn't* attend Saturday's party have heard that I spent it kissing Oliver on some form of vehicle, I know there's no way Ainsley isn't in the loop. I take a deep breath before turning to her.

She's smiling.

At the front of the room, Mrs. Nelson fiddles with a remote control. She's experiencing some technical difficulties with the movie we're supposed to watch about momentum and collisions. Apparently it gives the class license to talk, so Kaylie hops up from her lab table and drags her chair to us. "Hey, kids."

Ainsley and I both tell her hello. My tone is wary; Ainsley's is chipper.

"So how about that party?" Kaylie waggles her eyebrows up and down at me. She's about as subtle as Theo.

"I know, right?" says Ainsley. "Thanks for taking one for the team, June."

I stare at her, trying to figure out her angle.

"Oh, is *that* what that was?" Kaylie asks.

"Yeah, he got a little crazy about Theo and me," says Ainsley.

"Typical," says Kaylie.

"Thanks for distracting him," Ainsley says to me.

"He just needed his ego stroked?" Kaylie says.

"Yeah, his *ego*." Ainsley makes a suggestive gesture with her hands.

"Right." I pull out my textbook. "That's totally what it was about. Oliver's ego." Even with Kaylie's minimal intellect, I'm certain she can't miss my sarcasm. I shake my head and make a show out of opening my book. I ignore Ainsley and Kaylie. I shut them out.

I can feel rather than see the glances they exchange with each other. "What's *her* problem?" Kaylie whispers.

I keep my eyes firmly fixed on the page.

Ainsley and Theo deserve each other.

• • •

It turns out even a superfast athlete can be avoided if one leaps from one's seat and sprints away when the bell rings, especially if one then takes off in the opposite direction of how one usually goes, and hides in the girls' bathroom until after the next class has started, even though it means one is then counted as tardy. However, it *also* turns out that if, an hour after that, one takes one's lunch to the library and squirrels away into one of the study carrels, one might not be as hidden as one thinks.

I've just unwrapped my sandwich when the chair next to me clunks away from the adjacent carrel. Oliver drops into it. "Running, hiding, changing locations. It's clever. You're like a rabbit."

"Thanks." I don't think my voice shakes, but I'm not completely sure. "I was actually just leaving."

"No you weren't." He reaches over and turns my chair so I'm facing him. His smile is faint and his eyes are sad, and it's stupid but I feel dizzy, like I might fall off my seat and right onto him. "I'm aware that it's lame to ask if you got my message." I nod and Oliver spreads his hands wide. "So . . . ?"

"Sorry. I was just really busy yesterday." It's transparent and flimsy and awful, but it's all I've got. I feel exhausted, but like the exhaustion is happening in my brain instead of my body.

Apparently I'm not hiding it well, because Oliver leans toward me. "June, are you okay?"

"I'm fine." I don't want to do this. I don't want to think about how he kissed me, and how I kissed him back, and how everything was perfect and held such promise. I know—I *know*—that it doesn't matter, that none of this matters, that promises break and people lie and we're all going to be moving on to other places.

And I know that when I'm in that other place, Oliver's not going to be there.

"You deleted your account on Mythteries," he says, and I shrug, because that's an easy one to answer.

"I was spending too much time on it."

A look of relief washes over Oliver's face. "I was worried you didn't have wireless anymore or something."

Heat rises inside me, a mixture of embarrassment and anger and memories I want to erase. "Like we didn't pay our bill? Like we got cut off?"

"No!" It pops out of Oliver's mouth too loudly, and I hear a shush from across the library. Oliver lowers his voice. "I just meant it was weird, that's all." He swallows, leans in—"June, let's talk about it"—and I jerk to my feet.

"I have to go."

Oliver stands, too. He clasps his hand around my elbow, but gently, like he could break my bones.

Or my heart.

"I'm sorry," he tells me. "I should have asked before I kissed you. But with the lime and everything, I thought it was clear. I thought you wanted to—"

"I did," I say, but only because I'm aching at the thought of Oliver thinking I didn't want it to happen when I was the one who led him outside, who pretended to put a lime between my teeth, who tilted my head. "It's fine, it's nothing, I wanted to do it. Tequila and starlight are a powerful combination."

"Tequila and starlight," Oliver repeats. He stares into my eyes, searching for answers I can't give him. "How much tequila did you have before I got there?"

"I lost track," I lie. "And then you arrived and everyone's emotions were running high."

Now Oliver looks annoyed. "Are you talking about the thing with Theo? I told you I don't care about him and Ainsley. It wasn't about that."

I make a gesture of dismissal. "I meant the end of the year approaching. Teetering on the precipice of real life, adulthood, everyone leaving. It's like the days are turning sepia-toned all around us."

"You're saying it was *nostalgia.*"

"Nothing has to change. In fact, I should be thanking you."

"For what." The way it comes out of his mouth is flat, not a question. He's angry. Or hurt.

Or both.

"For Nico Vega," I tell him.

"Who?"

" 'Bang Bang.' It's a new song for our playlist."

"A song." Oliver crosses his arms. "You want a song. You think you get a *win* because of Saturday night."

"Of course. High school life means that even though you can mess around with the girl you drive to school"—I pause, because it's so hard to say, and yet it's so true that it must be said—"it doesn't have to mean anything. It doesn't have to mean anything at all."

And that should be it. That should put an end to all of it. All this investment, all these damn *feelings*—this should be enough to put them on a shelf and shove them away.

But Oliver is an athlete. He's used to pushing through the defense, to tackling in the final five, to several other football metaphors I don't understand. Even in the last minute of the game, Oliver doesn't give up.

And this is definitely the last minute of the game.

"That is bullshit." He stabs his finger at me, and the circles around his irises go coal black. "You're a coward. All this crap about how nothing this year matters, it's an excuse."

The fire inside me flames brighter, threatening to burn me alive. I picture my ashes dancing up and away in a giant black cloud of pain.

"You don't care about anything." Oliver raises his voice and I tense to meet his anger. "Not about traditions, not about memories, not even about the people who like you the most. That's your problem. It's not that you think high school doesn't matter. It's that you think *nothing* matters!"

"Which is way better than thinking that *every* tiny, stupid moment has to matter!" The vitriol explodes from me and I can't do anything to stop it. "God, you can't *blow your nose* without adding the tissue to your mental yearbook. Every move you make is the Most Important Thing!" Somewhere in the back of my fire-scorched brain, I clock the librarian—Miss Emily—standing up from her desk and moving toward us. But

I don't care. Oliver thinks I don't care about anything anyway. "It doesn't *count,* Oliver!"

"What the hell does that mean?" He glares at me, his muscles tightening, the tendons in his neck rising.

"Nothing can ever live up to your expectations, because what you think this year is supposed to be, it's too much! None of it is *real.*" It's an eruption now. All flame and smoke and heat. I'm furious and I'm letting all that fury blaze through me, right out at Oliver. "You're going to get your diploma and throw your hat in the air, and it'll all just be *done.* I don't want to be a part of that!"

"You don't want to be a part of *anything*!" Oliver yells back.

Miss Emily is now fluttering nearby. She is young and sweet and I think she has a toddler at home. Judging by the terrified look on her face, she has never dealt with two teenagers in an all-out verbal war.

"You have no *idea,*" I tell Oliver. "You literally know *nothing* about me."

"I know that you're a coward. I know you're so terrified of every pothole that you don't ever take the ride. Actually"—he stops, mouth open, palms facing upward—"you don't even learn to *drive the car*!" Oliver laughs, a harsh, bitter sound that rings out among the books. I part my lips to speak, to tell him what an ass he's being, or maybe to find a reset button so everything can go back to how it was, but Oliver is on a roll. An enraged roll. "When? When, June?"

"When *what*?" I spit out. "When will you shut up and go away?"

"In your superior estimation, *when* does it start to matter? College? Do you start giving a shit in college? Do you have any idea how many people *don't* use their college degree as adults? Tell you what, I'll look that up. I'll get an extra effing Aerosmith song because some percentage of the global population doesn't use their degree!"

Miss Emily makes a clucking noise and we both ignore her.

"You need to calm down," I tell Oliver, but he's not even close to listening.

"Look at my parents, June! They didn't start dating in high school. They got together in college. And now here they are, two kids later, and they're splitting up, making your opinion crap. You don't have a philosophy. You have a *permission slip*! It's your lame way of getting yourself off the hook for *anything* you do. It's license to be an asshole." He pauses, and it's like he's suddenly been doused with a giant, sobering wave. All his fire and heat cools down at once. "But, June, you're not an asshole, are you? Say it. Please say it." His eyes are killing me. "Say that you're not an asshole."

But I can't say that. I can't say it because I have to do something that is so much harder, so much more painful. I can't say it because my ashes are already blowing away, down the street and out into the world. Instead, I say something else. I say the thing that finally puts an end to it all.

"The night of the prank, when you had to drive your mom home, do you know what our moms were drinking?" The next words fly out of my mouth like arrows. "Several bottles of your dad's best wine."

There's no waiting. The realization breaks hard and ugly across Oliver's face. "You knew," he breathes. "You knew about my parents."

"I knew way before that." The nail slides into the coffin of *us* like it's going home. "Remember the morning you came to get me and you were eating something out of a napkin because your mother slept in and didn't make you breakfast, even though she *always* makes you breakfast, and you thought she was upstairs with a headache?"

"No," says Oliver, not because he can't remember it, but because he *can* and he doesn't want it to be true.

"She was at my house. That's the night she found out your dad was cheating on her. That's how long it's been. That's how long I've known. So I guess you're right, Oliver. You win, like you always win. I'm an asshole."

I watch as the debris of his rage washes out to sea, and the waves of what is left crash over him, one by mind-numbing one.

Disbelief. Realization. Acceptance.

Betrayal.

"I'm sorry." It's Miss Emily. She's stepped closer, and now she's cracking her slender knuckles and speaking in a voice just over a whisper. "You seem to be in the middle of something, but I have to ask you to take it outside."

"I'm going," Oliver tells her. "Sorry we disturbed the library." He turns back to me, and for just a second, I wonder if maybe someone *did* find that reset button, and maybe this can become a bad dream, a nightmare that never happened. But then Oliver's face twists with a new emotion, one I've never seen before when he's looked at me.

Disgust.

"You used the word 'literally' wrong," he spits out, and then he whirls and stalks away.

This time, I know it's for good.

It's for the best.

Chapter 31

Another rural intersection. Another student trudging up the bus steps, glancing around for an empty seat, dropping onto the hard vinyl, and staring out the window as the bus lumbers back onto the street in a cloud of exhaust. Same as it's been for the past forty-five minutes and will be for the next forty-five.

Same as it was yesterday.

Same as it will be tomorrow.

• • •

Just like I have for the past two weeks, I wait to go into the physics room until the very last second of break. If the bell is about to ring, there's no time for conversation with Ainsley.

Or with Oliver. Ever since the text I sent him from the bus on my first long morning ride, there's been nothing more to say.

When I walk in, Ainsley is at our lab table, poking around on her phone. I am agonizingly aware of the muscled blur in my peripheral vision. These days, Oliver also arrives at the last possible second. It's like we've come to an unspoken agreement about how to conduct ourselves around each other: we just don't.

Today I change direction. I head to Kaylie's empty seat, and when I plop down into it, Tyler gives me a startled look from the adjacent chair. "Change of scenery," I tell him.

The bell rings and Kaylie saunters in. She sees me in her spot and stops abruptly at the top of the aisle. Her mouth and eyes get all round, like she can't believe I would be so daring.

I gaze at her. No, it's more of a glare. A challenge.

What are you going to do about it?

It turns out the answer is nothing, because we both hear Ainsley's high, sweet voice from my old table—"Over here!"— and Kaylie whirls. She sits down by Ainsley and order is restored to the world. Two hot cheerleaders at a table together. Oliver the hot jock in the back.

Me next to a guy named Tyler, neither of us with anything to say.

• • •

I leave fifteen minutes before the end of class. I tell Mrs. Nelson I have to go to the bathroom, but then I take my backpack with me. Either she doesn't notice or it's the end of the year and she just doesn't care anymore.

The hall is empty, so, because I can, I fling my backpack down it. It flies through the air and lands with a satisfying whomp several yards away. It's only a tiny act of rebellion, but it feels great. I reach it and this time I haul off and slide it across the floor, like I'm back at Wolverine Lanes and it's my bowling ball.

My backpack skids all the way to the corner, and when I get to it, there's Theo Nizzola, squirting mustard through the vents of someone's locker. Because that's what he does instead of throwing backpacks down a hallway.

"Hafferty, you skipping?"

"No, Theo. I'm not skipping." Normally I would walk away and find another bathroom in another hallway, but today I don't feel like it. Today I lean against the wall and watch him. He finishes what he's doing and sets the empty mustard bottle on the floor before straightening and looking at me.

"What do you want?"

"Why are you such a dick?" I ask.

"Shut up." He starts to walk away.

I run to catch up and then to pass him. I jump in front, turning to block him. "Hey, Theo. Do you honestly, *truly* think I was giving Oliver sexual favors for rides to school? Me, a straight-A student with a bright future. And him, a hot popular dude with his pick of girls. Do you *actually* think that's what was going down?"

"Go back to class," Theo says. "You don't belong out here."

But I'm not done.

"No, really. Are you *that* much of a moron, or does *constantly* talking about sex make you feel like you have a bigger penis?" He doesn't answer, so I take a step toward him. My voice gets louder. "Seriously, why are you like this? What do you *get* from it?"

"You never liked me." Theo glares at me. "Why?"

That's a stupid question.

"Why *would* I like you? You're disgusting. Your only contribution to society is to say horrible things."

"I didn't always."

"Yes you did."

"Not when I first moved here." He crosses his arms over his thick chest. "Not in ninth grade."

"That's bullshit." I don't have a memory of Theo that doesn't involve him being a jerk. . . .

Except that I do.

Suddenly, I do.

It *was* ninth grade.

Ninth grade was when Theo became a horrible person.

It was the beginning of the year. Geography class. Mrs. Carter asked Theo to read aloud from a chapter. Something about resource consumption in the United States. He started haltingly. Pausing before long words. Pronouncing things incorrectly. And Mrs. Carter stopped him, correcting him every single time. Making him repeat the words.

At first it was only awkward, because Theo read so slowly and messed up so many times. But eventually, someone snickered. Then someone else did. And then every time Theo pronounced something wrong, people laughed again. And *still* Mrs. Carter didn't put an end to it. She just kept Theo reading and reading, with him pronouncing words wrong and her correcting him while people laughed.

Until Theo started saying things wrong on purpose.

He mispronounced words to sound gross or sexual. "Resource" became "re-*whores*." "Sustainable" became "sus-*taint*-able." "Country" . . . well, it didn't change that much.

The class laughed more, but now they were laughing *with* him instead of *at* him. Mrs. Carter finally got fed up and sent him to the office. As he was packing up his things, she asked me to finish Theo's chapter. Out loud. So I did. With perfect diction. Because that's how I roll.

Now I stare at Theo, looming before me in the hallway. "You act like this to me because I'm good in school?"

"You think you're better than me."

I gaze up at him, unable to refute it. I *do* think I'm better than him. But it's *because* he's such a jerk. There's no win here. It's an endless circle of awful, and if it's ever going to be better, someone has to be the first one to make a move. If I'm going to think of myself as the better person, I'm going to have to act like the better person.

Somehow, moving against all the history between Theo and me, I manage to make my mouth form into a tentative smile. Somehow, I say the words. "I'm sorry."

Theo scowls down at me. "I told you to go to class." He turns to the mustard bottle and gives it a kick. It flies down the hall, spattering tiny yellow drops as it goes. Theo grabs his backpack and, without another word, walks away.

At least I tried.

• • •

Oliver drives past my house in the behemoth. I know this because I'm out on the porch swing, ostensibly flipping through one of my mom's decorator magazines, but in reality hoping to see him. Wondering if Theo told him about our exchange.

Guess I'll never know, because Oliver doesn't look at me. He doesn't even turn his head in my direction.

He just drives by.

Chapter 32

Lily is showing me photos of her midnight-haired punk boy when Darbs bangs up the bleachers at high speed, skipping every other step. "You guys!" she yells when she's still a good dozen away. "Hey, you guys!" By the time she reaches us and plops onto a bench, she's out of breath and has to take a minute before she can talk.

"What's your guess?" Lily asks me.

Since Darbs looks happy, I go with "Yana?"

"Good one," says Lily.

Darbs nods and her turquoise hair flops all around her shoulders. "Guess what I found out?"

"She's a bisexual Christ-hugger like you after all?" Lily says.

"No!" Darbs beams. "She's a *lesbian* Christ-hugger!"

I blink at her. "Seriously? After this entire school year of pining? You could have been with her all along?"

Lily whaps her. "Are you guys a *thing* now?"

Darbs scrunches up her face and shakes her head. "Ew, no!"

Lily and I exchange glances. "Uh . . ." says Lily.

"I'm dating Ethan," Darbs says. "But get this, you guys. We *prayed* together!"

It takes me a second, but then I put it together. Darbs found someone who is more like her than like everyone else at school, someone who embodies two things that other people have a hard time believing can exist within the same person.

"It's like I've found a unicorn," says Darbs, and she and Lily laugh.

I laugh along, but it's hollow.

Like me.

• • •

Itch is in the stairwell again. Apparently the most recent girl to waltz through the revolving door of his love life is Akemi Endo. She and Itch are in a corner, leaning against the wall, gazing into each other's eyes. By all appearances, the school could explode around them and they wouldn't notice, which is strange. Something is different about this girl—about the way Itch *is* with this girl.

It's the gazing.

Itch's tongue isn't in her mouth. His hands aren't roving over her body. They aren't even holding hands. They're just *looking* at each other.

There's a twist in my gut, a painful squeeze that holds and then goes away, leaving me even emptier than before.

• • •

I turn the corner into the main lobby as, across the crowded room, Oliver comes down the stairs. I pull back to wait him out, but as I do, sadness washes over me. Sorrow that isn't for me, but for him.

Oliver's hair is combed neatly and he's wearing a suit, but that's not why I'm sad. It's because of his tie. His maroon tie. It's a "power color."

Oliver is going for an interview at the bank. He's letting his soul be crushed by the immense weight of his future.

A future in which I am nowhere to be found.

• • •

"What?" I look at Shaun, surprised, as he turns the wheel to guide us out of the school parking lot. "When did he do it?"

"A couple weeks ago."

"But it was such a big deal," I say. "It meant everything. Why didn't you tell me?"

Shaun shrugs. "It was anticlimactic."

We pull onto the main road and head toward my house. "Spill," I command Shaun. "What happened?"

"Kirk sat down at the dinner table for chicken casserole. He said he had something to tell them, and everything got really quiet. His dad put down the serving spoon and his mom clasped her hands together, and they waited. He said that was awful, the waiting part." Shaun smiles. "Kirk said it all came out of his mouth in a babbling stream, about how someday he wants a house in the suburbs and some kids and a dog, but that he's not going to want a wife. He'll want a husband."

Even though I've never met Kirk, I can picture it. The tablecloth, the silverware, the hush of his parents. "What did they say?"

"Kirk thought there'd be some sort of Lutheran hellfire raining down, but it was nothing like that. His parents looked at each other and smiled, and then his mom said, 'Thanks for telling us, honey.' His dad said he'd better bring up his grade in math if he wants to afford a house in the suburbs. And that was it."

My shoulders relax. "They already knew."

"Yeah."

"Kinda like if you asked him to prom," I say. "Not a big deal at all."

Shaun shakes his head. "It's been too long. We missed our chance."

"Have you even *mentioned* it? Did you tell him the date?"

"No."

"Then how do you know?"

"Why do you care? It's not like you're going." Shaun slides a look at me. "Unless maybe you are . . . ?"

"Don't change the subject. You should at least *ask* him. You're not giving him a chance to say yes or no. You're not giving him a choice."

Shaun is silent the rest of the drive. When he pulls up in front of my house, he turns to look at me. "Oliver doesn't have a date."

"Oliver hates me," I tell him. "Thanks for the ride."

• • •

Lily and I had plans to go to the mall after school so I could help her find accessories to go with her prom dress. She said she wanted something that straddled the line between cute and ironic, so we were hoping to find skull earrings decorated with rhinestones.

Sadly, I'll never know what treasures awaited us at our local

286

retailers, because instead, Lily and I are in the shadows underneath the bleachers, and she's sobbing against me. "Why?" she keeps asking.

"I don't know." I stroke her dreadlocks. "It's not fair."

Lily's punk boy broke up with her today . . . in a text message while she was in chemistry class. A week before prom. It definitely is *not* fair.

"Did he give an explanation?" I ask when Lily is finally wiping the tears from her face.

"I called him during sixth." It surprises me, because that's when she has private violin practice, which she never, ever skips. "I said I had a migraine."

Apparently that's what we do when we have boy problems.

"What did he say?"

"That he needs to be free. That Juilliard girls are too entrenched in their prescribed world. That we're too rigid. Too—" She breaks off, then gets control of herself again. "Too focused. He says he wants *anarchy* in love. What does that even *mean*?"

It means he's an ass. I don't say it with my mouth, but my face must be expressive enough, because Lily starts crying again. I pat her. After a second, she pops her head up. "Do you think I shouldn't go to Juilliard?"

"No!"

"But I could play violin somewhere here. Like kids' birthday parties or something."

"Lily, you can't help it if a boy changes you, but you don't let him change your *plans.*" I neglect to mention that kids don't want violinists at their parties. "You *are* going to Juilliard and you will be an amazing famous violinist, because now you have suffered for your art." I look into her dark, sad eyes. "That stupid punk-ass boy hurt you and that sucks, but years from now, you will be in a giant stadium, and thousands of people will be *shattered* by your playing, because your music will be so full of truth and heartbreak and mystery and . . . *What?*"

Lily is smiling at me through her tears. "Violinists don't play in *stadiums.*"

"Where, then?"

"Concert halls. Symphony spaces. Auditoriums."

"Then those," I tell her. "You'll play in those and you'll kill it."

She considers. Nods. "I just want to fast-forward to that part," she says. "The part where it doesn't hurt anymore."

"I know," I tell her. "I do, too."

Chapter 33

All anyone can freaking talk about is how prom is tomorrow. In homeroom, it's Shaun and Lily. He convinced her that the best way to deal with a broken heart is to occupy herself with other things, so now she's going to prom with him. Lily says she might only stay for an hour, but at least she won't go through life wondering how things might be different if she'd attended her senior prom. When she says it, she and Shaun both turn and give me pointed looks.

I roll my eyes at them. "Subtle. Very subtle."

"Just come," says Lily. "We'll dance together."

"I'll let you pick songs," Shaun adds.

"Nope." I can't explain how prom sounds like an exercise in agony. Like a special kind of torture chamber where you have to pretend the pain isn't happening.

• • •

It was Señora Fairchild's fault. I was on my way to the bleachers when she rushed past me, hugging a giant pile of folders against her pregnant belly. We greeted each other with *"hola,"* and that's where it should have ended, except one of her folders slid out from her arms, creating an avalanche situation, and I ended up on my knees beside her, helping shuffle them all back together. *"Gracias,"* she said. "Can I ask you for a favor?"

Since a teacher's "asking" is in actuality a command, of course I said yes.

"Come to my room at the end of lunch," she told me. "I have more things that need to be taken to the office. I'll give you extra credit."

"I already have an A."

"Right," she said. *"Bueno."*

That's why I hustled to finish eating, and why I'm hurrying through the center of campus while everyone else is still having lunch, and why I see what's happening at the sundial. I stop to stare, because it's so entirely weird.

The usual Beautiful People are hanging out, eating and chattering and laughing. That's not the weird part. That's totally normal. What's strange—no, what makes absolutely no sense in my brain whatsoever—is that among them are Ainsley and Theo and Oliver.

Together.

Theo is sitting on one of the benches with Ainsley draped over him. His arm is around her waist, and her fingers are twined in his hair. Oliver is on the other end of the bench, and as I watch, Theo leans toward him and says something. They both laugh and Theo kisses Ainsley.

Like nothing ever happened.

Like none of it mattered.

At all.

If I was still driving to school with Oliver, if we weren't

avoiding each other, if my heart didn't hurt, I would run over and slam one of my songs in his face. I would crow about it, about how he himself is living proof that high school is a drop in the bucket of emotion and importance. He would be his usual combo of amused and chagrined, and I would triumphantly choose something by Joy Division or Ume or Wax Fang. Tomorrow I would blast that new song as loud as the behemoth's speakers would allow. Oliver would smile tolerantly as I sang and danced in my seat, and maybe I even would catch him nodding his head along to the music.

Instead, everything inside me hardens. I turn to leave. . . .

But not before Oliver glances in my direction. Not before our eyes meet.

• • •

When I come out of Spanish, he's leaning against the hallway wall with his arms folded over his chest. The sight of him jerks my body to a frozen halt and my heart into a racing sporadic beat. He doesn't smile, but he does edge his chin upward slightly in my direction. It's a move done by guys in bars on TV. It's a gesture that represents everything I hate. It's the smallest possible motion one can make to acknowledge another person.

But because this is Oliver and because he has repeatedly defied my expectations, I excuse it. I excuse him. I merely drop my backpack to the floor where I'm standing, right in front of the open door. Other students jostle me as they stream around both sides of my body, but I stay still, a stony outcrop in a rushing path of water.

Oliver peels himself off the wall and ambles over. He stares down at me and I stare up at him, and no one says anything for what seems like way too long. He doesn't look happy and I have no idea how I look, because my insides are trembling and my thoughts are jumbled, so it's anyone's guess how that mess translates to my face.

"I'm a decent guy," Oliver finally says, and waits for a response. When I don't have one—because it's neither a question that requires an answer nor something I'm willing to dispute—he continues. "I honor my promises. I'm supposed to drive you to school."

"I'm the one who told you not to," I remind him.

"In a text message. Thanks for that." He folds his arms over his chest again. "I thought you'd want to know that you were right."

"About what?" It comes out of my mouth in a whisper.

"The playlist. I've been reassessing some things, and you were right about the music I've been listening to my whole life. It's crap. It's overly produced and fake, just like Flaggstone Lakes. In fact"—he pauses, running his fingers through his hair—"you were right about all this stuff being crap." He spreads his arms in a gesture that encompasses himself, the school, everyone around us. Me. "You win, June. None of this matters. It doesn't matter at all." He crooks a smile at me, but there's no joy in it. It's bitter, flat, lifeless. It breaks my heart. "Call me if you want a ride on Monday."

"I won't," I tell him.

"I know," he says.

But he keeps standing there, looking down at me. I can't tell what he's thinking, because his expression is so blank. He's not the Oliver I've gotten to know over this year: the one who's exuberant, who cares about soufflés and bowling and football games.

That Oliver—the one who cares about *everything*—is gone. And it's my fault.

Chapter 34
PROM DAY

I'm alone in the farmhouse, alone in my misery. Mom is on campus and all my friends are getting ready for prom tonight, so I play games on my phone for a while. But not Mythteries. I don't play that.

Somewhere around lunchtime, I try calling Dad. He doesn't answer and I don't leave a message, but I do shoot him a text.

> hey dad, what's up?

Even though he didn't pick up when I called, he texts back right away.

> hi beautiful. in rehearsal, new play, amazing role.
> closes in july so def able to come out & help u
> move into dorms. what do u need for college?

I turn off my phone. I don't know what I need anymore.

• • •

Two long and boring and lonely hours later, I'm reconsidering my decision not to call Mom when I hear a familiar crunching coming from outside. It's accompanied by the low rumbling sound of an engine. Those two noises together can mean only one thing.

The behemoth.

I rush to the front door.

Except it's the wrong behemoth. This one isn't black; it's somewhere between beige and gold. And the person driving isn't Oliver. It's his mother, Marley.

Oliver's mom's white-blond hair is pulled into a high ponytail and she carries a giant designer bag. She's finally remembered to return some socks and pajamas she borrowed from Mom when she spent the night. "There's a book, too," she tells me.

I smile and nod and reach for the bag, assuming she'll drop it and run, but instead, she pushes past me into the house. "Can I borrow a pen?" she asks. "And some paper?"

I follow Marley into the kitchen and provide her with writing implements. She scribbles a note to Mom and glances up at me. "Hannah says you're not going to prom tonight?"

"I'm not into it."

"That must be a generational thing. Oliver is meeting some friends there, but he doesn't seem excited at all. I practically had to drag him to get a tux."

I have a sudden, overwhelming surge of desire to *see* Oliver in his tuxedo. I can imagine how he'll look, all tall and blond and old-school movie star—

No. I mentally pack the image into a box labeled "Nice Try" and stash it away. Instead of thinking about Oliver, I reach out my hand to his mother and accept the note she gives me. Then I walk with her to the front door, where she thanks me. "Sorry to barge in unannounced."

"No problem. Have a nice evening."

I close the door and glance down at the note in my hand. It's not anything exciting.

> *Hannah—*
> *Thanks for the read.*
> *Still on for coffee Monday?*
> *—Mar*

But for some reason, I keep staring at the note. And staring at it. There's something about it. Not *what* it says, but *how* it says it. The neat, slanted handwriting.

I pound up the stairs and into my bedroom, where I rush to the bulletin board hanging on my wall. Holding Marley's note up to it, I compare.

I was right. Marley's handwriting is the same—like, the *exact* same—as the handwriting on my father's birthday card. The one that came with the flowers he sent me. The one I cling to when I'm lonely or sad or angry. The one that was supposedly transcribed by the local florist.

Local florist, my ass.

Marley Flagg wrote that card.

• • •

Marley has already backed down our driveway and pulled onto Callaway when I slam out the front door. The behemoth takes off. I know it's pointless to try to catch it, but I try anyway, racing down the driveway and into the street, waving my arms and screaming, "Mrs. Flagg! Wait!"

It's the only way I'm going to find out the truth.

I chase her for a couple houses' worth of road before slowing to a stop, my breath coming in short gasps. I'm not sure if it's sweat or tears covering my face. . . .

And miraculously, ahead of me, the behemoth also stops. I drop my hands to my knees and try to catch my breath as the big car makes a slow U-turn and Oliver's mom comes back for me.

She's coming back with answers. Answers that I already know will break my heart.

• • •

"Did you write this?" It's the third time I've asked the question, but Marley still hasn't given me an actual answer. We're standing on the front porch and I'm waving the florist's card in the air.

"I'm calling your mom." Marley dives a hand into her huge bag and scrabbles around in it.

"No." I move to stand directly in front of her. "You owe me."

"What do I owe you?" Marley says, not in a snotty way but like she's confused, like she has no idea what I'm talking about.

"I covered for you. I knew about your marriage problems for months and I didn't say anything to Oliver."

"I appreciate that—"

"It ruined everything!" I'm getting more and more worked up with every passing second in which I am not given the simple courtesy of being told the truth. "You put me in a really bad position. Oliver is my friend and I should never have known more about his family than he did. That's messed up and it's not fair. It wasn't fair to me and it definitely wasn't fair to him, so please tell me the truth about why you faked that note from my dad. Enough, already!"

For a second, I think I've gone too far and Marley is going to yell at me, or tell on me, or ground me. But instead, she fixes those huge blue eyes on mine. "Oh, sweetie."

"What? 'Oh, sweetie' what?"

Marley steps closer. She reaches for my hand and I allow her to take it, because even though I'm mad, I'm also a little terrified of hearing whatever she's going to say next. "Your dad . . ." She stops and gives a little sigh. "Oh, honey, your dad is such a screwup."

Words of denial and defense leap to exit my mouth, but I clamp my lips together hard and I keep them inside. I keep everything inside.

And I listen.

"It's not your fault," Marley tells me. "It's not your mom's fault, either. Hell, it's probably not even *his* fault. It's just who he is—one of those guys who never sees what's right in front of him. He loves you, June. I believe that and so does Hannah. But your dad . . . he does the best he can. It's just that your mom's best is a lot better." She squeezes my hand gently. "We had lunch together on your birthday, your mom and me. Your dad texted while we were in the restaurant, asking your mom to pick something up. Something for you."

No. No-no-no-no-no.

"He had forgotten about your birthday until that morning."

Until I sent him a picture of my decorated locker.

"Your mom said she'd take care of it, and we went to a florist for the prettiest bouquet we could find."

Dad will visit. He'll visit. He said he would.

"I wrote the note so you wouldn't recognize your mom's handwriting."

He's better than that. I need him to be better than that.

This time, I'm 100 percent sure the wetness on my face is not sweat.

"Come here, honey." Marley pulls me into her arms. I let her rock me and stroke my hair before she pushes me back so she can stare into my face. "What can I do?"

"I want to go to the prom," I tell her.

• • •

Marley and I are sitting awkwardly on the art gallery bench when Mom and Cash emerge from her office. The buttons on Mom's blouse are fastened wrong, and Cash's hair is a little wonky, which makes sense, because the door was locked when Marley tried the knob.

Cash gives me an apologetic look. "June—"

"It's better for me if we don't talk about it," I tell him.

"It's better for me, too," he says.

"Well, I think we *should* have a healthy discussion," my mom chimes in.

"Hannah," says Marley, but my mom doesn't notice.

"When two adults are in a relationship, it's natural to—"

"Hannah!" Marley says again, and this time my mother shuts up and listens. "We have a more pressing matter than your sex life. June wants to go to her prom, which starts in an hour and a half. She needs a dress, accessories, hair, and makeup. I told her we could make that happen." My mother opens her mouth, but Marley raises a finger. "In other news, June knows about the flowers and how her dad's kind of a lovable loser—"

"Marley!"

I touch my mom's arm. "It's okay."

"Put it on your maternal to-do list for future discussion," Marley tells my mother. "Right now, we have one priority: to get June ready for her senior prom."

I see my mother consider, weigh, decide.

"We should call Quinny."

"On it," says Marley. "She's bringing options. Next issue: transportation. Is it too late to rent a limo?"

"I can take her," says Cash. "Nothing says 'prom' like a pickup truck."

"Actually," says Marley, "Oliver is flying solo—"

"No!" It explodes out of my mouth like a bomb, and everyone stares at me. I collect myself. "I mean . . . that would be weird. You said he already has plans with his friends. Besides, I have an idea. Where's my phone?"

• • •

I am a frothy lavender milk shake standing atop a chair in the center of the gallery. Mom and Marley and Quinny whirl around me, plucking at and tweaking the tulle foaming from my waist. Fortunately (for him), Cash was sent out for burgers. "Enough!" I throw my hands in the air. "I don't think this is the one."

"Next!" says Quinny, heading to the garment bags slung across the bench. Mom unzips the back of the milk shake dress

300

and Marley starts tugging it down. Over the last hour, since Quinny arrived with the dresses, I've lost all sense of modesty. The lavender is the eighth one I've tried on. Or maybe the ninth. One was okay, but the rest were either too poofy or too big in the chest or something. Quinny is a costume designer for the university theater and has all kinds of interesting stuff. I'm just worried she doesn't have something that will both fit me and look like what a reasonable person might wear to a prom.

"This one," says Mom. She's pulling a dress out of a bag. "Try it."

Four minutes later, I'm in a strapless steel-blue circle dress straight out of the fifties.

The sexy part of the fifties, that is.

The dress dips low in the back, gathering at my waist before blooming out all around me in a ballerina skirt that stops right above my knees. The fabric is textured but not too shiny. "Bengaline," Quinny tells me when I run a finger over it.

Best of all, she and Marley and Mom have somehow managed to rig an undergarment that hoists and maneuvers in such a manner that I actually appear to have boobs. It's perfect. . . .

Except the dress doesn't quite fit me.

Quinny hands my mother a tiny green-handled instrument. "You rip. I'll sew."

Next thing I know, my feet are back on the ground. Quinny pins the dress just as fast as Mom can rip stitches out of it. Marley brushes my hair and shushes Quinny, who keeps saying things like "Quit moving her" and "Hold still, Marls."

When Mom and Quinny are done with the ripping and pinning, they help me wiggle out of the dress. I end up sitting on the bench in a crinoline and my T-shirt while Marley plays with my hair and, nearby, Mom hot-glues rhinestones to earring backs. "It's convenient having an entire art studio at our disposal," she says.

I don't say anything.

I am mute with gratitude.

• • •

I stare at my own image looking back at me from my cell phone screen. I'm wearing the blue dress and peep-toe pumps on tall, slender heels. Sparkly earrings dangle from my lobes, which are visible because my hair has been swept into a glamorous updo. My eyes are lined and my lips are red. I'm a sleek, pinup version of myself.

A cluster of tiny roses appears between me and the phone screen, and I get a whiff of their delicate aroma. Cash is holding them with a bashful smile. "I got the wrist kind so you won't have to put a pin through Quinny's dress."

Although nothing else has made me tear up, this does. "Don't!" says Mom. "Your mascara will run!"

"Thank you," I tell Cash, and hug him. Then I touch my on-screen image, sending it speeding through the galaxy toward my father. It's accompanied by a message.

Don't just scratch the surface.

He won't get it. He won't understand that because of his choices, he has a daughter in name only, a series of images and messages translating to a relationship that doesn't really exist.

302

He can't begin to comprehend it, and that's why I am able to forgive him. Because he really, truly doesn't understand.

I forgive him, but that doesn't mean I need to keep pretending he's going to show up. I've pretended for way too long.

Mom pulls me away from everyone else. "Hey, Marley said you might have some questions for me."

"Just one," I tell her. "Will you teach me how to drive?"

A big smile breaks over her face. "Of course, honey."

• • •

My ride arrives later than I hoped, but I don't care. After all, it took quite a bit of convincing for us to reach an agreement at all.

"Are you sure about this?" my ride asks.

"Very sure," I answer. "You and I have really, really good reasons to go to prom tonight."

We pose for photos, I thank everyone who was involved in the Xtreme Cinderella-ing, and then we're off.

• • •

The car jams to the curb and I hop out before the valet can reach my door. I'm in the biggest hurry of my life and I don't care who knows it.

I'm alone when I run up the front stairs, and I'm alone when I cross the vast empty lobby of the hotel and step into the glittering ballroom. Hung with twinkling strands of light and dotted with white-draped tables, it is crowded with people I have known for years. My ears are flooded with indie punk music, and that's the moment I feel the most alone of all: when I enter my senior prom.

It's my own fault, of course. Sure, it was a boy who broke my heart, but I am the one to blame. I am the one who broke a promise.

Still, I hold my head high, because I have a reason to be here. I have a grand romantic gesture to make, an epic speech to give, a heart full of regret to bleed out over the scuffed vinyl.

My ride catches up to me as I'm scanning the dance floor. I know everyone here, or even if I don't *know* them, I know their face, or their name, or some small fact about them. Despite all my attempts to deny it and to pretend I am different, now that I'm here, I have to admit the truth: these are my people.

Maybe I'm not alone after all.

Maybe I never have been.

And then I see Itch. He's standing on the edge, swaying back and forth in that way guys do when they don't want (or know how) to dance. He isn't looking for me, but that makes sense, since he's here with Akemi. She's right beside him and their fingers are twined together.

Nothing about tonight is going to be easy.

I turn to say that I need to speak with someone, but my ride is frozen, staring into the distance. "Go," I say, and then I also go. I make a beeline toward my ex-boyfriend.

Itch and Akemi stare at me when I barrel up to them. "I'm sorry," I tell them. "But I need to talk to Itch."

"No way," Itch says.

"I get it. I'm not exactly the first person you want to hang out with tonight."

"You're actually the last," he says. "The dead last."

"Be nice." Akemi elbows him in the ribs. I shoot her a grateful look and she shrugs. "I'm secure," she tells me. "Besides, I have to pee." She rises on her tiptoes and gives Itch a peck on the lips. "Remember. Give to the world what you want it to give back to you."

It's the kind of statement Itch and I would have mocked just a few months ago, but it no longer sounds mockable to me. In fact, it sounds sort of deep and real. Who *am* I?

As Akemi sails off, the current music fades and an old Elton John song swells up in its place. I grab Itch by the wrist. "This one time, you are going to dance with me like a cheesy high school joiner," I tell him, and yank him onto the floor.

Shockingly, Itch allows it. I place his hands on my hips and set my hands on his familiar, narrow shoulders. We sway together, arm's length apart, his eyes hard and angry on my own. "What, June?"

"I'm going to say out loud why you're so mad. Okay?"

Itch doesn't answer, exactly, but he does tilt his chin down a tiny bit. An almost imperceptible acknowledgment.

I take a deep breath. "At first, you were probably mad because of a bunch of things, because that's how breakups work. People get mad when relationships end. But in most cases, people then get over it." Itch's stony gaze doesn't falter. "But you *couldn't* get over it, because I never *let* you, because I made you feel like our breakup wasn't important. Like it didn't matter, like maybe our entire relationship didn't matter, because it wasn't even worthy of a *mention*."

Itch's fingers tighten on my waist, just a little, and for the briefest of moments, we're back in time, back in the stairwell, and we belong to each other all over again. I don't want to be back there with him now, but I couldn't be more thankful that it happened.

"Someday, there's going to be a Grown-Up Me," I tell him. "That Grown-Up Me is going to have High School You to thank for a little part of who she is. Future Grown-Up Me says thank you. Thank you so much for helping her turn into herself."

Itch stares back at me and I realize we've both stopped swaying and my fingers are gripping his shoulders. I relax them and feel him relax, too. "Tell her she's welcome," Itch says. "I mean, when you see her. When you see Grown-Up You, tell her I said you're welcome."

"I will," I say, and we smile genuine smiles at each other . . . until Itch's gaze drifts past me. His expression changes.

Akemi is back.

I turn so I can apologize to her, so I can explain that I'm not trying to do anything inappropriate with her boyfriend and that we're just talking . . . but it's not Akemi.

It's Oliver.

He is standing at the edge of the dance floor, watching us with a dark, furious look. He's seeing Itch's hands on my hips, my hands on his shoulders. I know Oliver saw our smiles and the way we were staring into each other's eyes. It must look like one more lie I told him: about being done with Itch.

Panic rises in me and I tug away from Itch but it's too late. Oliver is gone.

I whirl back to Itch. "I'm sorry," I tell him. "I have to go."

"Wait." Despite my need to find Oliver, I let Itch fold his arms around me. It's a hug that would have felt awkward when we were dating, but somehow, now that it's not supposed to be romantic, it's just nice. Itch feels nice. "If he doesn't want you, he's a jackass," Itch tells me.

"Thanks." I separate myself from him just as Akemi arrives.

"I'll take him back now," she says, reaching for Itch's hand.

"You should," I say. "You guys make a supercute couple."

• • •

I charge in the direction Oliver disappeared into the crowd but realize there are several doors leading out of the ballroom. I choose one and find myself back in the ornate lobby. A uniformed bellboy looks up when I race in. "Can I help you, miss?"

"Did a guy come through here?" I ask breathlessly.

The bellboy shakes his head. "Can you be more specific?"

"Tall, blond, really cute?"

He looks like he's considering. "There was this one dude, but I think he had brown hair. He was probably closer to my height, and I'm not that tall."

"Just now?"

"No. Ten minutes ago. Maybe more like fifteen—"

"Thanks," I say, not meaning it at all, and run back toward the ballroom.

• • •

An empty corridor. I almost turn back but then I notice the two doors leading to bathrooms. I rush up to the one that says MEN and pause. All my internal rules prohibit me from opening this door. I knock on it and wait, but nothing happens. I reach out, turn the handle, and am about to walk in with my eyes squeezed shut when the door to the women's room bangs open and Ainsley appears.

"June, what are you doing?"

If Ainsley was gorgeous in normal, everyday street clothes, right now she's an actual angel. Her skin glows bronze against her glittery white dress, and her green eyes are wider and brighter than usual.

"I'm knocking on this bathroom door." World's most obvious statement.

She sizes me up. "I thought you hated prom."

"I did." I don't want to tell her I'm looking for Oliver, because I don't want her help, or anything to do with her. That brief flash of friendship I had with Ainsley . . . it wasn't real.

And then the bathroom door opens, and of course Theo comes through it. "Was that you knocking?" His eyes ooze up and down my body before flicking to Ainsley. "I'd do a three-way. Since it's prom and all."

Back to this. Forever this. Some of us have the ability to change, to shed our skin, to move forward. And some of us . . . are Theo.

"I don't suppose there's anyone else in there?" I ask him.

"Nope," says Theo. "But if you want to go in and check, me and Ainsley will wait right here. Or, better yet, you could be the one to wait here and guard the door while the two of us go in and—"

"Shut up," says Ainsley, and for a second, I think she's talking to me. But her eyes are narrowed at Theo. "Get a new joke," she tells him before turning to me. "We dropped our car with the valet, but Oliver didn't. He parked in the lot behind the hotel, because he said he wanted to be able to make a quick getaway." She points back in the direction I came from. "Go left down that hallway off the lobby." Ainsley sees my hesitation. "I'm telling the truth," she says. "I didn't always, but right now I am."

"Thank you, Ainsley." It comes out sounding heartfelt, and I belatedly realize it's because I feel that way. "For real."

Ainsley cocks her head and regards me, like she's trying to figure something out. "You know that thing about keeping your friends close and your enemies closer?" she says. "I was doing that. Except you weren't ever an enemy, were you?"

"Only to myself."

"Fair enough." She makes a shooing gesture. "Hurry. Before he leaves."

I give her a last grateful look before racing off.

• • •

The bad news is that the parking lot—like most parking lots—is huge. The good news is that so is the behemoth. I see its dark shape towering over the surrounding cars and I hurry toward it. Maybe I'll sit on the hood or something until Oliver arrives.

Except that when I'm right in front of it, the headlights flare, blinding me. The engine rumbles to life, but I stand my ground, raising my arms to shield my face from the light. He'll have to run me over if he wants to get out of here.

Standoff. I wonder if he'll honk, because that would be a very Oliver thing to do, but he doesn't. He only kills the engine. The lights cut off and the glare is replaced with darkness. After a minute, he gets out. I can't see him, but I can hear his voice.

"June, what are you doing?"

He doesn't sound mad, which is what I expected. He sounds tired, and that might be worse. I know I need to say something important and epic and romantic, because this is a moment that requires an important, epically romantic gesture, but the words aren't there. Instead, all I have is the overwhelming fear that I've already lost the one person I most want to find.

So I blurt something out—something that hasn't always come naturally to me.

The truth.

"I'm going to learn how to drive."

"Congratulations," he says. "Very independent. You don't need me anymore."

Well, *that* came out wrong.

My vision adjusts to the lack of light in the parking lot, and Oliver comes into focus before me. His eyes are hard. Cold. Angry.

"No, listen. My dad was supposed to teach me." I try to explain, the words scratching raw against my throat. "It was going to be this fun thing we'd do together, the way his dad taught him, in parking lots and on farm roads. He kept saying he was coming, but then he'd always have a reason why he couldn't, and I always acted like it didn't matter, because I needed to pretend that was true. Because otherwise it mattered *so much* that he never, ever did what he said he'd do. That I was always disappointed. That he made me feel like *I* didn't matter. And, Oliver"—I draw in a deep breath and let it out all in a rush—"it mattered. You were right. It all mattered. What your dad did and what mine didn't. All the traditions and moments and choices. You taking this stupid bank internship that we both know will crush your soul. Ainsley and Itch. Everything."

I stop and wait, but apparently my speech isn't nearly epic or romantic enough, because Oliver doesn't sweep me into his arms. The only thing he does with his arms is fold them in front of his chest. "Great revelation," he says. "And nice timing, since just now I saw you and Itch *mattering* to each other."

"We were *talking*. You know that."

"How would I know that?" Oliver glares at me. "You didn't tell me when you broke up with him. Why would you mention it if you got back together?"

"Oliver." I know I sound desperate, but I don't care. "Please. We've already talked about this."

"It was the ultimate *screw you*." Oliver's voice is icy. "We were friends and it was great, and then I thought maybe we were more than friends but I didn't want to mess it up. I was with Ainsley and you were with Itch and it all seemed manageable that way. Like at least we wouldn't ruin it by trying to have something more than friendship, even though I knew—I *knew*, June—that you and I together was so much more special and interesting than either of us with anyone else."

I stare at him. He's not just mad. He's furious. "Oliver—"

"I'm still talking," he says. "When you didn't even tell me you broke up with Itch, that's when I knew I had made it all up in my head, that there was nothing else there. We really *were* just friends like I'd been lying to Theo all along. So I went with it. Because I really—*really*—liked you as my friend. And also because otherwise, the world didn't make sense."

I wasn't crazy. All that stuff I was feeling between us—it was *real*. I open my mouth to tell him so, but he's on a roll.

"And then there was Kaylie's party, when I thought it all changed, when I kissed you the way I'd wanted to kiss you for *months* and . . ." He pauses. Swallows. Recovers. "And suddenly everything in the world seemed like it was *right*."

"It *was* right," I break in. "It was—"

"It was bullshit!" he thunders. "Just tequila and starlight and nostalgia—"

"I only had the one shot!"

"—and I was the closest guy around."

"That's not true!"

"What's not true?" Oliver surges closer to me. The light from the hotel plays over him and now I can see him in his tuxedo. He looks classic. Sharp. Agonized and beautiful. "The part where you broke my heart or the part where you pretended it never even happened? I have no idea *what* you're trying to say. What are you trying to say, June?"

I broke his heart.

I broke his heart.

No, it's *my* heart that's breaking. It's cracking inside me, fracturing into an infinite number of tiny jagged pieces, and if I open my mouth to say a single word, they're going to fly out and rip apart everything in sight. Or maybe just me. I'm the only thing that will rip apart.

A year ago, a month ago, a *week* ago, that fear would have been enough to keep my mouth shut. But now something has changed, and that something is Oliver Flagg, and I have to tell him that.

"What?" I hear it in the word. I see it in the tense way he's

312

holding his mouth, in the way his upper body is leaning toward me. It's *hope*.

So I answer it. I answer it with a hope that is just as strong.

"This is the moment." That doesn't make much sense, so I elaborate. "It wasn't the night of the senior prank, Oliver. It's *tonight*."

"What's tonight?"

"The night I'll come back to, the one I'll replay over and over and over again like a song in my head." I smile through my tears. "The one when I tell you the truth."

He's standing in a way that makes me think of that deer we startled on our drive to school. Like if I make the wrong move, if I say the wrong thing, he could bolt and I'll never see him again. "What truth?" he asks.

I take a slow, careful step toward him. I reach out to touch him. His muscles are tensed beneath the tuxedo jacket as I slide my hand down his arm and rest my fingers lightly against his. I open my mouth, and when I speak, all those jagged little heart pieces pour out. "The truth is that this is the single stupidest thing I've ever done, showing up right before everything changes and our lives turn upside down and time runs out, but I have to, because I've finally figured out that some things are uncontrollable, and one of those things is my heart and the fact that it absolutely, without question, loves you." We stare at each other and I watch his eyes widen. Just in case I wasn't completely clear the first time, I tell him again. "I love you."

"I got that part," he says. One corner of his mouth is twitching up, just a little. I take it as an encouraging sign, but even if it's not, I'm too far gone to stop the rest of it.

"And it matters," I tell him. "It matters because *you* matter and I love you."

The words hang between us. My heart stops beating and the world stops turning and every twinkling star in the sky freezes into a bright pinpoint of white-hot light.

And then Oliver smiles, and I feel it everywhere, like he's touching me everywhere. "Well, obviously I love you, too," he says. "So now what?"

The tiny jagged pieces of my heart coalesce into laughter. The laughter bounces off the hood of the behemoth and rings out over the parking lot.

"Now we go to prom," I say.

• • •

I'm walking into my senior prom, onto the dance floor, where it seems like everyone I've ever known is jumping up and down to some sort of Beatles house remix. It's like a thousand high school dances I haven't attended, except that this time I *am* attending and I'm doing it while holding hands with Oliver Flagg. Our fingers are interlaced, like they were always meant to be that way. As we wend our way through the craziness, we see Darbs. She and Ethan Erickson are holding hands and bopping around in a group with Lily. Nearby, Yana Pace dances with a girl in red sequins.

Oliver pulls me to a halt in the middle of the crowd. A few people glance at us, but Oliver doesn't seem to notice, because apparently, I am the only thing he notices. In fact, his eyes are roaming all over me. "You look kind of amazing," he says.

"Thank you." It seems weird to tell a boy he looks beautiful, so instead, I slide a finger down the lapel of his tuxedo. "You look like a spy." One of his eyebrows arches up, so I attempt an explanation. "An international spy. A dashing, handsome international spy who sort of has this *thing* about him that makes all the girls crazy and . . . *What?*"

He's smiling that blinding smile down into my eyes. "It's another one of those moments," he says.

"Which moment?" I ask, even though I think I know the answer.

"The one where I kiss you."

"I'm pretty sure you're right," I answer, my heart speeding up. I want him to kiss me *so bad,* but I'm also a little terrified of it—of how it's going to make me feel. "We haven't had any tequila. . . ."

"Good," he says, and then his mouth is on mine. I was right to be terrified, because Oliver Flagg's kiss destroys the entire world. Everything around us drops away, and all I know is the feel and the taste of him. I don't care who's looking or who's surprised or what administrative official could run up and tell us to knock off the public display of affection. Oliver is *everything,* and it's even better than when we were on the hood of the behemoth, because this time I'm not pretending about anything. This time, I'm just me. With him.

And it's so real.

After a moment (okay, a few moments), Oliver pulls away and gazes down at me. I suspect I look the same way he does—a little rattled, a little exhilarated, a lot in love. "We're going to do more of that," he tells me. "When we don't have an audience."

"I can't wait." And yet I can, because I'm going to savor every last second of this prom.

Oliver slides his hands down my arms, linking his fingers with mine again. "Hey, guess what."

"You're trading in the behemoth for a smaller, more fuel-efficient vehicle?"

"Oh, that's right. I had forgotten how bad you are at guessing." He leans over and pecks me on the lips again. "I got that summer bank internship—"

My heart falls. "Oliver . . ."

"—and I turned it down. Instead, I'm taking woodworking classes at a studio off State Street. Dad's not thrilled, but he's busy trying to handle things with Mom, so he's dealing."

I beam up at him before breaking away. "I have to do something. Wait here."

Leaving Oliver on the dance floor, I run up to the deejay booth, where I fling my arms around Shaun. "You look like you're having fun," Shaun says after he pries me off his body.

"So do you." I shove my phone at him. "I have a deejay request."

Shaun glances at the song scrolling across my screen. He rolls his eyes. "Who *are* you?"

"I know, right?" I grin at him and he grins back. He looks happier than I've ever seen him. He looks like how I feel.

A minute later, I'm back with Oliver on the dance floor. After kissing me again, he motions to the deejay booth. "Who's the guy with Shaun?"

I follow his gaze. "Oh, that's Kirk. He drove me here."

"Cool," says Oliver.

"*Very* cool," I say, and then the next song—the one I requested—rises from the hotel's speakers. We hear powerful drumbeats followed by power chords. In fact, it's definitely the drummiest, power-chordiest song that has ever graced the airwaves.

"Seriously?" says Oliver with great satisfaction.

"Seriously," I assure him as I slide my hands up his chest and over his shoulders so I can link my fingers together behind his neck. He circles his arms around me, dropping another kiss onto my lips as "When It Matters" pours out from the speakers. "Look, you just won," I tell him. "You won the playlist."

"I won something better than the playlist."

"That's super cheesy," I say, and he grins down at me.

"But now you embrace cheesy."

"Now I embrace *you*," I clarify.

"*That's* super cheesy," he says, and then we're swaying back and forth, like Itch and Akemi, like Shaun and Kirk, like everyone else. Because even though this moment is cheesy and weird and antiquated, it means something.

It matters.

SUMMER

Epilogue

"You know I'm not supposed to have boys in my room," I tell Oliver, right before giving him a gentle shove toward my bed. He sits down on it, pulling me onto his lap.

"You're also not supposed to consort with boys from rival schools," he reminds me. "And yet here we are."

"Consorting away." I give him a peck on the mouth. I'd like to give him more than a peck, but we have a job to do. "I guess we're going to have to make some exceptions to the rules."

"Shaun will appreciate that, too."

"I consort differently with Shaun," I tell him.

"Well, I would hope so." Oliver tries to start the kissing again, but I pull away and hop up.

"Later," I promise him. "Now come on. Get up."

He groans but allows me to pull him to his feet.

Mom and Cash are still drinking coffee in the kitchen when we make our last trip downstairs. They must hear us clomping on the steps, because Cash calls out, asking if we're *sure* we don't need any help. "I'm sure," I answer, right before my box tumbles out of my arms and lands on the floor with a thump.

"Allow me," says Oliver with a bad British accent. I roll my eyes but let him get my box along with the one he's carrying. He lifts them both—his muscles doing all kinds of things under his T-shirt—and catches the way I'm eyeing him. "What?"

"Just appreciating the Oliver Flagg thing," I tell him, and we grin at each other.

Outside, he loads both boxes into the overflowing bed of Cash's truck, and we secure it all with a tarp. "Do you need to say good-bye to your mom?" he asks.

I shake my head. "I already did, and she's going to come by the dorm later."

"I hope she knows that boys are allowed in *that* room," Oliver informs me, then quickly shakes his head. "Correction: not *all* boys. Just one."

"Definitely just one," I assure him. "The one who's only going to be three hours away."

"But who will visit a *lot*." Oliver leans over for a fast kiss . . . and this time, it turns into a slow kiss. He pulls away long enough to glance at the house—no one's watching—before crowding me against the truck so he can take his time.

It doesn't matter how long I've been dating Oliver; when he kisses me like this—all deep and deliberate—I forget everything. I just melt.

When we break, I smile up at him. "I might let you carry everything into the dorm after all," I tell him. "Because now my knees are weak."

"Yeah, mine too." He pulls Cash's keys out of his pocket. "Ready?"

Oliver opens the driver's-side door and I clamber aboard. I'm grateful Cash is letting us borrow his truck to move my stuff, but it's even more unwieldy than the behemoth. Oliver swings around the car to sit in the passenger seat beside me. He hands me the keys, and as I crank the engine, he nudges my arm. "You sure you don't want me to do that?"

He's kidding, and he knows I know it.

"I would," I tell him. "But you can't drive a stick shift."

"You could teach me." Oliver leans across the seat to kiss my neck. I try to bat him away, but I don't try very hard. "I should at least get to pick the music," he murmurs into my ear.

"Be my guest." I motion toward the console, which features an old battered radio with no jacks or wireless connections. "But our playlist isn't going to work in here."

"That's okay." Oliver gives me a last kiss. "I don't need the playlist anymore."

He turns on the radio and scrolls through stations until some pop song I can't name comes on. "That's terrible," I tell him.

"Awful," he agrees.

"Turn it up."

He does. I back onto Callaway and shift into first gear. I touch the gas and the engine revs. Its power becomes *my* power: there all along, just waiting for me to notice.

I let out the clutch, and we head down the road, happy to listen to any song that plays.

Sunrise Songs Playlist*

"When It Matters"—*Emotional Resonance***
"Making Love out of Nothing at All"—*Air Supply*
"Gone Daddy Gone"—*Violent Femmes*
"Here I Go Again"—*Whitesnake*
"Cry for Love"—*Iggy Pop*
"(I Just) Died in Your Arms"—*Cutting Crew*
"Heaven"—*Warrant*
"London Calling"—*The Clash*
"I Wanna Be Sedated"—*The Ramones*
"Angel"—*Aerosmith*
"Luv Luv Luv"—*Pansy Division*
"I'll Be There for You"—*Bon Jovi*
"Chase It Down"—*Ume*
"This Is Usually the Part Where People Scream"—*Alesana*
"Love Bites"—*Def Leppard*
"Hearts Are Made for Beating"—*Wax Fang*
"You're So Vain"—*Carly Simon*
"The Search Is Over"—*Survivor*
"Bang Bang"—*Nico Vega*

*All playlist songs exist.
** Except this one.

Acknowledgments

So much gratitude to the following:

Anyone who's reading this now. You are the reason. Thank you.

My exceptional book agent—Lisa Gallagher—for her endless passion and support and enthusiasm.

Chelsea Eberly, both for her mad editorial skills and for the gift of collaboration. This book came about through a magical alchemy where one person says a thing, and the other person says a thing, and then they come to a whole *different* thing that is far better than either of the original things. That happened a lot, and it was both extraordinary and extraordinarily fun.

Michelle Nagler, for letting me talk about ideas, and for listening, and then for taking a chance.

Alison Kolani and Barbara Bakowski in Copyediting, Jocelyn Lange in Subsidiary Rights, Heather Palisi in Design, and the entire Sales, Marketing, and Publicity teams at Random House Children's Books, who are too numerous to name but are fantastic champions.

Barrett Gregory for the fun photo sesh and great new head shots.

Elise Allen and Nina Berry—my fantastic author friends who took time from their *own* books to read my initial pitch pages.

The writing and support staff of *Grey's Anatomy,* season 12 . . . with an extra-special thanks to Andy Reaser for "PMGO."

Sara Rae Dodson—who was the first Real Live Teen to read this book—for her breakneck pace, insightful thoughts, and fearless honesty.

Nicole Desperito, for joining my chaotic village, for reading early drafts, for helping bring order to the chaos, and for letting me learn through teaching.

Countless numbers of friends and family, who are my cheering squad, my necessary distraction, my loves.

About the Author

JEN KLEIN lives in Los Angeles with her husband and a menagerie of little boys and animals, all of whom are unruly and ill-behaved. When she's not writing YA novels, Jen is an Emmy-nominated television writer, currently writing on the series *Grey's Anatomy*. Visit her online at jenkleinbooks.com and follow her on Twitter at @jenkleintweets.